THE BROTHERS' BAND

LIZA MALLOY

To the man who serenaded me with his favorite U2 songs all those years ago...
To the friends who accompanied me to countless concerts in the 90s...
And to all the amazing musicians out there, constantly motivating me with upbeat melodies, fast-paced rhythms, and inspiring lyrics...
This book is for you!

NOTE ABOUT THE PUNCTUATION

In a literary world where some readers staunchly defend the Oxford comma and others call it outdated, I've dared to spark my own punctuation debate involving an apostrophe. Though there is some differing of opinions amongst formal style manuals and grammar experts, the vast majority of my readers preferred Thomas' over Thomas's when polled. Therefore, throughout this book and the sequel, I will be using a single "s" when using the possessive form with the name Thomas. This is intentional and not a typographical error, but I apologize to all who prefer the alternative. Who knew grammar was so controversial?

PROLOGUE

*A*s I look back on what I've written, I'm surprised. For the first time ever, my journal resembles a love story and not a harried travel blog. I suppose some would call it a tragedy, but really it was just a different type of adventure. It's a tale of two brothers, one woman and five guitars. It's an account of two very different addictions—one overcome and one that still wakes its victim each night, with a dry mouth and a hollow aching in the chest. It's also a story about music and family and the insurmountable way passion blurs the fine line between love and hatred. But mostly, this is the story of how I met the love of my life.

So let me begin.

1

CHAPTER ONE

"It snowed last year too: I made a snowman and my brother
knocked it down
and I knocked my brother down and then we had tea."
~Dylan Thomas

I've always loved rainy days. I've always relished warm, sunny days where short pop-up showers unexpectedly interrupt a crystal clear sky, only to disappear just as hastily, leaving glistening dew on everything in their path. No, I was never one of those women with perfect hair that magically bounced back after a sprinkle, and actually, I was usually the unlucky one wearing a white tee shirt over a polka-dot bra.

Still, there's always been something magical and mysterious about the rain. When I was five years old, my dog Casper returned home out of the blue in a rain shower, nearly a week after he went missing.

Twenty-one years after that, I met Dylan, in what felt like the exact same storm.

I had worked late the night before, waiting tables at Echo, a chic club in the Chelsea neighborhood of New York where up-and-coming bands often performed. I wasn't due at my regular job at Skyward Bound Travel Agency until eleven, but I'd left my apartment around ten, intending to stop for coffee and allow plenty of time for the caffeine to fully permeate my core.

The sun shone brightly when I left my apartment. The air was fresh and light, and my short, flowing lemon-colored skirt and turquoise blouse matched the atmosphere perfectly. I'd always been a subway girl, but my apartment was only a half mile from the closest station, so I could safely remain a cute-shoe girl too. I didn't splurge much, but as a single girl in New York City, trapped inside most days and nights, sometimes a shiny new pair of bright blue peep-toed heels was all that got me through the day.

I retrieved my worn copy of *Anna Karenina* from my purse once I selected my seat. I loved a good romance, especially the classics. My fellow subway riders, comfortably seated with their smart phones and tablets, eyed me suspiciously, as though I held an abacus. I never could explain the feeling of a physical book touching my fingers as I read, the smell of the pages after they sat on the shelf for years, or the way my tears smudged the ink when I reached that fateful scene that broke my heart each time, no matter how many times I read it.

I turned the pages hungrily. Karenin had just confronted Anna, refusing to separate and threatening to take their son if she wouldn't leave Vronsky, and, suddenly, it was time for me to exit. I blinked, struggling to separate my mind from the book and to prepare myself for the sudden burst of sunlight as I emerged from the darkened subway. To my surprise, the sun had faded.

My coffee shop was a block from the station, and as soon as I reached the street level, I felt the rain. It fell in sheets, soaking everything and everyone in its path. It was a quiet shower, not just in the way it barely made a sound as it pelted the concrete and metal comprising Midtown West Manhattan, but also as it seemed to mute the normal noises we New Yorkers expected of our surroundings...the honking, the chatting, the clanking of machinery.

I smiled at the beauty of it, but once the first drop hit my hair, I shrieked and ran as fast as my Louboutin heels could carry me. Traffic forced me to stop at the next light, but I resumed my dash as soon as the intersection cleared, weaving haphazardly amidst a crowd of people holding everything from newspapers and briefcases over their heads. I was comforted only by the fact that clearly, no one else had thought to bring an umbrella today either.

Finally, with the coffee shop in sight, I smiled again, only to have the heel of my shoe stick in a drainage grate.

I grunted, apologized to the people whose path I was blocking, and tugged, but the shoe stuck firmly. I needed a better angle to unwedge the shoe, and the only way to achieve that would involve stepping out of the shoe and placing my bare foot on the dirty sidewalk. Unable to stomach that option, I futilely wrenched harder. My clothes and hair were already drenched, and the water pooling around my forehead was starting to drip into my eyes and obscure my view of the trapped shoe. My pride had taken a hit, but I had to retrieve my shoe without harming it. Sure, it was last year's design that I'd bought on sale, but any Louboutin, even one on sale, was a chunk of change.

Suddenly, the rain stopped. I glanced up, as though expecting to see that God himself had performed this valued miracle, but instead, I simply saw an umbrella held firmly over my head. A man, the bearer of the umbrella, crouched down beside me.

"Let me try," he offered, in a dreamy British accent. With a quick twist of his wrist, the shoe popped free. I stumbled backwards as the shoe came loose, and the man steadied me gracefully, a quick "whoopsie daisy," escaping his lips.

I smiled, trying to remember when—if ever—I'd heard an adult use that phrase.

"Thank you," I said, wiping the water off my forehead and eyes. I glanced up at the umbrella man and froze, mouth agape. He was, without a doubt, the most gorgeous man I'd ever seen up close, but more surprising was the overwhelming feeling that I knew him from somewhere.

A teenager bumped into me from behind and I startled, having forgotten I was in the middle of a busy sidewalk. Mr. Handsome guided me by the elbow off to the side, out of the path of oncoming foot traffic. "Are you alright?"

I nodded, unable to speak. Obviously, the rain was messing with my head, because I could have sworn I was standing inches away from Dylan Parker, lead singer of Sierra, my all-time favorite British rock band.

"You're quite sure of that?" he asked.

I nodded again, now staring unabashedly. He was tall and slender, but well-toned. He was dressed like a normal non-rock-star person, with dark wash jeans, brown work boots that he hadn't bothered to tie, and a gray tee shirt. I suppressed the temptation to lean closer and see if he smelled as perfect as he looked.

He smiled back at me. "It was a lovely morning before this shower, wasn't it? Didn't quite see that coming."

"But you have an umbrella," I pointed out, my voice recovered.

"I'm from London. I always have an umbrella."

"You're not who I think you are, are you?"

He laughed softly. "I'm afraid I can't answer that. I'm not a mind-reader, love."

"Would you sing me something?" I asked, and as soon as the words left my mouth, I cringed. Had I actually just said that out loud? What kind of person says that? My face instantly felt hot, and I hoped the shadow from the umbrella hid my blushing cheeks.

He grinned now, clearly uncertain what to make of me. "Ah, but you were running. You must be in a hurry."

I shook my head slowly. "Just trying to get out of the rain."

He glanced at my book, peeking out of my bag. "Some light morning reading?"

I shrugged nervously.

"You should try *Resurrection*. Fascinating look at the government."

"You read Tolstoy?"

He smiled and locked his dark mahogany eyes with mine. "I also drink coffee. Care to join me?"

I glanced around. The rain was still pouring down around us. "You're the only person with an umbrella in all of Manhattan. I have no choice but to follow you."

As we walked the final ten yards to the coffee shop, he placed a hand on the small of my back, sending shivers up my spine. We each ordered black coffee, then sat at a table in the corner of the café.

I ran my hand over my hair, desperately trying to tame the frizzed mess that was likely appearing. Dylan's hair, of course, looked perfect. It was short, much shorter than I'd seen it in photos, and a rich brown. He extended a hand.

"Dylan Parker."

"Lily Mitchell," I replied, noting that the thick silver band on his ring finger was on his right hand. Of course, his watch was also slung loosely around his right wrist, so I had to wonder if that was another cultural thing, like the driving on the opposite side of the road.

"Pleasure to make your acquaintance."

I smiled and sipped my coffee. I didn't know why I was eying his ring anyway. It wasn't like this was a date, and it never would be. I didn't date musicians. Well, technically I had dated musicians, three of them to be precise, but those experiences provided more than adequate support for a new rule.

"Not many people recognize me," he said suddenly.

"That surprises me." They weren't the Beatles by any means, but Sierra had more than its fair share of hits. Plus, Dylan was hot. Even someone who wasn't a fan of his music could at least appreciate his good looks.

He leaned forward. "And no one has ever asked me to sing to them on a street."

I knew I was blushing again. "A girl's gotta try, right?"

He drank his coffee quietly, a hint of a smile on his lips.

"I saw you in concert seven years ago." I said.

"Our first tour in the states was five years ago."

"I saw you then, too. The first time was at a local club, Echo. I think you've switched out some band members since then."

Dylan frowned. "Just the drummer. That was a long time ago. Are you a musician?"

I laughed, recalling my failed attempts at multiple instruments. "No. But I worked at Echo all through college, and now I still do a few evening shifts."

He relaxed back in his chair, crossing his arms across his chest. I noticed a pair of thick sunglasses clipped to the collar of his slate gray tee shirt and immediately gazed up at his dark chocolate eyes. "So you see all the bands before they make it. Tell me then, Lily, do I need to fear the competition?"

My heart thudded uncontrollably at the way he said my name. I wasn't sure if it was the accent or the way his voice was dripping with confidence. Or maybe it was his full, moist lips, surrounded by a thin layer of dark brown stubble.

"I wouldn't be too concerned if I were you," I finally said.

"What do you do, then, when you're not watching bands or reading of suicidal lovers?" He paused and his face paled. "Shit, I've ruined the ending for you."

"I've read it before," I said, watching the relief wash over him.

"I'm a travel agent. I work at Skyward Bound, just down the street."

"And what brings a person to do that?"

I shrugged. "It's a job. And I love traveling. Or I think I would, if I ever went anywhere. I get great discounts on trips. I'd love to see Europe sometime."

"So why don't you?"

"Well, it's just discounted, not free. And I don't really have anyone to travel with now." I sipped my coffee while he contemplated this response. "What brings you to New York?"

"I live here."

"Oh. I just assumed you lived in England."

"I have a flat in London, but I spend most of my time here."

"Are you from London originally?"

He shook his head slowly, his eyes clearly on my lips. "Ipswich, in Suffolk County. It's northeast of London. About an hour by rail."

I swallowed nervously. Being this close to someone so beautiful, with such a sexy accent, was making my palms sweat.

"What does one study at the university to become a travel agent? Sales?"

I laughed at the thought of myself studying anything business-related, although I suppose technically both of my jobs were in the sales arena. "I studied literature at NYU. I double majored in Comparative Lit and English Lit."

"That seems...redundant."

"It was wonderful," I replied, wistfully recalling those magical days where people actually expected me to sit around and read all day. Now, on the rare occasions where I had a slow day at either job, people grimaced at me whenever I pulled out a novel.

Dylan glanced at his watch.

"I'm keeping you from something," I guessed.

"I have an early lunch date," he said, adding, "with my manager."

"Well, it was nice talking with you. Thanks for the coffee and the umbrella." I paused. "Maybe you'll see me at your next concert."

He leaned forward. "I'd rather see you before then. Could I have your number?"

I couldn't help but smile. Not only was his request enormously flattering, but in all honesty, goosebumps spread down my arms at the mere thought of spending more time with a man as sexy as Dylan. But I knew what I had to do. "That's probably not a good idea," I said.

Dylan frowned and tilted his head as though he couldn't figure me out. "You're married," he finally said.

Somehow, his cockiness was cute. "No. But I don't date musicians, and I'm afraid if I spend any more time with you, I'll be tempted to make an exception."

"All musicians? That's quite the broad generalization."

I smiled and shrugged.

"What about a concert pianist? Or an opera singer?"

Now I giggled.

"Seriously, what's the basis for this rule? Did one bad guitarist ruin it for all of us?"

I held up three fingers, one for each of the mistakes I'd made.

I'd always been drawn to the temperamental, artistic type, which is part of why I loved working at Echo. But working there had also led me into one too many relationships with troubled musicians that I met at the club.

"Ouch. That might be a little harder to overcome. What is it about us musicians that makes us off limits?"

That was an easy one. "You smoke, drink, party, travel, and stay up all hours of the night. You're broody and moody and just a little too arrogant."

"Fuck, you've dated my brother, haven't you?"

I laughed, and he joined in.

"I don't smoke," he said finally, his eyes darting quickly to the other side of the café, where a teenager was taking a photo of him on an iPhone.

"Good. It's a terrible habit."

He nodded. "Horrid." He kept staring at me and smiling, then finally sighed and picked up his umbrella. "Fine. You win. But what if you change your mind?"

It was a pointless question. I knew I'd change my mind the second he left. Hell, I already regretted telling him I wouldn't date him, but I knew how things would turn out. It might be fun for a while, probably lots of excitement, romance, and terrific mind-blowing sex, and then I'd end up hurt, alone, and even more emotionally damaged than I already was.

"Can I see your phone?" he asked, interrupting my thoughts.

I handed it to him, confused.

He snapped a photo of himself and then typed something in. "Now you have my number. Delete it if you want."

I smiled. He handed my phone back to me, his hand lingering on mine. Our eyes locked again, then he leaned in and kissed my cheek. My entire body tensed in response.

I watched him leave and then realized it had stopped raining. I caught my breath, then started off towards the travel agency.

* * *

As soon as I got off work that day, I called my best friend Jill. We had been close since freshman year of college, when we were assigned as roommates. On the surface, we were far from an obvious match. She was rational, calm, and fully in control of her life, not to mention obsessed with fitness. I, on the other hand, had always been the romantic, emotional dreamer ready to do anything on a whim. Even our majors were polar opposites—Jill studied business and I spent my days reading novels. But despite our differences, we just clicked.

Even now, our lives were starkly different. Jill had married her college sweetheart and worked a normal nine-to-five job in her chosen career. I bounced from loser to loser, seemingly incapable of learning my lesson, and I worked two different jobs, neither of which even remotely resembled the actual career I'd dreamed of in college.

Still, we managed to get together as often as possible, although lately our hangout spot tended to be the gym, Jill's favorite place in the world. So, that evening, we met up for a spinning class and analyzed my entire encounter with Dylan over post-workout smoothies. She pretended to agree with my decision not to give him my number, but I saw the look of horror in her hazel eyes as I spoke.

"Maybe he's different," she said. "You could call him and give him a chance."

I responded with an exaggerated eye roll.

"Okay, so he's probably not. But you could approach this differently. Don't look at it as a potential relationship so much as a chance for fun. You deserve fun."

"I deserve fun that doesn't end with me crying and fasting for days."

"Yeah, you don't deal with breakups well. What if you just meet up with him for sex once or twice?"

"I'm not desperate."

"I hardly think shagging Dylan Parker counts as desperate."

I smiled. "Shagging?"

"That's what they call it in the UK, right? How was the accent?"

"So sexy."

She bit her lip. "God, I'm jealous."

"You weren't jealous when Michael left me at that dive in Jersey," I reminded her. Michael was my most recent musician boyfriend. He liked me to watch his concerts, which was generally fun, until the night where, about a month into our relationship, he forgot I'd come with him and left with a groupie, ditching me at a sketchy bar hours from home.

She offered me a sympathetic look. "True. Most of the time, I'm glad I married young. But when I hear about you meeting a hunky British rock star, I can't help but want to live vicariously through you." She glanced at the clock for about the tenth time since we'd sat down, and I knew she was eager to get home to her husband.

"Tell Scott I said hi."

Jill nodded. "Keep me posted."

Eager to start my online research on Dylan, I opted to forego the shower until I got home. I ran a quick internet search on my phone on the subway, but couldn't get too focused. Once I was safely in my apartment, I pulled out my laptop and resumed my snooping. I lingered on a few separate photos, my personal favorite being a shot from two years ago where he was shirtless and staring off into the distance, guitar case in hand.

I snapped the computer shut when I heard a key in the lock. My current roommate, Carrie, was nauseatingly nice, and while we were certainly on cordial terms, we weren't exactly close friends. Carrie was extremely conservative, and she tended to be judgmental about the men in my life, so I didn't want her to see me stalking a British rock star.

I greeted her pleasantly, we swapped generic details from our day, and she moved into her bedroom to review her Bible study discussion notes.

I opened the computer again, and with renewed determination, I typed "Dylan Parker drugs and women" into the search box. I held my breath as the results popped up. Initially, I was pleasantly surprised. No scathing photos popped up, no recent news articles of his arrests, not even a sign that he was guilty of the requisite hotel-trashing.

As I scrolled down further, I found what I'd been expecting. The story was three years old, and brief, but it said that police had been called to his hotel room for a domestic disturbance. His then-girlfriend ultimately didn't press charges for assault and battery, but the police found cocaine in the room.

To some extent, I felt vindicated. I'd been right to be wary of him. But no sooner did that thought cross my mind, and I realized I could be jumping to conclusions. The article just implied he hit his girlfriend. There was no real proof, certainly no conviction. And the drugs could've belonged to the girlfriend. Or a friend.

"Stop it, Lily," I said aloud, scared of the growing disappointment I felt at my new discovery. Before I could do anything stupid, I pulled out my phone, cringing as I deleted Dylan's contact info and photo. I dumped the laptop on my bedroom floor and went to shower.

* * *

TWO DAYS LATER, I was at work, eying the beautiful day jealously. Thanks to my limited budget, I'd brought my lunch like I always did, but that didn't mean I couldn't escape the office for lunch. Surely there was a vacant bench somewhere nearby where I could enjoy the sunshine. Although I did virtually all of my work over the phone, we occasionally had appointments or walk-ins. So, I buzzed Bridget, the receptionist, to confirm that I didn't have any meetings.

"Sorry," she replied. "I was just about to tell you, but some guy called a little while ago and asked to meet with you."

Two other travel agents were in the office today. There was no reason he couldn't meet with one of them. "Well, have Marcus or Cindy handle it."

"He specifically asked for you. He wanted to know if you were working today, and if he could meet with you."

I groaned. It was probably some old fart that wanted to see if I could get him a cheaper rate on a state park inn or something equally ridiculous. I was all in favor of easy commissions from repeat customers, but sometimes, it just wasn't worth the time. "What's his name?"

"He wouldn't tell me."

Super. "What time is he coming?"

"He called about an hour ago and said he'd be here between twelve and one."

"Okay, send him back whenever," I mumbled, disconnecting. Hopefully, he'd come soon, and I could still eat my crappy sandwich in the sunshine. I sighed, reapplied lipstick, finger-combed my long, brown hair, and checked the flight prices for another customer while I waited.

A few minutes later, I heard a gentle tap on the wall of my cubical. It was Bridget, escorting my appointment back. I stood to greet him, then gasped as she stepped out of the way. It was Dylan.

"Thanks, Bridget," I said, trying not to blush when she mouthed "he's hot" in response.

She stepped away, and I motioned for Dylan to sit.

"You don't take rejection well," I guessed.

He flashed a sexy grin in response and my breath caught in my throat. Dylan looked even more amazing than he had the other day. He still hadn't bothered to shave, but his jeans lacked the holes of the pair he'd worn last, and his shirt, albeit untucked, had buttons. I suspected this counted as dressed up for him.

"This has nothing to do with that," he replied. "You're the only travel agent I know in town."

"New York is full of travel agencies. And don't you have someone else who makes your travel arrangements for you anyway? Like a manager? Or a personal assistant?"

"I'm rather picky about my travel needs," he said. "I like to oversee the details."

His accent was so cute that I couldn't help but smile. Clearly, he interpreted that as an opening. "You didn't call me," he said.

I shrugged.

Dylan leaned closer, so close that I was suddenly overwhelmed by the tantalizing smell of his cologne. For a minute, I panicked that he was going to kiss me, but then he pulled back, a small object in his hand. It was my phone. He tapped it and grinned. "It looks like it works." And then he gasped. "You deleted me? I can't believe you actually deleted me."

I wasn't sure what to say. He looked genuinely hurt.

"I'm sorry," I finally mumbled. "You seem really nice, and I'm sure you're nothing like the other musicians I've dated, but I just can't risk it."

He shook his head. "Of course." He cleared his throat. "Now about my travel plans."

"Oh. You're actually taking a trip?"

He nodded. "I'm going to Los Angeles. I'll need a plane."

"A plane ticket? What date?"

"No, a plane. A small jet."

I hesitated. "We don't have any contracts with private jet rental companies. You could probably get a better deal dealing with them directly."

"Clearly you weren't a business major. You're not very good at sales, are you? You work on commission, right?"

I smiled.

"See? You do like me. You're concerned about my finances." He handed my phone back to me, and we locked eyes.

"I'm awfully hungry," he continued. "I think I could focus better once I have some food in my stomach."

"I'm not falling for this," I said. "I have a busy afternoon."

"Your lovely receptionist said you don't have any more appointments today."

Every ounce of my being yearned to go with him, to keep hearing that perfect melodious voice, but it was a terrible idea. "Why me?" I asked.

He raised an eyebrow. "You intrigue me. You work in a

cubical all day because you love traveling. You think Tolstoy is fun. You refuse to associate with musicians, as they're all too serious and dangerous, yet you spend your evenings in a club surrounded by musicians. You, my dear, are a living, breathing, paradox. A puzzle just waiting to be solved."

I couldn't fault him for that response. At least he was honest.

He narrowed his eyes. "I would back off, but evidently, I don't take rejection well. And I'm quite certain you were flirting with me at the coffee shop. Are you really not attracted to me in the slightest?"

A loud chortle escaped my lips. "Oh come on. Everyone is attracted to you, with your perfect hair and that adorable accent and those lips…"

"What about my lips?"

"Nothing," I said, certain I was blushing.

"Then what's the problem? You can't really be serious about the musician rule."

"I am serious. I considered the possibility that you might be different and I looked you up. But you're not any different, so then I deleted your number."

He raised an eyebrow, but didn't speak, so I continued.

"Can you tell me what happened in a London Hotel room three years ago?"

He glanced down. "No, I don't recall."

I sighed. "I think you should contact the jet companies directly. I'll jot down some numbers for you."

He reached out and placed his hand over mine. "I can't remember any of it because I was stoned. I don't know what happened before the police came, I don't know what happened right after."

I frowned, both caught off guard by his honesty and disappointed that his confession confirmed my suspicions about him. "What about your girlfriend? She was there at the time."

"Yes, and so was my bloody brother. We were all high, not a

one of us could tell you what happened. But that was a long time ago and both my brother and I have done a great deal of maturing in the interim." He checked a text on his phone. "I know what you read and I could tell you I didn't do any of it, but the truth is I don't bloody know."

He paused again. "Look, I'm not asking you to marry me. I just thought you might like to have lunch."

I considered his words, and the next thing I knew, I was standing, purse in hand, ready to go.

"Did you finish your book?" he asked as soon as we stepped out of the office.

"Yeah. Turns out she killed herself. Real tragic."

He laughed.

"I have to admit I was surprised that you know Tolstoy."

"What, you mean the other musicians you know don't read the classics?" he teased, casually slinging his arm around my back as though we'd been together for ages.

"Fine, so I might generalize. But if you knew about the other losers I've dated, you'd understand." I bit my lip, realizing his admission to being high that night at the hotel meant he did have something in common with my ex-boyfriends, not that any of them would have been honest about it. And at least he'd had the sense to be remorseful over it, and not to brag about his past drug-induced adventures, like my ex Michael would have.

Dylan led me into a small Italian restaurant a few blocks from the travel agency. Over the span of an hour, I told him my pathetic tales of past musician-lovers, and he told me about his aversion to reptiles, his love of reading, and how his mother taught him the violin when he was four. I left lunch feeling guilty, having wrongly judged a man for his profession.

He followed me back to my cubical, and I rented a jet for his L.A. trip. There was a quiet moment, and I knew he was about to kiss me. I felt my whole body begin to tingle, but then, he pressed his lips gently into the top of my hand. I was disappointed, and he knew it.

I glanced down, jotted my number on a post-it note, and handed it to him.

He smiled. "When can I see you again?"

I shrugged coyly.

"How about dinner Saturday? Or do you work then?"

I shook my head. "That sounds perfect."

He slid the post-it note back to me. "Address?"

"We could just meet there."

This amused him. "I haven't decided where I want to take you yet."

"You have a car?"

He nodded.

I sighed and jotted down the address. "I wouldn't leave your car in front of my building though. It's a crappy neighborhood."

He grinned and stood. "Duly noted. Seven o'clock?"

I nodded.

Dylan winked, and left.

I was still smiling a moment later when my cell phone rang. I didn't recognize the number, but I answered anyway.

"Change of plans," the familiar British voice began. "How's six o clock? And don't dress up. Jeans and flats."

"Flats?"

"The shoes. That's what they're called, right?"

"Oh, right." Suddenly, I felt silly. What had I thought he meant, an apartment? I made a mental note to brush up on my English, er, British, before the date.

"Excellent. See you then."

"Um, Dylan?"

"Yes?"

"You were just checking that I gave you my real number, weren't you?"

He laughed. "See you Saturday."

CHAPTER TWO

"She had an eye to see and an ear to hear:
he could show her things and tell her things, and taste the bliss of
feeling
that all he imparted left long reverberations and echoes he could
wake at will."
Edith Wharton, *Ethan Frome*

On Saturday, I was ready by five thirty, in case there was another change of plans. Logically, I knew that since Dylan was male, he'd be at least fifteen minutes late, and since he was a musician, another fifteen on top of that. So, I was whole-heartedly expecting to not leave the apartment until at least six thirty.

I'd selected a pair of cropped aqua-colored skinny jeans and a slinky, white scoop neck tank. I paired them with my silver sequined ballet flats, as per instruction. I couldn't decide between my two favorite necklaces, so I wore both, along with a slew of bangles on my wrist. I ran the straightening iron over my hair an extra time, in case the evening humidity was rough, added a light layer of lip gloss, and swiped on two coats of my favorite mascara.

I'd been blessed with olive skin, thanks mostly to my Italian heritage. My thick, dark brown hair generally cooperated when I wanted it straight, and I'd worn it below my shoulders since before high school. Full, black lashes accented my dark brown eyes.

I was slightly taller than average, and slender, a pleasant side effect of the fact that I couldn't afford the kinds of food I'd like to be eating. I had perky breasts which seemed to satisfy my past boyfriends, but, personally, I wouldn't mind going up a cup size. I wasn't particularly fond of exercise, but my best friend was a gym junkie. Since she insisted virtually all social outings revolve around the gym, I was in decent shape, despite my protests.

I'd never had a problem attracting male attention. Unfortunately, it wasn't always the right kind of attention. Lately, my potential suitors seemed to fall into two stereotypical categories —drunken patrons at the club or bored construction workers I passed on the street.

I had just curled up on my bed with my dog-eared copy of *Ethan Frome* when my phone rang. It was Dylan. My heart sank, certain he was calling either to cancel or postpone. I answered tentatively.

"How rough is your neighborhood exactly?"

"Huh?"

"You said I shouldn't leave my car here. Normally, I'd come up to your door, but if my car won't be here when we return…"

I smiled. He was here! "What kind of car is it?"

"A Porsche 911 Carrera S."

I bit my lip, thrilled to get the chance to ride in that. I might have even kept my license up to date if I'd known I'd come into contact with a Porsche. "I'll come down," I said.

I said goodbye to Carrie, and rushed downstairs. I felt giddy at the sight of Dylan. He was leaned against the sleek, silver car, his legs crossed at the ankle. He was wearing jeans, of course, and a black button-down short-sleeved shirt. Oversized sunglasses covered his eyes and prevented me from seeing his full expression, but he broke into a wide smile when he saw me.

"Nice car," I said, leaning in to allow him to kiss me on the cheek.

Dylan grinned and scanned his eyes over my body. "Nice everything."

My entire body tingled with excitement at the compliment.

He opened the passenger door and I climbed in. I plopped my oversized bag on my lap as he took his seat, and he reached for the gearshift, pausing and glancing into my purse.

"You brought a book," he said incredulously, lifting *Ethan Frome* from my purse. "You actually brought a book. On a date. Do I bore you?"

I smiled. He was unbelievably sexy when he teased. "I like to be prepared for anything. And besides, I was at an exciting part."

"And I'm sure you don't know how this one ends either?"

I shrugged.

He smiled and pulled away from the curb. "I have a cousin named Ethan. Dreadful little child, he was. Almost would've wished a sledding accident on that one."

So he'd read Edith Wharton too. I was impressed. And confused.

The thing was, people just didn't surprise me. My first impressions of people had always been right. I wasn't particularly talented in any useful aspect of life, but I'd always been able to read people. I knew right when I met Jill that we'd be friends for life. I knew as soon as I saw Carrie that she'd be a perfect roommate. And I'd known from the start that each of my last few disastrous relationships would turn out horribly... not that I'd resisted diving into them regardless.

And, as of earlier this evening, I'd known for certain that

someday, Dylan would turn out to be just like every other musician I'd dated, and I'd get hurt, probably sooner than later.

I prayed that for once, I'd be wrong, that we'd have a great date or two, and then he'd go off on tour and we'd separate amicably, with nothing but good memories and a sweet nostalgia.

I realized suddenly that he was watching me. "Did you say something?"

He shook his head. "No, but I'd love to know what you're thinking."

"I was thinking about how most people are fairly predictable."

"Is that so? Then tell me, what do I have planned for tonight?"

I bit my lip thoughtfully. "Dinner. Or maybe a concert. Or perhaps even a party."

As soon as he grinned, I knew I'd guessed wrong.

"Fine, then where are you taking me?"

"Brooklyn."

I laughed. "Can you be more specific?"

"You'll just have to be surprised," he taunted.

His hand dropped to my thigh and a flash of heat shot throughout my body. Why did musicians have this uncanny ability to turn me on? I hardly knew anything about this man, but the sheer sensation of his hand on my body made me consider jumping onto his lap at the next stoplight.

Maybe Jill was right, maybe it had just been too long since I was last with a man. It hadn't been that long, really, but I was at the point in my life where I no longer enjoyed the thrill of spending the night with a relative stranger, and since my last relationship had ended four months ago, well, yeah. It had been a while.

"You're doing it again," he said.

"What?"

"Being mysterious."

"I'm mysterious? You're the one who won't tell me where we're going."

He laughed, and we talked comfortably for the rest of the ride. When we reached our destination, I was indeed surprised. He had taken me to Coney Island.

"Have you been here before?" Dylan asked.

I nodded. Growing up in Jersey, it had been an annual summer outing for me and my family. "It's been a while, though," I said.

He smiled, clasped my hand, and led me to a ride. We went on a roller coaster and the bumper cars before the sun began to set. Two people approached Dylan and asked for his autograph, which he politely gave, with little discussion.

"I thought you said no one ever recognized you."

He shrugged. "I only meant that it's unusual. Maybe five a day. Nothing unmanageable. When I'm with my brother, it's worse."

I nodded, imagining that the two strikingly handsome Parker brothers side-by-side would be quite a sight. "Are you two together a lot, I mean, when you're not working?"

"More often than not, actually," he said, pulling me towards the beach.

"What's next?"

"Now we walk," he said.

"Walk where?"

"Nowhere, love. It's sunset, on a beach. Just enjoy it."

And I did. We walked about a half mile up the beach before stopping. He stripped out of his top shirt, leaving only a dark green undershirt, and spread the button-down on the beach for me to sit on.

"But now your shirt is going to get all sandy," I said.

"It'll survive," he said, sitting close and wrapping his arm around me. We were mostly quiet as we watched the sunset. I was anxiously waiting for him to kiss me, growing more and more nervous by the second. When my phone buzzed suddenly, I nearly fell over.

I glanced down at my phone. It was Jill, texting me for a status report on the date so far. I subtly wedged my phone back into my purse.

"What, you're not going to answer? To tell her how I'm exceeding your every expectation?"

I smiled at his arrogance and snuggled in closer to him. After another minute, Dylan stood. "Shall we walk back?"

I nodded and followed. We played a few games, Dylan winning me the requisite stuffed teddy bear, and then took a romantic ferris wheel ride once it was completely dark. As our car sailed higher and higher, the noises of the festivities below grew quieter, and the sparkling lights seemed almost magical.

"This is beautiful," I said, again wondering when he'd kiss me.

"You're beautiful," he replied.

I turned and saw that Dylan was staring at me. He leaned in slowly, placed his hands on my cheeks, and pulled me in for the kiss. His lips brushed against mine lightly at first, then relaxed into the kiss slowly. It was a polite kiss, the kind where I could tell he was holding back. Dylan ended the kiss before I was ready, while my entire body still ached to taste him. He'd offered me just enough to convince me that our chemistry wasn't limited to conversation. His hands dropped from my cheeks, and he squeezed my hand in his. I blinked and tried to control my breathing.

"You're terrible," I finally mumbled, smiling.

He grinned in response.

"I mean, really. A sunset walk on the beach, a kiss at the top of the ferris wheel... So cliché."

"And you love it," he said.

"I do," I admitted, glad he hadn't taken my statement as an insult. I loved romance, and there was no denying that certain things were romantic. There was obviously a reason they became clichés.

"Are you hungry?" he asked when we deboarded.

"I could eat. What did you have in mind?"

He glanced around. "Hot dog and cotton candy?"

I laughed. Leave it to the wealthiest guy I'd ever dated to buy me an amusement park hotdog on our first date. "Works for me," I said.

We talked while we ate, wandered around some more, then stopped along the beach again to watch the fireworks. The sandy expanse was more crowded now, so we stood along the edge of the boardwalk. Dylan's arm was around me, and the heat from his body was driving me crazy. I glanced over at him every so often, and a few times our eyes met, and he'd smile. It was an eager, school-boy smile, not a seductive, about-to-ravish-someone smile. I wondered if his hesitation about kissing me had to do with being recognized, maybe some fear of hidden paparazzi photographing him with a regular old American girl.

I didn't have to wonder long, because before the fireworks ended, Dylan pulled me close and kissed me again. My heart pounded in time with the explosions above us. This time, he lingered long enough for our tongues to meet, but not long enough to satisfy my thirst for him.

"Are you cold?" he asked, whispering in my ear.

I shook my head, confused, and then realized I was trembling. I knew my shivering wasn't from the temperature, but Dylan stepped behind me anyway, wrapping both arms tightly around me until the fireworks ended.

We walked back to the car, hand in hand, mostly quiet.

"What now?" I asked as we stopped by the Porsche.

He opened the door for me, waiting while I lowered myself into the seat. "Well, I could be a gentleman and take you home." He shut my door and walked around to let himself in.

"I don't have a curfew," I said, surprised at my own brazenness.

He grinned. "In that case, I could take you out for a proper meal."

I was torn. I really wasn't hungry, at least not for food, but I wanted to spend more time with him. I knew that the responsible thing to do would be to let him drive me home now, before I let my emotions and heightened sex drive get the best of me. I knew we should quit while we were ahead, while the date was still perfect, while he still clearly wanted more of me.

Of course, that was what I meant to say. Instead, I heard myself mumble "okay."

We drove to a small sushi restaurant, drank some Saki while we waited for our food, and made small talk. When our food arrived, I ate a few bites, but mostly I was just fascinated by his stories about England and the rest of his travels.

"Something wrong?" he asked, gesturing to my plate.

I blushed. "No, it's great. I'm actually just not that hungry." My eyes wandered down his perfect body as I spoke, and I again wished I could control myself.

Dylan nodded knowingly and motioned for the check. "So I guess now I should see you home," he said. "You and your dating stereotype rules, you probably have rules about sleeping with immigrants."

I laughed aloud. "You're hardly what I picture when I hear the word immigrant."

"So does that mean you'd make an exception, then?"

"I have a three date rule. For all men, regardless of citizenship status or national origin."

He paid the bill with cash and we walked out towards the car. "I was never a mathematician, but it seems we had coffee on Tuesday, lunch on Thursday, and a whole evening together tonight."

"But Thursday wasn't a date. It was business."

"If it had been business, you would have paid."

"I don't have an expense account," I said.

We had reached the car. I hesitated, assuming he'd want to open the door for me again. Instead, Dylan suddenly pushed me against the Porsche and kissed me. He placed his arms on either side of my head and the length of his entire perfect body pressed into me, effectively trapping me. It was the kiss I'd been craving all night, possibly all year.

Dylan's lips were warm and smooth, and his tongue caressed mine skillfully. I eagerly reached for his hips, twisting my fingers around his shirt. It was clear what he wanted, and I knew I wanted it too. By the time his lips left mine, I was dizzy and breathless. Dylan calmly kissed me on the forehead and skipped around to the other side of the car.

I struggled to catch my breath and then plopped into the car. I glanced at him as he climbed into the car and knew I was only fooling myself if I tried to resist further. "I think you're right," I said, realizing that to him, it was a foregone conclusion.

He laughed confidently, and moments later we were pulled up alongside a large building. I'd been too distracted during the drive to pay attention to what side of town we were on, and I had no intention of stopping to ask questions now. Dylan tossed his keys to the valet, greeted the doorman, and led me to the elevator. He used a key to reach the floor, leaving me to assume his residence occupied the entire level, but when we arrived, I saw there were actually two apartments on either end of the hall.

"Thomas—my brother—he lives there," he explained, as though reading my mind.

Dylan led me to the other apartment, unlocked the door, and before we'd even made it all the way in, his lips were on mine and I was wriggling out of my shirt. He pushed me against the door, his mouth wandering to my neck, behind my ear, then back to my lips, while my hands slid up his shirt along his smooth, firm stomach. Every touch made me desperate for more of him.

His hands caressed my breasts, groping at the silky bra before reaching around my back and unclasping it. I helped him out of his shirt and began unbuttoning his jeans. We both kicked out of our shoes, and then he carried me across the room, delicately placing me on a couch and climbing on top of me.

His mouth found my nipple and I groaned, louder than I'd intended. He sucked harder, his other hand unfastening my pants and sliding down the front, his fingers trapped between my panties and the soft denim. I writhed against his hand, my own fingers grasping desperately at his hips and butt. Dylan climbed off of me, tugging my jeans until they were on the floor. He stared at me for a moment and smiled, and suddenly, I felt completely at ease. I lifted my hips so he could take off my panties, and then he kissed my chest and stomach again before moving lower and lower.

The dull throbbing between my legs intensified, and the moment his tongue reached its goal, I felt certain I'd explode. The sensation of his mouth against my already damp flesh was too intense, and I wasn't ready for our fun to end yet. I reached for Dylan's arms, desperately pulling him back up to my face and we kissed again. Except his tongue worked just as powerfully against my mouth as it had lower on my body, and even the kissing made me more eager to have him inside of me.

I fumbled for the button on his pants and he backed away, disappearing in the darkness and leaving me alone and naked on his couch.

He returned quickly, a foil packet in hand. He stepped out of his jeans and my breath caught in my throat as he slowly lowered his boxer briefs. Dylan was larger than my last boyfriend, but at this point, I didn't care. I was ready to go and I needed him now. He slipped into the condom and rejoined me on the couch without wasting a single moment.

He kissed me again then pulled back and smiled. God, even just that cocky grin was an aphrodisiac. I couldn't remember a man ever looking at me quite the way Dylan was now. Even though we were in the midst of what I was sure would prove to be an entertaining but brief one-night stand, the look in his eyes made me feel cherished and revered.

I lifted my hips, guiding him into me. We moaned in unison as our bodies joined, then we paused, both of us relishing the delicious sensation. The relief I felt from the sudden fullness was fleeting though, as the moment Dylan shifted his hips, the tension inside me began to build.

We fell into an unrelenting rhythm and I was caught off guard by how quickly I felt the warmth of my impending climax start. It spread through me, building momentum with every passing second, and I dug my teeth into his shoulder to soften my cries when it hit me. Dylan followed suit shortly after, then collapsed on my body, both of us breathing hard.

Dylan lifted his head finally, and our eyes met. I smiled, still dazed. He kissed my nose and climbed off of me, disappearing again for a moment, but returning still nude. "That was fun," he said, sitting at the end of the couch and lifting me up towards him. "We should do it again sometime."

"Now?" I asked, more out of confusion than anything else.

He laughed. "Give me a minute, love. I'm not Superman."

I relaxed against him, gently tracing my finger along the path of his necklace.

His breath quickened. "You are spectacular," he said.

I smiled, certain no one had bestowed that particular compliment upon me before. "And you're worth breaking rules for. So far," I added.

"So far?" He shook his head. "Jesus, you're bloody difficult." He kissed me again, and his thumb casually brushed back and forth across my nipple. I inched away just enough to be able to reach his lap, and I gently nudged his chest backwards before taking him in my mouth. Within seconds, he responded appropriately, but I continued the rhythmic motion until his breath quickened and his fingers pulled more frantically in my hair.

I grabbed a second condom from the table beside the couch and pulled it over him before swinging my legs onto either side of his body. His mouth was level with my breasts now, and he caressed and licked them freely as I tilted my head back excitedly.

I shifted my hips slowly at first, increasing the speed as the pressure in my groin grew. Dylan's hips rose to meet mine, and our eyes met briefly then locked.

This time, we both climaxed together.

I sighed contentedly. "I feel better now," I said.

"I hadn't realized you were feeling bad."

I rolled my eyes. "Oh please. You know exactly how to drive a woman crazy."

He smiled proudly. "You're hardly any better. You've been taunting me all week."

I shrugged and scooted off his lap. He stood and returned a moment later. He tossed me a thin, blue bathrobe and stepped into his jeans before heading to his kitchen.

I sniffed the bathrobe curiously, pleased to find a distinctly masculine soap smell on it. I wasn't naïve enough to believe I was the first woman he'd brought back here, but it was still comforting to not be offered a spare bathrobe last worn by a nineteen year old groupie.

"Would you like some tea?" he asked, filling a kettle with water.

I laughed, but accepted the offer. I slowly inched off the couch, shrugged into the robe, and joined him in the kitchen. "So this is your apartment," I said, glancing around.

He nodded, and I took that as an invitation to tour.

It was a large space, with massive windows lining two walls of the main room. The kitchen was small, but modernly equipped with stainless steel appliances and sleek granite countertops. The living room had a massive flat-screen TV mounted to the wall, two sofas, an armchair, an oversized coffee table, and two end tables. The furniture was all chocolate and beige, with crisp modern lines, sort of an expensive version of Crate and Barrel. The other half of the room was set up like an office, with a desk and several bookshelves. There was no clutter, and hardly any personal belongings.

There was a hall off the side of the living area, leading first to a bedroom, furnished in similar style to the rest of the loft, and a large bathroom, with a Jacuzzi tub and separate ceramic-tiled shower with two showerheads. The last room was clearly built as a second bedroom, but had been arranged, not surprisingly, as a music room. There was a piano, drum set, several other pieces of recording equipment, and five guitars. Album covers and awards lined the far wall.

I sensed Dylan behind me and turned quickly. He offered a mug of tea to me and I accepted. "Five guitars?"

"You'd be surprised how often strings break."

"I thought musicians were supposed to be superstitious. Don't you have a lucky guitar you have to use each time?"

He kissed the side of my head, inhaling the scent of my hair. I hoped it still smelled like vanilla and lavender and not like hotdogs and carnies. "And just when I hoped you'd stop generalizing about us musicians," he said. He ambled across the room and began opening each of the guitar cases.

"They're identical," I observed. He nodded.

I gestured to the piano. "Do you play?"

He sat at the bench. "What do you want to hear?"

"Surprise me."

Without pause, he started into a beautiful song. I'd heard it before and suspected it was Chopin, but couldn't be certain. His fingers moved effortlessly across the ivory keys, his eyes staring straight ahead, closing for long periods. There was something so peaceful about the way he played, and yet so unnerving all at the same time. Dylan was a rocker; he wasn't supposed to know classical music, let alone to feel it so deeply.

I stepped closer, set my tea on the table beside his, and slipped onto his lap facing him. He smiled, and his hands fell away from the keys only briefly before resuming the song. I smiled at his impressive trick, playing without any visual on the piano, and he leaned in for a kiss. The music stopped and his hands pulled at the edges of the robe, revealing my breasts.

He ran his hand down the center of my body and I arched backwards against the keys. He kissed my neck, his warm breath tickling behind my ear, and then his fingers slipped into the robe, resting gently along the small of my back. He pulled me closer and we kissed.

It was a long, familiar kiss, and it was this kiss that convinced me I was doomed. Before, when our tongues met and my entire body quivered, I could blame my reaction, my neediness, on sexual tension. Now, there was no such excuse. I was fully satisfied and still wanted nothing more than to be in his arms.

"It's late," he finally said.

I scooted off his lap, assuming that was my cue to get dressed and head out.

"Stay," he commanded, motioning for me to follow him to the bedroom. I hesitated, but really had no interest in leaving a moment sooner than I needed to. I felt oddly comfortable, here with Dylan.

When he stepped into the bathroom, I went to retrieve my purse from the kitchen. In addition to a book, I'd packed a toothbrush, deodorant, makeup, a folding hairbrush, and clean underpants. Obviously, I liked to be prepared. I took a turn in the bathroom when Dylan emerged, then went to join him in bed.

I paused before climbing in beside him, something peeking out of the nightstand drawer catching my eye. "You said you don't smoke."

He followed my gaze and pulled the pack of Lambert & Buster cigarettes out of the drawer. It was unopened, which made me feel a little better. Still, it was definitely too early for the lies to be coming out. "I don't," he insisted.

I rolled my eyes. I hadn't noticed any ashtrays or any cigarette smell on Dylan or any of his things, but still, nonsmokers didn't stash cigarettes in their bedrooms.

"I did smoke, in England, but I don't here."

"Then why do you have this in your bedroom?"

"In case I wanted one."

I frowned, but he simply shrugged. "It doesn't have to be all or nothing. For you Americans, it's either two packs a day or none ever. In England, you can smoke one day a week and not the others. It's the same with food. Here everybody has to overindulge or starve themselves, there's no just enjoying things for what they are and then leaving well enough alone. It's all about moderation."

"It's different. Nicotine is addictive, regardless of the culture."

He shrugged. "Some cultures are more susceptible to addiction because of their obsessive behavior," he said.

I shook my head. It was three o'clock in the morning. I wasn't about to argue with him about the merits of the American way. I climbed into bed beside him and lay back.

He rolled over to face me and pouted. "I'm sorry," he said. "You can't go to sleep upset with me after the perfect night we had. I didn't mean to mislead you. I just don't consider myself a smoker." He tore open the carton, climbed out of bed, and shook the cigarettes into the wastebasket before sliding back under the covers.

I laughed. "I'm not upset." And it was the truth. Part of me suspected I should be, but I was just too damn happy.

He kissed me again, until I forgot any of it had ever happened, and then I fell asleep on my side, his torso pressed against my back, his arm tightly clutching me.

When I awoke, he was gone, as I'd known he would be. Another thing I'd learned about musicians is that they didn't sleep, at least not at normal times.

I glanced at the clock and realized maybe I was wrong. It was nine o'clock. He could've slept all night at my side, and simply gotten up at a more respectable hour. I went into the bathroom and attempted to make myself presentable, but considering I'd left my clothes in the kitchen, that was quite a challenge. I was about to leave the bedroom when I realized I heard voices.

I grimaced, pulled the robe tighter, then inched the door open, peering tentatively into the living room. Dylan and another man immediately turned in my direction. I smiled sheepishly.

"Good morning," Dylan said, coming to the door. "Are you hungry?"

My eyes darted across the room to the other guy, who was still staring. "My clothes," I whispered, quickly looking away.

Dylan grinned, jogged across to the kitchen, and returned with my jeans and tank top. I glanced at the clothes and we both realized my bra was missing at the same time.

The other guy cleared his throat, and to my horror, I saw that my bra was wedged underneath the couch, right by his shoes. He bent down, and held the bra up, dangling it between his fingers.

"Thanks," Dylan said, retrieving it for me.

I blushed, and darted back into the room to get dressed.

When I reemerged, Dylan handed me a cup of coffee. It was then that I got a better look at the other guy and recognized him as Dylan's brother. He was slightly taller, but with similarly impeccable posture and good looks. Thomas had the same lush dark hair as his brother, but fierce emerald eyes instead of rich brown like Dylan.

I smiled politely at him, trying to forget the awkward moment from earlier. "You're Thomas, right?"

He nodded, then turned to Dylan. "You're right, she is gorgeous," he said, as though I wasn't standing there.

"Thomas was just leaving," Dylan said pointedly.

"No, I wasn't. We need to finish this before Monday."

Dylan replied to him, and as both of their voices grew more animated, I was struggling to follow. Initially, I thought they'd transitioned into a foreign language, but then I laughed, realizing their accents were simply thicker when they spoke with each other than with me.

They both paused and turned to me as I laughed. "Sorry. I should be on my way anyhow, so don't let me keep you from your work." I retrieved my purse and started to the door.

"What was so funny?" Thomas asked.

I stared at the ground, embarrassed. "Nothing. You just both sound much more English when you're arguing with each other."

The brothers glanced at each other, and Dylan approached me. "You don't have to go," he said.

I smiled because the look on his face told me he actually meant what he'd said. "You could call me later."

He sighed. "At least let me drive you back."

I shook my head. "You're busy, and besides, I like the subway. It'll give me a chance to read."

He leaned in and pressed his forehead against mine. "I had a lovely time last night," he whispered.

"Me too."

He kissed me then, and I couldn't help but kiss him back, until the point where it grew uncomfortable knowing his brother was in the room, watching. I pulled back and waved at Thomas. "Nice to meet you," I said.

"Pleasure's mine," he replied.

I made my way out of the building and onto the street before realizing I had no idea where I was, or where the closest subway station was. I pulled out my phone to check, but before I'd opened my map app, the doorman was at my side.

"Ms. Mitchell?" he asked.

I nodded.

"Mr. Parker asked me to see that you got a ride home." He motioned and a cab pulled over instantly. He asked my address, and I told him, and before I could protest and insist that I was fine with the subway, he had bent down and was speaking with the driver. I was just starting to panic about the cost of a cab when the doorman retrieved cash from his pocket, paid the driver, and held the door for me. "He'll take you home, and the fare has already been paid."

"Um, thanks," I stammered. I relaxed into the back seat, but instead of reading, I quickly dialed Jill to give her the recap.

I was dying to hear from Dylan the rest of the day, but willed myself not to call. I joined Jill at the gym that evening, determined that Booty Boot Camp was the best way to distract myself.

* * *

STILL DESPERATELY IN need of something to take my mind off of Dylan, I returned to the gym for cardio kickboxing the next morning. I had just exited the locker room, ready to head into work Monday morning, when my phone rang.

It was him. Finally.

"Are you working today?" Dylan asked.

"Yes, why? Do you need another plane?"

He laughed. "My bed felt very empty last night."

I smiled, but was too distracted by thoughts of Dylan's bed to craft a witty reply.

"Lily?"

"Yeah, sorry. Did you and your brother finish up whatever you were working on?"

"Hard to say. We'll know soon enough. We start recording today."

I was impressed. I'd known many performers, even some who wrote a few of the songs they performed, but none that had actually recorded their own albums. Sure, I'd known that Dylan wrote songs and recorded albums before, heck, I even owned two of his albums, but actually hearing him say it was thrilling.

"That's exciting," I finally said.

"I hate recording," he replied. "It's a tedious process that sucks all the life out of a song."

"Really? I would never guess that from listening to your music."

"It takes hours of production to make each minute of song sound seamless and raw."

"Are you recording a whole album?"

"Fuck no. That would take ages. We do one song at a time. We've got the studio three days this week, so we'll work till we've got one song done, then we'll start with the next the following Monday."

"So you're not free till Thursday."

"Sweetheart, I can't wait that long to see you. What about tomorrow night?"

"I work then."

"Tonight?"

"Won't you be working late?"

He hesitated. "Meet me at the studio. I'll introduce you to the band."

"Are you sure?"

"Of course."

"What time?"

"Seven?"

I quickly agreed, and then I heard voices in the background on his line. British voices. We said our goodbyes, and I practically skipped the whole way to work.

CHAPTER THREE

"He could not be mistaken. There were no other eyes like those in
the world.
There was only one creature in the world who could concentrate
for him
all the brightness and meaning of life. It was she."
Leo Tolstoy, *Anna Karenina*

I was excited about meeting the remaining members of
Sierra, thrilled at the prospect of hearing them record
some, and out of my mind with anticipation over more sex with
Dylan. He hadn't given me any direction as to the wardrobe, but
figuring he'd be tired after recording all day, I was confident we
wouldn't go anywhere too fancy.

I went with jeans and a fitted black v-neck. I added a long,
layered necklace and sparkly red pumps for a splash of color. I
took the subway to the station closest to the studio he'd named
then made the rest of the trip by foot. I arrived a little before
seven, like I'd planned, hoping I'd be able to watch a few minutes.
I pulled open the thick door and was momentarily dazed by the
blast of cool air rushing out.

A woman about my age greeted me at the desk.

"Hi. I'm supposed to meet Dylan Parker here."

"They're in studio four. Hold on," she said. She left her desk and returned quickly. A moment later, a balding man in a business suit appeared and came towards me.

He offered his hand, which I shook politely as he introduced himself. "I'm Ari Steiner, Sierra's manager."

"Hi. I'm Lily. Dylan asked me to meet him here."

He nodded as though he already knew that. "They're still going," he said.

"Can I watch?"

He considered this for a moment, then led me to the sound room. There were two guys in jeans working the equipment and another man in suit pants, his jacket draped over the chair. None of them acknowledged my presence. Ari pointed to a seat, so I plopped down and immediately felt myself grinning as I looked out the large window.

Dylan was singing, but I could barely hear him. The bass guitarist was the central sound coming through to the booth.

Ari scooted forward. "We do multi-track recordings, where each person's part is recorded separately then blended later. That way you get a finished product where everyone sounds their best."

I nodded, unable to take my eyes off of Dylan. He seemed tense, and was clearly concentrating. His head was tilted down towards his guitar, and even when he raised his face, I saw that his eyes were closed. When he opened them, he smiled, and I realized he could see me just as clearly as I could see him. His hands left the guitar and he blew me a kiss, the rest of the band continuing to play. The three other guys in the booth all turned to me, as if they'd just realized someone else must be in there.

Another moment passed, and then the guy to my left interrupted them. "Got it. Go back to the chorus and we'll do the next verse one more time."

Dylan stepped forward, flicked off some switch, and then we saw the band members converge and talk.

"Why can't we hear them now?" I asked.

Ari laughed. "Because they don't want us to. They turned off the sound." He paused. "They're talking about you," he added. "They say shit about us all day without the courtesy of muting the mics."

"You're American," I observed, in lieu of responding to what he'd just said.

He nodded. "So are you."

There was a buzz as the band flipped the mics back on. "One more time then it's all for today," Thomas said, his accent so thick that it took me a minute to determine what he'd said.

Somehow, the last run through took a full ten minutes, even though they were only covering one line of the song. Still, I was fascinated by every minute of it.

When they finally stopped, Ari motioned to the door. "You can go in there now," he said.

I thanked him and made my way into the studio. Dylan plopped his guitar into the case and smiled at me.

"Your presence was a little distracting for all of us," he whispered in my ear before kissing me.

I gasped. "I'm sorry. I didn't mean to interrupt, I just…"

He shook his head. "No, you didn't interrupt. I only meant that we're not used to recording with a beautiful woman staring back at us."

I suspected I was still blushing, but he wrapped an arm around me and started to introduce me to the rest of the band. "You know Thomas, and here's Owen, Gavin, and Dave."

"Nice to meet you. I'm a big fan," I said.

They all mumbled various responses and then continued packing up their stuff before shuffling out of the studio.

"One minute," Dylan said, heading to the hall to speak with Ari.

I turned and saw that I was alone in the studio with Thomas. He smiled warmly at me. "You looked like you enjoyed watching," he said.

"I did. It was amazing. I've never seen the recording process."

He raised an eyebrow. "I hope you don't regret it later."

"Why would I?"

"Sometimes seeing the mechanics of it, well, it kills the magic. You can't hear the music anymore without seeing the equipment."

I smiled and got a good look at him as he packed up his guitar. He was maybe an inch taller than Dylan, probably five pounds heavier, and had longer hair, but otherwise strikingly similar features. I got the impression he was the more responsible of the pair, but I wasn't sure if that was just because I knew he was a year older than Dylan or something about the way he carried himself.

Thomas rose, guitar case in hand. "You seem like a nice girl," he said. "Be careful with my brother." His eyes darted towards Dylan, but before I could ask what he meant, he left.

I stood alone in the studio, trying to decipher his words. Clearly, he was concerned. But what I didn't know was whether he was worried about me or his brother. Was he cautioning me not to hurt his brother, or warning me that Dylan might hurt me?

Fortunately, the uneasy feeling left me as soon as Dylan returned. "Are you hungry?" he asked.

I nodded.

We drove to a quiet steakhouse, valet-parked the Porsche, and were seated immediately without a reservation. Clearly, there were perks to dating a celeb. We ordered drinks, a vodka and cranberry for me, a whiskey on the rocks for Dylan, and he requested a refill before we'd even selected our entrees.

"You must be tired," I said.

"I'll manage. So tell me what you thought of the band."

I did, and we spent the first part of the meal talking about how he got to know each of his bandmates and Ari. We ordered another round of drinks while he asked me more details about my work, my college days, and even my family.

He hung on my every word, seemingly oblivious to the other patrons in the restaurant. I found myself similarly mesmerized, eying his lips hungrily as he spoke, eagerly anticipating the touch of his skin against my own.

When the waitress came by to ask if we'd saved room for dessert, we both laughed. She seemed confused, but I knew both Dylan and I were thinking the same thing. He paid the bill quickly and we made our way to the valet stand. He leaned in and kissed me while we waited, ending the kiss too soon, as always.

"Sexy shoes," he whispered, his breath tickling my ear.

"I didn't think men noticed shoes," I said.

"They're Wizard-of-Oz red, Lily. It's hard not to notice."

He tipped the valet and off we drove. We followed the same routine as before, making love on the same couch we'd been on the last time.

After, I stretched out on top of him, and he draped his arms over me, his hands planted firmly on my butt. "I like your view," I said, gazing past the edge of the couch out his window. The city was all lit up for the night, but within the quiet, sterile apartment, all the lights seemed muted.

"This view's not too shabby either," he trilled, eyes locked on my breasts.

"I should probably leave soon," I said. "So you can get some sleep before you start up again tomorrow."

"You could stay here forever," Dylan mumbled, lifting one hand to caress the back of my hair.

We remained still for a while longer, and I wondered if he'd maybe fallen asleep. I lifted my head to glance at him and saw that he was wide awake. "You feel cold," he said.

"A little."

He scooted out from under me. I expected Dylan to grab a

blanket and return, but instead, I heard the bath water running. He emerged from the bathroom with a towel draped around his waist. He went into the kitchen, poured himself a large drink and offered me one. I slipped into the tee shirt he'd been wearing and joined him in the kitchen. I selected a bottle of water and then turned to see that he'd retrieved *Gone with the Wind* from my purse.

He motioned for me to follow him to the bathroom. He tossed the towel and climbed into the tub, placing our drinks and the book on the ledge beside the tub. "Come on. I'll read to you," he said.

I pulled his shirt off over my head and stepped into the tub. He shut off the water and I settled back against his chest, relaxing into the hot water. We soaked quietly for a moment, and then he began to read, his dreamy voice rendering each word even better than it had been written.

I sighed. I was done for, and I knew it. Two real dates and I was falling in love with a man who was, at least on paper, all wrong for me. Nothing good could come from this relationship, I thought, convinced the ominous feeling in the pit of my stomach was based on hard facts that I was a fool to ignore. But I was equally positive that as long as Dylan wanted me, I would be powerless to leave.

He reached the end of a chapter and I slid the book out of his hands, placing it on the edge of the tub. "I like you all slippery," I said, wriggling up against him.

A deep breathy laugh escaped his throat in response. I heard the ice clink from his glass and I turned just as he finished the last of his drink. He took a washcloth and dipped it in the soapy water before gently rubbing it across my stomach and chest and then wringing it out so that warm water trickled across my nipples.

He dropped the washcloth and moved in with his hands, first focusing on my breasts, then sliding them down my body and working his magic between my legs. I felt my heart beat faster and heard my breathing go more frantic, and then he stopped, slipping out from behind me, pulling the drain on the tub.

As the water slowly drained from the bath, he traced his mouth along my body in the same pattern his hands had followed. By the time he reached my inner thighs, only a few inches of water remained. He closed the drain then dragged his tongue along my body, expertly maneuvering it until I couldn't stand the pressure anymore and felt myself explode into wave after wave of pleasure.

Dylan smiled proudly and kissed my stomach. Still dizzy, I sat up, nudged him backwards, and inched closer in the water to return the favor. His hands twisted through my hair while I kissed and licked him, and I knew he was close when his fingers, now tangled in my wet locks, pulled more frantically.

My hair was sopping wet by the time we finally got out of the tub. I rubbed it with a towel as best I could, then paused at the edge of the bathroom door. "What time do you start recording tomorrow?"

"Ten."

"Are you sure you want me to stay? I have to work in the morning too." Technically, I knew I was supposed to be in by nine, but since I was more frequently scheduled to come in at ten or eleven, I figured no one would care—or even notice—if I showed up at ten. I wasn't a full time employee, and since we were never too busy, the only real issue was ensuring I worked enough hours to qualify for my health insurance.

Dylan stepped closer and cupped my breasts in his hands like they were delicate produce. "I am positive I want you to stay."

I borrowed a sleeveless undershirt and shimmied back into my panties before climbing into bed beside him. I nestled into his body, my head resting on his chest and my leg draped over his. He wrapped an arm around my back and pulled the sheets up to my waist. I kissed his chest and he kissed my forehead in return.

I thought about how comfortable this felt, already, as though this was exactly the way the two of us were supposed to be at this moment. I'd never been a big believer in fate, but nothing else explained the coincidental meeting, the instant chemistry, or the eerie feeling I had that I'd been waiting for Dylan my entire life. And then I recalled his brother's statement.

"What's the deal with you and Thomas? Have you two always been close?"

Dylan took his time answering. "No. We were quite competitive as children."

That was easy enough to picture. Two brothers, especially so close in age, would of course have some squabbles as kids. As an only child, I never experienced the camaraderie or competition firsthand, but most of my friends had siblings.

"Our father left when we were young, and we never seemed to accept that our mother had enough attention for both of us. But after..." he paused, and his eyes closed for a moment. "Nevermind."

"Were you a lot alike as kids?"

"We looked alike, 'cept Tom was taller. We both played music and football, or soccer as you'd call it. He always got better grades, and we both spent our fair share of time in the headmaster's office."

I smiled, imagining them as kids. "Why didn't you get better grades? You must have had the aptitude for it. I've never met anyone outside of college that is as familiar with the classics as you are."

"I have a good memory," he said with a laugh. "And I liked reading and writing and books. I've never liked listening or doing as I'm told."

I kissed his chest again, certain that he was just being modest. Soon, I felt my eyelids flitter shut as I listened to the rhythmic beating of his heart.

I awakened the next morning around eight, and miraculously,

Dylan was still asleep. *Wrong again*, I thought, deciding none of my musician generalities applied to him. I crept out of bed and snuck into the bathroom to assess the condition of my hair. Surprisingly, it had dried tamely, falling into soft waves with less frizz than I'd expected after the hot bath the night before. I washed my face and put on my makeup and deodorant, brushed my teeth, and then realized I needed to go home to change into clean clothes before heading in to work.

When I emerged from the bathroom, Dylan was awake and typing something on his phone. When he saw me, he quickly set the phone face down on his nightstand. I stepped closer to tell him I needed to leave, and he pulled me onto the bed, quickly flipping me onto my back and scooting on top of me. We kissed, and I still smelled the whiskey on his breath from the night before. He slid his hands inside the sides of the shirt and I squirmed at the tickling sensation.

As I wriggled away from him, his phone buzzed, and I glanced over at it. I noticed then the half-empty glass his drink had been in the night before. "Have you been drinking this morning?" I asked, more curious than anything else.

He shook his head at this ridiculous notion. "I couldn't sleep last night, so I got up and made another drink. But then I missed you and came back to bed." He started to lift the shirt up over my head.

"We can't do that now. I have to go. I need to get home, put on some decent clothes, and get back to work."

He glanced at the clock. "I'll be quick."

"Gee, as tempting as that is…"

He flashed an adorable pouty face and I couldn't say no.

Fifteen minutes later, we were on our feet, feeling much more relaxed.

"I should go," I repeated.

He sighed. "Someday, I'll make you breakfast."

I smiled and leaned in for a kiss before quickly dressing in my prior night's outfit.

"Was the taxi ride okay the other day?" he asked.

I nodded. "It was. Thanks. You know, your doorman paid the driver though."

Dylan grinned. "I reimbursed him. And I already paid for today's, so no taking the subway."

* * *

I COULD BARELY CONCENTRATE at work that day. I kept ambling to the Keurig in the break room in hopes of the excess caffeine and yummy scents helping me focus, but it was useless. All I could think about was Dylan—his smooth voice, that seductive accent, his dark eyes, and that perfect, skilled body of his. Desperate, I slipped in headphones and tried listening to Sierra's latest album. Within minutes, I saw that my office phone line was ringing.

"Good morning, this is Lily Mitchell. What can I do for you?" I asked, cringing when I realized it was well past noon…hardly morning.

"I had a travel question." The caller needn't say his name—I knew immediately it was Dylan.

"Hey there, aren't you supposed to be recording?"

"We're taking a break. Thomas needed a throat lozenge."

"Ah."

"About my travel question. You know that plane you booked for us?"

"Uh huh."

"None of us are familiar with the company. I thought we'd feel better if our travel representative accompanied us on the flight."

"Um…" I frowned. I had no idea what the protocol was on that, or even why that would be an issue.

"Lily?"

48

"Yeah, I'm just not sure..."

His deep gravelly chuckle interrupted me. "Lily, I'm just inviting you to Los Angeles with me. I need a date for the awards show. I thought if you went as our travel agent, you could get off work easier."

I smiled. He wanted me to go to Los Angeles with him. On a private plane. To an awards show. I tap-danced my feet around the plastic floor covering beneath my desk chair. "Let's see, you're leaving on Saturday and returning on Tuesday, right?" I glanced through my calendar. I'd have to take the whole weekend off at the club, but it would be worth it. "Okay, if you're sure."

Dylan laughed. "Of course I'm sure. I asked you, didn't I? I better go now. I'll ring you later."

He hung up quickly, leaving me doe-eyed as I realized I'd need to find a dress by the weekend.

I immediately phoned Jill, hoping to recruit her for some lunchtime dress shopping the following day. She agreed, and I went back to being unable to focus on my work.

* * *

JILL AND I met at the mall the next day at noon. By that point, I'd gone nearly twenty-four hours without talking to Dylan and was beyond eager to at least talk about him. Jill focused on the dresses, eying each price tag with horror as I fingered the soft materials, certain I could find the right dress by touch.

We both paused by the perfect gown. It was a rich plum-colored evening gown, with a plunging neckline and delicate beading around the bodice. It was breathtaking. I was already picturing my shoe collection to determine if I'd need to purchase a matching pair when Jill swatted my hand away.

"Stop touching it," she cautioned. "I read somewhere that the longer you touch the material, the more likely you are to buy it."

"But it's stunning," I said.

"And nine hundred dollars," she said, tugging me along.

I grimaced. That was two weeks' pay at the travel agency. If I added in the new shoes, I was probably looking at my weekend pay from the club too. "Jill, come on. It's worth a splurge. When am I ever going to have an opportunity like this again?"

She rolled her eyes. "Lil, that's my point. It would be a reasonable expense *if* you'd have another opportunity to wear it, but for one night, that's insane! Let's go look at prom dresses. You could easily squeeze into a Junior's size."

I stood firm and snatched a 4 off the rack. "Just let me try it on," I urged.

That earned me another eye roll from Jill.

I hurried into the dressing room before she could discourage me. Generally, I'm Ms. Negativity in those tiny, poorly lit stalls of hell, but even I couldn't pretend that this dress didn't accentuate my every asset while hiding all of my flaws. It was a match made in heaven. I waltzed out of the dressing room, a huge I-told-you-so grin plastered on my face.

I twirled around in front of Jill and she nodded, much more calmly than I would've liked. She should've been jumping around with me. I mean, what were the chances—finding the perfect dress on the first try?

"It's beautiful," she finally admitted. "But you are the most gorgeous woman I know, so you'll look great in a two-hundred dollar dress."

I handed her my phone. "We'll let Dylan decide. Take my picture."

She begrudgingly agreed. I quickly texted him the photo along with the message "For the show Monday...worth the splurge?"

I changed back into my work clothes while I awaited a response. I wasn't sure if he'd respond at all, since they were still in the middle of recording, but I got a response before Jill and I even reached the shoe department.

It said "You're stunning. Won't match the red shoes though."

I laughed and showed Jill. She sighed, defeated. Then my phone buzzed again.

"Where are you?" this text read.

I replied, just as I found the perfect pair of shoes. They were a metallic charcoal color with just enough shimmer to compliment the dress perfectly.

"Let's put it all on hold, go get some food, and then if you still want to buy, we'll come back," Jill suggested.

I conceded. I knew I wouldn't change my mind, but this way I could appease Jill. The saleslady was on the phone as I approached, jotting something on a piece of paper. I waited patiently, then asked her to hold the items for me. She nodded, pulled out a hold tag, and asked my name.

"Huh, that's good timing," she said, a peculiar look on her face. "I just got a phone call from a gentleman asking me to put whatever you purchased on his credit card."

My eyes widened. Jill and I exchanged excited grins. "A British guy?"

The saleslady nodded. "Still want to put them on hold?"

I laughed. "No way, I'll take it!"

Purchases in hand, we meandered to the food court. "See, that's why I like him so much," I said as we sampled the bourbon chicken.

"Because he buys you expensive stuff?"

"No, because he's always surprising me. He's just so sweet in such unexpected ways."

Jill smiled. "Plus he buys you expensive stuff."

"Yeah," I grinned. We both knew I wasn't with him for the money, especially based on my history of only dating broke guys, but anyone who said they didn't like a free dress was either lying or insane.

We both decided on chicken sandwiches, and soon we were seated at the table.

"So tell me more about him," Jill urged. "I haven't gotten any details since the day after your first date."

"We're calling that our third date, remember?"

She grinned, knowing exactly what I meant. As my best friend, she was privy to all the juicy details.

"Honestly, I think I'm falling in love with him. At first it was just physical attraction, well, and that accent, but he's just so charming." I closed my eyes and remembered him playing the piano for me. "He's perfect."

Jill slurped her Diet Coke loudly.

"What?"

"Nothing."

"You don't believe me that I'm falling in love?"

"No, I do," she insisted. "You always fall in love with guys when you barely know them. And then they just continue being perfect in your mind long after they start being horrific in reality."

"He's different."

Our eyes locked and she smiled warmly. "I hope so."

* * *

THE FLIGHT to L.A. was nothing like I'd expected. Instead of being romantic and mysterious, it was stressful and loud. Apparently, the band still had to figure out exactly what they were doing for their performance and I ended up trying my hardest to tune them all out while reading.

Once we arrived, though, things were better.

Dylan and I spent the afternoon exploring the town. He'd been there before, of course, so he was showing me all the highlights he thought I'd enjoy, saving time for a romantic L.A. meal and perfect sex back at the hotel. The next day, the band had to do a dress rehearsal for the awards show, leaving me with a few hours to myself. Like any rational broke girl, I spent the time shopping on Rodeo Drive. I didn't buy much, but it felt amazing to even be shopping in the same stores that I'd seen Julia Roberts explore so many years before in one of my favorite movies of all time.

Dylan was affectionate when we were together, more so than any of my past boyfriends. He held my hand when we walked, kissed me in front of other people, and actually looked at me when I spoke.

But the awards show was an entirely different story. I'd expected glamour, and while the fashion was thrilling, the atmosphere at large was anything but glamorous.

Dylan had started drinking hours before the show, a fact which visibly stressed Thomas, who was already a nervous wreck. And as soon as the show started, I was seated with strangers while the band waited backstage for their performance. The band's single-song performance went smoothly, despite Dylan's inebriation, and then he was able to sit with me during the rest of the lengthy show.

By the time we left the theater, I was exhausted and ready to switch into my PJs, but apparently, we were scheduled to attend a party. It was mostly musical people there, and a few C-list actors I wasn't familiar with, and there was tons of drinking, smoking, and probably drugs. Dylan, the apparent party boy, fit right in, flitting from one group of people to the next, sharing a drink with nearly everyone he reached.

After I while, I stopped following him around, content to simply sit on a couch and chill. I even lost track of him for fifteen minutes or so, but when he returned to me, he was even more animated than before, despite the late hour.

When we left the party, Dylan was still manically hyper. I tried to be excited for him, figuring he was just wound up after the performance, but I was tired. We made love back at the hotel, and then I fell asleep, aware that Dylan had already snuck back out of the room to write new songs or whatever he did in lieu of sleeping.

The next day, Dylan was groggy and cranky, but I couldn't really blame him. The man had hardly slept. After some coffee and breakfast, we were both good to go, and had one final day to enjoy the beautiful L.A. day.

CHAPTER FOUR

"You should be kissed and often, and by someone who knows
how."
Margaret Mitchell, *Gone with the Wind*

*T*he week after we returned from L.A. was idyllic. Dylan
and I were in that honeymoon stage of a new relationship, where we were still perfect in each other's eyes and still
spending exorbitant amounts of time in bed together, but past
the awkwardness of the initial getting-to-know-you period.
Floral arrangements magically appeared on my desk at work,
text messages ranging from sweet to seductive to downright
pornographic kept my phone buzzing, and I returned home at
night to find the Porsche idling in front of my apartment.

We saw each other whenever we could—grabbing breakfast
together before I went to work or sneaking long lunches at mid-
day. One night, Dylan even came with me to the club, although
aside from talking with my boss briefly, he hid out at a back table
in the corner, probably hoping to avoid recognition. It was late

when I finally got off work, but he was still there, waiting patiently in the corner.

"I thought you'd leave by now," I said with a smile as I untied my short black apron.

"Why would I leave alone when I'd have a chance to leave with you later?"

I leaned in and kissed him. He broke off the kiss, slid his sunglasses over his face, and wrapped his arm around my waist as we headed out the door.

"What'd you think of the band?" I asked. The band playing that night was a regular, or at least as regular as we ever got. They'd played at the club three other times and seemed pretty decent to me.

He shrugged. "I wasn't here for the band, sweetheart." He flashed me a look that told me exactly what he was there for, and suddenly, I'd lost my train of thought.

We made it all the way to the bedroom this time, and within an hour, we'd had great sex, showered, and returned to bed. I started to slip into a tank top and panties when his hand reached for mine.

"Why don't you sleep without that?" he suggested, tossing the clothes onto the floor. "I love when you sleep naked."

I smiled. "It's cold."

He pulled me into bed. "I'll keep you warm."

I couldn't exactly argue with that. We cuddled in bed, both of us enjoying the knowledge that we didn't have to be up early in the morning. We talked extensively, his deep voice soothing me close to sleep. There was a lull in the dialogue and I thought he'd fallen asleep, but then he spoke.

"I can't stand the thought of a month away from you," he mumbled. "You're all I think about now and I see you all the time."

That roused me fully. I flipped over so my chest was pressed against his, propping my head up to face him. "Where are you going? A full month?"

He smoothed my hair back. "England. Not for a couple more weeks though."

I couldn't hide my disappointment. I recognized this moment well—the point in a relationship where my knight in shining armor started to bum me out. "Are you going on tour?"

"Not really. A couple of concerts, and some filming for music video."

I sighed. It wasn't like he was ditching me because he wanted to, but still…I'd been with one too many guys who spent more time out of town than in it, and I didn't want that again. Especially not now, when we were so happy.

I tried not to focus on the reality of the situation. I'd always known any relationship I had with Dylan could never be more than a fling, but I had yet to accept the fact that the fling might be ending so soon. Obviously Dylan wasn't planning on maintaining a long-distance relationship with me while he spent a month abroad on a glamorous rockstar work trip.

"A month is really long," I finally said, hoping the answer didn't sound too pathetic but unsure of what else to say.

"You'll miss me," he teased.

"Of course I will."

He wrapped his arms around my back and scooted my body until I was fully on top of him. "You could come with me."

"I'd get fired," I said gloomily, without even considering the invitation. "And you'll be busy and won't want me around."

"I always want you around," he said. "Surely you have some vacation time saved up?"

I laughed. I was pretty sure the club didn't offer vacation time, and while the travel agency did, it was a meager two weeks per year.

"Fine, then fuck the concerts. I'll just stay here. I can't stand seeing you this sad."

I smiled. I suspected he was kidding, but still, it was flattering.

"You'd love London," Dylan mused. "And the English country-side is gorgeous this time of year. Besides, I'd make a great tour guide. And just think of all the depressing British romances you could read on the plane. *Wuthering Heights, Jane Eyre…*"

At the first mention of a Brontë sister, I lifted my head to face him. "You really want me to come?"

He nodded. "I can't last that long without you, Lily. You have to come. I'll send you our itinerary tomorrow and you just tell me what days you want to come and go. You can stay as long as you like, and I'll pay for everything."

"You're serious?" I was already picturing myself strolling around the streets of London, my arm looped around Dylan's.

"Dead serious."

"Then okay. I should be able to come for two weeks." I relaxed against him, every drop of tension leaving me as fast as it had appeared.

Then I realized another possible problem. "Except…"

"What?"

"Well, I usually go see my parents and eat dinner with them a few Sundays a month, and they already know I've been seeing someone since I've blown them off a couple times, and I didn't tell them about L.A., but I know I couldn't keep a whole trip to another country secret, and…"

"Lily, you're rambling."

"Oh. Sorry. I just meant that I'll have to tell them about you because they'll ask why I'm finally traveling abroad and who I'm going with and then they'll want to meet you."

"Okay," he interrupted calmly.

"Okay what?"

Dylan looked confused. "Didn't you just say you wanted me to meet your parents?"

I nodded, although he certainly was more concise than I'd been.

"Well, okay to that. I'm free Sunday."

I smiled again and kissed him, certain I must be dreaming.

* * *

THE NEXT MORNING, I called home.

"Oh Lily, how are you?" My mother asked, before I'd even said hello.

I opened my mouth to answer, but she continued. "You just have to come see my begonias soon. They are just spreading like wildflowers this year. I think it must be because we didn't plant any petunias. Your father always says, 'don't plant too many begonias, those petunias are prettier to look at,' but he just doesn't know what he's talking about."

I paused at the break in her rambling, uncertain whether she was done.

"Lily?" my mom said, clearly suspecting I'd hung up.

I laughed. "I'm good, Mom. That's great about the flowers. Weren't they blooming the last time I visited a couple weeks ago?"

She scoffed. "Why no, I'd only just planted them then. You'll have to come back now. You know your father will give you money for the train."

"Actually, that's why I called, to see about visiting."

"You know us. Anytime is a good time. Just let me know in advance, and I'll make a pot roast. And some of those potatoes you like. You still eat potatoes, right? I keep reading about these silly low-carb diets where you lose weight by not eating potatoes and bread. Sounds like the sort of thing you'd see a lot of in New York."

"I still eat potatoes, Mom."

"Well, good."

It always amused me how my parents spoke of New York lately, often implying I lived in some far away galaxy where everyone wrote backwards and eschewed shoes. In reality, my parents met in New York City. At the time, my father was a banker working in Manhattan and my mother was studying for her real estate license in her family's home in Brooklyn. When they married, they migrated to Queens. When I was born, they skipped just across the border, to Jersey City. When I left for college, they relocated to their current home, in Patterson, New Jersey.

"So how about Sunday?"

"What about it?"

"Would that be a good time for me to come by?"

"Sure, sure. I'll make the pot roast. Maybe I'll see if your grandmother wants to come too."

My dad's mom lived in a nursing home in Queens. She was healthy as a horse, but mentally not quite all there lately. I loved her dearly, but sometimes she turned simple family dinners into a fiasco.

"Actually, Mom, would it be okay if I brought someone with me? I wanted to introduce you to someone. Then we could invite Grandma another time."

My mother was quiet for a minute and then I could just hear her cheeks widen into a smile. "A friend? A coworker? Or a date?"

I rolled my eyes. We both knew exactly what kind of a "someone" I meant. "My boyfriend, Dylan."

"I didn't know you had a boyfriend. Why haven't you mentioned him before?"

I think we both knew why. The last boyfriend I'd introduced them to, Rex, had offered to meet me at my parents' house after playing a gig in Atlantic City the night before. He'd shown up two hours late, clearly hung-over, and the whole ordeal was like watching a train wreck.

"I'm telling you now." I sighed. "We haven't been dating that long. I really like him, though."

"Where did you meet him?" This was my mother's subtle way

of ascertaining whether he was another struggling artist I'd seen at Echo.

"Outside of a coffee shop. It was raining and I didn't have an umbrella, and my…"

"Why didn't you have an umbrella? Do you own one? We have plenty of umbrellas. I'll leave some out for you to take Sunday. You should always have an umbrella."

"Mom, that's really not relevant to the story. Can I finish?" I paused before continuing. "As I was saying, my shoe got stuck in a drainage grate and along came Dylan with an umbrella and he helped me get my shoe free and then bought me coffee."

"Well that's nice. Is he employed?"

Clearly, my parents don't have a lot of faith in my taste in men. "Yes. He has a job, a nice apartment with no roommates, and a car."

She had no snappy response to this, so I smiled, victorious. This weekend, I would finally know what it felt like to have my parents approve of someone I dated.

"Is he a native new Yorker?"

"No, he's from England."

"England, North Dakota?"

"No, England, the country, near Ireland. Wait, there's a town called England in North Dakota?"

"I think so," she paused. "Maybe it's New England, North Dakota. What's an Englishman doing in New York?"

"He's been really successful at his work and New York City is just the best place for his career right now."

"What career is that?"

And here came the tricky part. I knew that as soon as I told her he was a musician, she'd make the same mistake I had and assume he was like all my other boyfriends. I had to phrase it perfectly, and talk fast.

"Actually, he's a songwriter and recording artist. He and his brother Thomas sing and play guitar for the band, Sierra. He's not like the other musicians I've dated, though. He's a really hard worker and they've produced actual albums, with terrific sales, they have music videos, they go on concert tours. He's the real deal."

My mother was quiet for a moment, and then summed up everything I'd said. "Your new boyfriend plays in a band with his brother."

I sighed. "Just give him a chance, Mom. I really like this one."

"You really liked all of the others at the start, too. Let me guess, he hasn't started touring yet, but he's assured you it'll all still work out when he does?"

"He's different. You'll see that."

"I hope so. Does he like cheesecake?"

"Everyone likes your cheesecake, Mom."

"No, remember that one you brought home a few years ago, what was his name? The one who said dairy made him gassy?"

Ah, yes. That would be Rob. Another embarrassing page from my dating history. "I'm sure Dylan will love whatever you make, Mom. We'll see you Sunday."

CHAPTER FIVE

"I only know that I love you. That's your misfortune."
Margaret Mitchell, *Gone with the Wind*

*W*e arrived at my parents' house at quarter till six on Sunday, earning major bonus points for being fifteen minutes early. My father was immediately impressed by the Porsche, interrogating Dylan on the ins and outs of its engine and maximum speed before I even had a chance to formally introduce him. My mom came out a few minutes later, wearing a spotless apron over her Sunday dress.

She smiled warmly. "You must be Dylan. We've heard so much about you. Welcome to our home. You can call me Beth."

He leaned forward and kissed my mother on the cheek, catching her off guard. Then, he handed her a bouquet of flowers. "I brought these for you," he said, "But they can hardly hold a candle to those gorgeous begonias."

My mom's hand rose to her chest as if he'd just told her she won the lottery. I wasn't sure if it was the accent, the flowers, or the compliment that had the biggest effect on her. She took the bouquet and then insisted on dragging him around the house for a tour of her other garden beds. I pried my dad away from the Porsche and we made our way inside.

The dinner went smoothly, with Dylan cheerfully eating all the food my mother had prepared, all while gushing about how tasty it was and what a treat a homemade meal was these days. He told amusing anecdotes, laughed convincingly at my dad's less humorous ones, and even offered to help my mom with the dishes, which she of course refused, insisting I assist instead.

I loaded the dishwasher while my mom hand-washed the pots, pans, and serving dishes. Dylan and my father retired to the back porch with coffee.

"It seems like Dad and Dylan are getting along," I said nonchalantly.

"Mmm hmm," she replied.

I sighed. "And what do you think?"

"About what, dear?"

"About Dylan."

"What about him?"

I slammed the dishwasher shut. "Just admit it already. You like him. I can tell."

My mother calmly folded the dishtowel beside the sink and turned to me. "He seems like a nice man. Not at all what I was expecting."

I smirked.

"Do you think he liked the meal okay? I would've made something fancier if I'd known he was so well off."

"I'm sure he loved the pot roast."

"What is it they eat in England? Mutton? Fish and chips? Black pudding? What is in that, anyway? I know it's not really a pudding."

I laughed. My mother's train of thought was on a remarkably screwy track, but she gave me the perfect lead in for what I needed to tell her.

"I'll have to find out," I said. "Dylan invited me to go to England with him in a couple weeks."

"Ooh, that will be nice. What's the weather like there now?"

I frowned. "Um, I don't know. Probably hot. I would think about the same as here. It's summer, anyway."

"Well, of course it's summer; it's not Australia." She paused, pouring herself another cup of coffee. "You won't have any trouble missing work?"

I shook my head, although I wasn't entirely positive of that fact yet. "I'll only miss two weeks. I never take time off anyway, so it's fine. Dylan has to be there for five weeks."

She raised an eyebrow. "Is his family still there?"

"His mother is. His brother lives in the same apartment building as him."

"Where's his father?"

I shrugged. "He left when Dylan was little."

"That's too bad. And his mother never remarried?"

"Guess not."

"Humfh."

I wasn't sure how to interpret her final grunt, but the dishes were done, and I was eager to rescue Dylan from my father. But when I reached the porch, I saw that my haste wasn't warranted. Dylan, who was laughing jovially at some oddball story my dad was telling as much with his charade-like gestures as with words, winked at me.

I squeezed onto the creaky porch swing beside him, and his arm reached around my back. My dad continued his monologue, unfazed even when Dylan's other hand came to rest on my thigh. I felt my heart flutter and knew this was a first—my parents both actually liked someone that I also liked.

My mother joined us on the porch and the surreal pleasant-ness continued. But I was nervous—there was no way this could go on indefinitely. Sooner or later, someone was going to say something to offend or horrify someone else, and the evening would be ruined. I stood abruptly.

"I have to work in the morning. We should get going," I said.

My mother frowned, and Dylan bit his lip—clearly trying not to laugh at me. My father nodded amicably though, shook Dylan's hand, and sent us on our way.

"Your family is exactly what I expected," Dylan told me as we drove off.

"Is that a good thing?"

He laughed. "Yes, of course. Your mother and father are both lovely. And everything about them is just so normal."

I winced, dozens of examples of abnormal behavior on the part of my parents jumping to mind.

We reached a red light and Dylan turned to me, grabbing my hand. Our eyes locked.

"I love you, Lily," he said.

I felt my eyes widen. I hadn't been expecting that at all. I was always the first one to say it in relationships, always. And honestly, it usually seemed like the guy just said it to pacify me, but Dylan said it with complete sincerity.

"I love you too," I said, leaning in for a kiss.

A car honked loudly, and we both glanced up. The light was green.

Dylan waved and cruised into the intersection. I laughed.

"What?" he asked.

"I can tell you're not from here. A true New Yorker would've given them the finger."

He shrugged. "I must just be in a good mood."

I smiled contentedly.

"I hadn't meant to tell you like that, you know," he said. "I planned to tell you during a boat ride on the Thames, or maybe at sunset on the top of Primrose Hill, but I just couldn't wait."

"You could tell me again then," I said, not wanting to admit that my subpar geography skills left me less than certain that those were London locations.

He nodded. We made small talk the rest of the drive, but my heart kept pounding wildly.

"Did you ever wish you had a sibling?" he asked me as we walked up to his apartment, hand in hand.

"Constantly. Whenever I was bored, I wished I had a brother or sister to play with." I laughed at the memories. "I used to pretend I had a twin sister, sort of like an imaginary friend, I guess."

He smiled. There was a lengthy silence before he spoke again. "I sometimes wonder if it would have been easier, being an only child."

"But you and your brother are so close," I said. I couldn't fathom a scenario where it would be better in any way to not have that. I glanced at Dylan and noticed a sadness in his eyes.

"Yes," he finally said, his voice uneven. He opened his mouth as though he intended to say more, then stopped.

I just knew there was something he was considering telling me, and a big part of me wanted to ask. But, I was determined not to be the naggy girlfriend, so I kept quiet. When we got to his apartment, we made love, but then I still sensed something off with Dylan.

He kissed my forehead. "You have to work tomorrow," he remembered. "You should get some sleep." He climbed out of bed.

"You're not going to sleep?"

Dylan shook his head. "I think I'm going to work for a bit," he said. He turned back at me and smiled. "I love you."

I grinned and snuggled down under the covers. Dylan left, and a moment later, I heard the clinking of ice in a glass, followed by the clicking of the door to his studio shutting. And then there was silence, so I fell asleep.

When I awoke to the buzzing of the alarm, I was smiling. He

loves me, I thought, sighing whimsically. I rolled over to face Dylan's side of the bed, which was empty and clearly untouched. I stretched and went to the bathroom before shuffling out to the living room, expecting to see him asleep on the couch. But he wasn't there, or in his studio, or anywhere in the apartment. In the kitchen, I found an empty bottle of bourbon laying on its side near the sink, but no note or other indication of Dylan's whereabouts.

I switched on the coffee pot and decided to shower and get ready for work, assuming he'd return soon. When he still wasn't back after I'd dressed and dried my hair, I briefly panicked, then reached an obvious solution—calling him.

He answered on the fourth ring, right when I expected voice mail to pick up. His voice was hushed and deeper than usual.

"Hey there," I said. "Where are you? I woke up and was all alone."

There was a shuffling sound, then a muffled "hang on," followed by silence. I grabbed a banana from the fruit basket while I waited for him to respond. There was a clicking at the door, then it started open. I hung up the phone and turned with a smile for Dylan, but it wasn't him.

Instead, Thomas poked his head in the door, a nervous look in his eyes. Dylan's cell phone was clutched in his hand. When he saw me, he pushed the door fully open and placed the phone on the counter.

"You had Dylan's phone?"

Thomas nodded. "He's at my place. Are you okay?"

I frowned. "Yeah, of course."

He seemed oddly relieved.

"What's he doing at your apartment?" I asked.

Thomas avoided eye contact with me. "Sleeping."

I poured myself a cup of coffee and offered him one. He accepted. Then I noticed he looked a little tired himself. "I'm sorry if I woke you. I just had no idea where he was, and I was about to leave for work."

He nodded. "I can lock up."

I slipped into my shoes and surveyed the room to find my purse. "Were you guys working together last night? What time did he come over? I didn't even know he left."

Thomas frowned. "Uh, he came over around two, maybe three. He was pretty tired."

"Then why didn't he just come to bed? Is he avoiding me?" I knew that I was starting to sound like a paranoid girlfriend, but it was a little suspect. He told me he loved me and then left his own apartment so he could sleep with his brother instead of me? Why wouldn't he just come back to bed with me?

Thomas sighed, and I could tell he was uncomfortable. I really didn't understand him anyway. I thought I was a likable person, and most people tended to agree, but Thomas clearly wasn't my biggest fan. Whenever he was near me, Thomas seemed nervous or agitated. And he rarely made eye contact with me.

"He was drunk," Thomas finally said. "He probably just didn't want to bother you."

I turned quickly so he wouldn't see my disappointed look, took another sip of the coffee and loaded the mug in the dishwasher. "I guess I'll see you later," I said, starting out of the apartment before I started to cry.

"Lily, wait," Thomas said.

I paused but didn't face him.

"Dylan really likes you," he said after a long silence.

I rolled my eyes. "Right."

* * *

DYLAN SENT a text while I was at work, telling me they'd be recording or rehearsing or something until late that night. No apology, no explanation for his odd behavior, nothing. He called Tuesday and invited me out for Tuesday evening, but of course I was scheduled to work then. And frankly, by that point, I'd had nearly thirty-six hours to overanalyze his weird behavior Sunday night and I was leaning more towards irritated than confused.

"I miss you," he said.

There was a lengthy silence.

"Are you mad at me?" Surprise filled his tone.

I wasn't sure how to answer this. His complete oblivion threw me. "Dylan, you said you loved me and then you disappeared for the night."

"I was only at my brother's."

"I know, but...you started acting strange right after you said it. If you want to take it back, you can."

There was a pause, and then he laughed. "I don't want to take it back, Lily. I love you. I apologize if my behavior made you question that. I didn't mean to act strangely, but I was thinking about work and once I start thinking about that, I find it hard to focus on anything else."

"You could've come to bed when you finished."

He didn't answer, so I continued.

"Thomas said you were drunk."

"Sometimes I drink when I write."

I sighed. I wanted to move on. He said he loved me again, and it wasn't like I suspected him of doing anything too clandestine in the night. "What were you writing?"

"I can't tell you."

"Dylan."

He laughed, in a sexy deep voice. "It's a surprise, Lil."

"What kind of surprise?"

"The kind I think you'll love when it's finished."

I grinned. "Okay, I can live with that."

"Are you really working tonight?"

"Yeah."

"Come over after?"

I was tempted. I knew it would be late, and I'd be tired. Then

I'd be even more tired by Wednesday at Skyward. But I didn't have to be in until noon Wednesday, so it could work. "Okay."

"I can pick you up."

"You don't have to. It'll be late."

"I know. I'll listen to the music this time."

Somehow, knowing I'd see him later made the rest of my day pass more quickly.

I looked for Dylan each time I made my rounds through the bar, delivering drinks and wings, collecting empty bottles. At a quarter till twelve, he still wasn't there, so I assumed he'd changed his mind.

Not a big deal, I told myself. I'd just walk home.

Then, I felt a hand on my shoulder and turned quickly, eager to see the man who loved me.

But instead, it was Ryan, the drummer for the band that had just finished their first set. They had played at the club numerous times, and were planning to record an album and attempt a small tour around the northeast in the next year. We had a comfortable friendship by this point, based largely on frequent heavy doses of meaningless flirting.

"How did we sound tonight?" he asked, squeezing my hip in an overly familiar way.

I smiled. "A little raw. I like the last song. I hadn't heard that before."

"Raw, huh?" He seemed to consider that. "Yeah, I guess that's about right. It's new, the last song," he added.

"You want a beer?"

He shook his head. "Now if you were offering a body shot, I might be tempted…"

"Yeah, well, not tonight."

"You got plans later? Me and the guys are going out for coffee and pancakes after our last set."

I nodded. "That sounds good. I'll have to see when I'm finished here tonight. Good luck," I said, and I returned to my work. It was mid-week, so the club wasn't exactly busy, but I still didn't want to fall behind.

"So that's who you'd leave with if I didn't show up?" Dylan asked, startling me as he spoke.

"When did you get here?" I asked as he pulled me in for a long, inappropriate kiss.

"Just in time to hear you make a date with the little drummer boy."

I couldn't tell if he was jealous, teasing, or angry. The accent, especially in the noisy club, made it harder for me to decipher his tone. "His name's Ryan, and it wasn't a date. He's not my type."

"Yes he is."

I laughed. "Come on, I'll get you a table."

The next hour was calm, so I actually sat down and watched a few songs with Dylan, and then I just needed to close up my tables before I could go. The band began clearing off the set and packing up their stuff as the club was emptying.

I saw Ryan across the club as he spoke to the guitarist, then he caught my eye and started across the room to me.

"You guys sounded really good at the end there," I told him.

His face lit up. "You think? We're really struggling with some of the new songs."

I shrugged. "I couldn't tell."

"So, it looks like you're done here," he said. "You coming with us?"

I opened my mouth to speak, then felt a hand on the small of my back.

"Sorry, but I think she'll be coming with me," Dylan said.

I watched Ryan's face morph from irritation to excitement as he recognized the face, or possibly even the voice. "Oh my god, you're Dylan Parker. Nice to meet you, dude."

Dylan politely shook Ryan's hand. "Pleasure," he replied coolly.

"Wait, did you hear us play?"

Dylan glanced at me uncomfortably, then nodded. "You have good control," he said. "Your bassist needs to slow down, though."

Ryan nodded, seemingly processing this random tip. Then he turned to me. "You didn't tell me you knew Dylan. Are you two like, dating?"

It was a pointless question, since Dylan had wound his arm so tightly around me by this time that the only possibilities other than us being romantically involved were a three-legged race or a kidnapping attempt. But I simply smiled and nodded.

"We better get going," I said. "I'll hang out with you guys some other time."

Ryan nodded and we walked away.

"No you won't," Dylan whispered in my ear.

"I don't like jealous men," I told Dylan as we walked out.

"Good. I don't like women who make me jealous," he replied.

The look in his eyes told me he meant it.

CHAPTER SIX

Help your brother's boat across, and your own will reach the
shore.
~Hindu Proverb

On Saturday night, Dylan asked me to call him before I left work. I did, and he promptly insisted on picking me up. I suspected he might still be worried I'd head home with Ryan if left to my own devices, but I agreed anyway, desperate to spend as much time with Dylan as possible before he left the following evening. Dylan sent me a text when he arrived, so I hurried out and climbed into the Porsche.

I leaned in to kiss him and he laughed, wrinkling his nose.

"Gee thanks," I mumbled, certain I smelled like fried chicken and beer from waiting tables on one of the club's busiest nights of the month.

"You're still gorgeous."

"Can I shower as soon as we get to your place?"

"Only if I can join you," he replied.

We made a beeline for the bathroom when we reached his apartment, peeling off our clothes between kisses. I stepped into the shower first, rinsing my hair, then turning to face the streaming water. Dylan climbed in behind me, grabbed the bar of soap, and began gently sudsing up my arms and stomach before slipping his soapy hands up over my breasts.

His thumbs tickled my nipples and I groaned. He stepped closer and his groin pressed into my lower back, showing me just how happy he was to see me. Dylan kissed my neck and ear while his hands continued working their magic. He slowly worked one hand downward, his fingers gliding across my thigh before landing firmly in between my legs.

I felt my heart rate increase, my breathing grow frantic, and the pressure in my groin intensify. And just when I had to have been at most a minute away from the most pleasurable sensations imaginable, Dylan swiveled me around to face him.

We kissed for a moment, and I eagerly nudged his hand back into place. Dylan smirked, clearly loving the effect he'd had on me, but shook his head. He lifted me off the ground, pressing my back into the wall, and my legs wrapped around his waist. But just as he was about to push into me, I broke off the kiss.

"We can't do this here," I said, breathless.

"Why not?"

"No condom," I said, struggling to focus since he'd resumed kissing my neck.

"One time won't matter," he replied.

"It only takes once."

He sighed, then hoisted me up a few more inches until he could reach my breasts with his mouth. "I promise I won't get you pregnant."

Normally, I'd laugh at this type of impossible assurance, but that hadn't even been my primary concern. I mean, Dylan was a rock star; I'd seen the groupies firsthand. He seemed like a clean, loyal man, but we hadn't exactly talked about our sexual histories yet. I was on the pill, but despite that, I was a cautious person in that department, essentially assuming every man I kissed had an STD until he'd proven otherwise.

Dylan's tongue raked along my nipple and I lost all willpower. My body was aching to have him inside me, and the second he glanced up from my breasts, our eyes met, and I had no interest in fighting him.

"You're bad," I breathed when we finished.

"That's funny, I would've guessed from the way you were shrieking there that I was good."

"I don't shriek," I said, hoping it was true. "And you are good at that. Very, very good. Too good. But we still shouldn't have done that."

He handed me the shampoo bottle. "I disagree. That was by far the most fun I've had all evening. And see? I was right. You're not pregnant." He patted my blissfully flat stomach.

"I better not be," I retorted. "But you have no way of knowing that."

He stared at me, his eyes like pools of melted chocolate. "I do so. And I never break a promise."

I washed my hair as he watched. When he stepped out of the shower and began drying off as I conditioned my hair, I decided to breach the other topic.

"Have you, um, been tested lately?"

"Tested?" He sounded confused, but as he turned towards me, I saw the look of recognition wash across his face. "Oh. Well, not since I started seeing you, but before then, yes, and I'm fine."

"Don't you want to ask me?"

"No. I trust *you*."

"Dylan, come on. I trust you too."

"Clearly not."

I could tell he was only pretending to be offended, but still, it hurt. "Anyway, I don't think you do trust me. What about the other night, when I was talking with Ryan?"

"Is he that guy from the band?"

"Yes."

"You weren't just talking with him, you were planning to leave with him. Is that how you get home when I don't pick you up?"

I turned off the shower and Dylan tossed me a towel. He had already dried off and tied his towel at his waist, but drops of water from his hair still glistened on his shoulders. I gently wiped the droplets off him. I thought about what Dylan was asking and decided I couldn't really blame him for being jealous. If I saw him flirting with a groupie at one of his concerts, it would drive me insane.

Besides, he wasn't too far off base. I'd certainly had a few instances where I left the club with one of the musicians who'd played there, hence my checkered past with relationships involving musicians.

"Is that why you picked me up tonight?"

"I wanted to see you," he said firmly. "But keeping you away from scalawags like Ryan was an added perk."

"I wasn't going to hook up with him," I finally said.

Dylan stared at me longingly. "I know that."

"Then what's the problem?"

"I worry about you. You act like New York City is this magical place where nothing bad ever happens. But you can't just walk home from the club in the middle of the night all alone, and you can't assume that every guy you leave with just to hang out has the same intentions as you. You're oblivious to the way that men look at you."

"I can take care of myself."

"But you don't have to." He made his way into the bedroom. "Do you work any this week?"

"Thursday, Friday, Saturday," I replied, sitting on the bed beside him. "And next Tuesday." And then I'd be on my way to England!

"If I asked you to take a cab home, would you?"

I turned to face him, and was struck by the way he was looking at me. Just by gazing into his deep, brown eyes, I could tell exactly how he felt about me. And I couldn't deny my feelings for him, especially when—just minutes after making love, he was already eying me as though he couldn't stand another minute without having me all over again.

"Yes."

"Good. I'll leave you cash for it." He smiled and kissed me before I could refuse the offer of payment. "Want your surprise now?"

"It's ready?"

He grinned and pulled on his jeans. I glanced around the room and grabbed the first clean-smelling article of clothing I could find, which happened to be the button down shirt Dylan had been wearing when he picked me up at the club. By the time I'd partially buttoned it, Dylan was back with his guitar.

I leaned back against the oversized pillows lining the head of his bed and listened happily as he serenaded me with his new song, "When Lily Smiles."

I was speechless when he finished. It was hands down the most romantic, thoughtful thing anyone had ever done for me.

"What do you think?" he asked. "I'm still tinkering with some of the notes, but…"

"I love it," I gushed, crawling over the bed and tackling him.

After we made love a second time, I made him play the song again. And again. And then, finally, I let him sleep.

We spent the better part of the next morning in bed, and then I helped Dylan as he frantically packed. Before I knew it, it was time for him to leave for the airport, and Thomas was waiting at the door along with one of the doormen, who was helping them transport their stuff.

"I know I'm forgetting something," he mumbled, glancing around the apartment.

"You could have her bring it to you when she comes if you think of it," Thomas said.

We had a dignified goodbye kiss, nothing like the dramatic and passionate farewell I'd hoped for, and then Dylan was gone.

* * *

THREE DAYS AFTER DYLAN LEFT, he remembered what he had forgotten to pack. It was a small sketch book where he'd apparently jotted down his notes for the music video sequences they were filming. I didn't have a key to his apartment, but he assured me the doorman would let me in and asked that I call him when I was there if I had any trouble finding it.

The doorman unlocked the door and asked me to return the key on my way out. I agreed, locking the door behind him. Dylan's apartment seemed cold and lonely without him there. I tried not to think about him, or the fact that I still had another week before I'd see him again, knowing it would just make me feel even more pathetic if I dwelled on how much I missed someone I'd only been dating for less than two months.

Dylan had said the notebook was in the desk drawer in his studio. I walked in and immediately spotted the table with two drawers next to his piano. I tugged open the largest drawer, but didn't see a notebook. There was loose sheet music, some pencils, and a whole slew of guitar picks.

In the smaller drawer, there was a single notepad. I retrieved it and began to flip through it, hoping to confirm it was the correct book, but it wasn't. Nothing had been written in this notebook.

I started to place the notepad back in the drawer when I realized something had fallen out of it.

I bent down and picked up the item. It was a 5x7 photo of a young girl. She was maybe four or five at the time of the photo. She was holding a daisy and smiling at something off in the distance. She had long dark brown hair, bright blue eyes, and features which were undeniably Dylan's. I flipped the photo over, hoping for a name or date, but it was blank.

A slew of emotions washed over me. I held my breath and blinked several times, trying to process this new information. How had I not known Dylan had a child? Why hadn't he mentioned her? I assumed she didn't live in New York, and maybe she wasn't even American. Maybe she was in England. Maybe I'd meet her in a few weeks.

I had an urge to call him, to quickly demand information about this young child, but I suppressed it. After all, we hadn't been dating for very long. It wasn't like he'd lied about it—I'd really never asked. Clearly, he'd tell me when he was ready. But I couldn't help but wonder, if Dylan had secrets this big, what else didn't I know about him?

I took another look at the child and then placed the photo and notepad carefully back into the drawer.

Suddenly, I realized that I wasn't even looking in the right spot. Dylan had said it would be in the desk drawer, and here I was at a table, albeit it one with drawers. Now that I thought about it, I was certain the desk across the room was what he meant.

I stood and opened the main desk drawer, immediately finding what clearly was the book containing his notes for the video. I knew then that I should leave the apartment, but I couldn't. There was a small, almost hidden drawer at the table that I hadn't noticed when I initially glanced at it. I knew it was wrong to snoop, and worse yet, I suspected Dylan wouldn't even mind me going through his things if I asked.

But I couldn't help myself.

I pulled open the drawer. There was a collection of odd small items—more guitar picks, some gum, eye drops, a pack of cigarettes, a square locker-style mirror, and a tuning key for the piano. I closed the drawer, but something in the back of it was blocking it and preventing me from shutting it fully. I reached my hand back and felt around. I felt something plastic with my fingers and pulled it forward until the drawer shut. Then I inched the drawer back open slightly, gasping at what I'd found.

It was a dusty zip top bag filled with a white powdery substance. At least an ounce, if I had to guess. I opened the bag and sniffed it, although I don't know why. I already knew what it was, and if I hadn't, well, smelling it certainly wouldn't have clued me in. I quickly replaced the bag in the drawer and scooted back.

I racked my mind trying to think of any clues, but I came up empty handed.

All of a sudden, I was overwhelmed with the urge to search every inch of Dylan's apartment. Well, either that or to start angrily throwing all of his valuables across the room. Tears blurred my eyes and I knew I was no longer thinking rationally, so I quickly left.

I locked the door and scurried to the elevator. When I reached the lobby, I tossed the key to the doorman and made my way back to my apartment as fast as I could.

Dylan called a few hours later. I let the call go to voice mail, immediately wondering what he was doing awake, since by my calculations, it was roughly two A.M. London time. When I didn't answer, he sent a text. Knowing I couldn't talk to him tonight, I shot back a quick reply, telling him I found the note-book and would call the next day.

But by the next day, I was only angrier. I'd set my alarm for earlier than usual, to allow time for me to talk with Dylan before I had to leave for work, but I couldn't bring myself to call him. Just before I left for work, though, he called me. I took a deep breath, and answered.

He said he was glad to hear my voice, but then began narrating the details of his trip so far. As I listened to him speak, I felt that familiar ache to touch him, or at least to see him in person. I found myself wishing the previous day had only been a dream, and I had to keep reminding myself not to get even more attached than I already was.

"You're awfully quiet this morning Lily," he finally said. "Late night?"

"Not as late as yours," I said, remembering how late he'd called. "Were you out partying?"

"No, just seeing some friends." He paused. "Is something wrong?"

"I don't think I can visit you."

"Why not?"

"Because I don't want to. It's just a bad idea."

"Is this because of work?"

"No. But you and I hardly know each other, and it doesn't make sense for me to pick up and follow you to another continent when it'll only make me fall more in love with you."

He sighed loudly. "I'm sorry."

"For what?"

"I don't know. I don't understand what's bothering you, but you sound sad and I hate that."

"When I was at your apartment, I accidentally looked in the drawer in your table by the piano instead of the desk drawer."

"Okay, but you found the correct book eventually, right?"

"Yes, but I found something else first."

"What?" His voice suggested he still didn't have a clue.

"Dylan, can you think of anything you might have in that drawer that you wouldn't want me to know about?" I waited, optimistically praying he'd say no.

There was a long silence.

Finally, Dylan said "oh."

And then I waited again, patiently, so he could tell me it wasn't his, that it was years old, anything at all to clear his name. But he didn't speak, so finally, I did. "Well? Dylan?"

"Yes?"

"Don't you have anything to say?"

"I don't know what you want me to say." He sounded flustered, but not nearly as much as I felt.

"I want you to tell me it isn't yours, that it's been in that drawer untouched for years and you just forgot about it, that you're not a drug addict."

"I'm not a drug addict," he said softly.

"And the rest?"

He was silent. I forced myself to take a deep breath, despite the crushing sensation in my chest.

"Why didn't you tell me?"

"What was I supposed to say, Lily? It's not something you talk about. I believe it's still illegal."

I held the phone away from my face while I sniffled and wiped my eyes. I didn't want him to have the satisfaction of knowing he'd made me cry. "Dylan, I told you from the start exactly why I didn't want to get involved with another musician and you swore to me you were nothing like that. You lied. Snorting cocaine is about as typical scumbag musician junkie as you can get."

"Lily, I can't get into this now. I'm not a junkie, though. I think you're overreacting. Just come meet me as we planned and we can discuss it all then."

"Why do you have it if you're not an addict? Why don't you just throw it out?"

He sighed again. "If it'll make you feel better, Lily, you can go back and throw it out. Flush the whole damn bag."

I considered this. I didn't know the street value of coke, but based on the amount in the bag, he'd surely be losing a good chunk of change if I flushed it. Then again, he was rich and could just buy more. Or maybe he didn't want to buy more. Maybe I should give him the benefit of the doubt. "Have you used any of it?"

"From that bag? I don't know."

"No, Dylan. I mean have you ever tried it?"

He took his time answering. "Yes."

"More than once?"

An even longer pause. "Yes. But it's been weeks, Lily. Since before we started dating."

I shook my head, cringing at the way he said "weeks" as though that was any considerable measure of time.

"Dylan, I can't do this. I really like you, but I can't get more involved with you knowing all this. I already know what it's like falling for someone who drinks too much and I don't want to go through that all over. I can't be with someone who uses drugs. I'm sorry, I just can't." I hung up before he could convince me otherwise.

The pain in my chest was nearly unbearable, but I was certain I'd done the right thing. If my feelings were already this strong for Dylan, there was no telling how hard I would've fallen in another month or two. Even I, a naïve, newbie New Yorker, as Jill phrased it, knew that a relationship with a cocaine addict was doomed for failure. So even if it hurt now, I reminded myself that the hurt was inevitable, and that it would only be worse if I waited.

Somehow, I made it halfway through the morning at work. I avoided casual chitchat with Bridget, the receptionist, and focused on responding to email requests for quotes and trip itineraries. It wasn't until I received a phone call from Emerson, one of my regulars, who wanted to surprise his wife with a trip to London for their fiftieth wedding anniversary, that I remembered the notebook. I told Emerson I'd figure out some options for him and call him back that afternoon with the prices.

And then I sent a simple text to Dylan. "I'll mail you the notebook. What's the address?"

I bit my lip as I awaited a response. Less than a minute passed before my phone began to ring. Why couldn't he just text back like a decent human being? Fine, I'd get it over with. I took a deep breath, and answered my phone.

"Dylan, I can't do this. Just tell me the address. I don't want to hear any excuses or talk about it."

"What address?"

His voice sounded confused, and then I quickly realized that it wasn't his voice.

"Thomas?"

"Yes. What address do you need? And what notebook? What's going on?"

"Why do you have Dylan's phone?"

"He said he was going for a walk two hours ago and he left it here. I thought you might know why he was acting weird."

"Oh. He didn't tell you?"

"No."

This surprised me. I had the impression Dylan told his big brother everything. "I'm not coming to England."

"You're not. Why is that?"

"Well, I guess we broke up."

"Oh."

"He lied to me," I added, even though Thomas hadn't asked.

"Lily, I realize it isn't my business, but Dylan talks about you a lot to me. I know he really cares for you and I can't imagine him lying to you. Are you sure this wasn't a misunderstanding?"

"I'm sure," I said. "I guess it was more of a lie of omission though."

"What did he neglect to tell you, exactly?"

I hesitated. If Thomas didn't know, it wasn't my place to rat Dylan out. "He never mentioned his, uh, illegal hobby," I finally said.

"You mean drugs?"

"Yes. I refuse to get involved with a drug addict."

Thomas chuckled at this. "Dylan's hardly a drug addict. And I'd say you're already involved, aren't you?"

"It doesn't matter."

"Lily, I really don't think you need to worry about him. He's been a, uh, recreational user for years. I don't think he's going to suddenly transform into a doper. And I haven't even seen him touch anything for months. Why don't you fly on out here and work things out with him?"

"Why do you even care?"

Thomas paused. "Well, for one thing, he's my brother. I'd like him to be happy, and he's been extremely happy with you. And for another, he's gone missing. I'm sure he'll come back, but it certainly won't bode well for the rest of our trip. We've got real work to do, and it'll be bloody difficult if he's moping around in a piss poor mood all day."

I guess I had to credit him for his honesty. And then, I wondered if he'd be honest with me about something else. "Thomas, does Dylan have a daughter?"

I heard a bemused laugh. "Not that I know of. Why do you ask?"

"I found a picture of a little girl at his apartment. It has to be his daughter. She looks just like him."

Silence ensued. I glanced at my phone to check if the connection was lost.

"Thomas?"

"Was there a date on the photograph?" Thomas asked finally, his voice strained.

"No," I said, and then I realized that the girl didn't just look like Dylan—she looked like Thomas too. Maybe it was Dylan's niece.

"I'm sure it's not his child," Thomas finally said. "I think he would've mentioned something like that to me."

"Okay." I decided not to press the issue further. It didn't matter anyway, since Dylan was out of my life now. "Well, if you or Dylan could text me the address of where you'll be staying in a few days, I'll send his notebook to him. I guess it has some notes he wants for one of the videos."

"Lily, why don't you just bring it with you? You can't actually break up with a bloke overseas. It just isn't right. You could come here, listen to what he has to say, and then fly right back if you want. You've already got your ticket, haven't you? You could even just bring the notebook here, drop it off, and spend the time traveling alone. It would be a waste to ruin a chance to see England just because you're on the outs with Dylan."

This was a tempting solution. I mean, I did have the ticket, and I'd already taken off work. And I had been looking forward to this trip since the second Dylan mentioned it. I dreamed of traveling the world, and now I was going to let a stupid boyfriend's lies ruin that for me? Besides, mailing it was ridiculous. International post would take forever.

Then again, I knew I couldn't actually go to England and not see Dylan. And if I saw him, I'd be tempted to forgive him, which was clearly a bad idea.

"Did you like the song he wrote for you?" Thomas interrupted my thoughts.

"That's irrelevant."

He chuckled. "Can we still record it if you don't forgive him?"

"I didn't know you planned to record it."

"Why wouldn't we?"

I started to tell him that I had thought the song was just for me, something Dylan did to make me happy, but then I thought better of it. If I'd been his muse, clearly it was just for commercial purposes.

"I better get back to work," I said.

"Lily, just talk to him again," Thomas asked. "I'll tell him to ring you when he returns." He hung up before I could protest.

* * *

87

I WAS LEAVING work hours later when Dylan called. I answered the phone and started to tell him that I couldn't talk, that I was just exiting the subway, when he began speaking.

"Please don't hang up, Lily. Just hear me out," he began. He paused before continuing. "I should have told you about what you found earlier. It's not a regular thing for me, and I haven't used it lately, so it didn't really occur to me. It's just something I've tried in the past."

"When you told me about all of the things you've been through with old boyfriends, I was listening. I didn't speak up because I really don't think I'm like any of the other musicians you've dated. I could never treat you like they did, Lily. I would never hurt you. I meant what I said when I told you to throw it out. If my having that is going to cause you to worry, I don't want it around, even if I know I won't use it either way."

I couldn't let him ramble on anymore. "Dylan, stop. It's none of my business. You can do it if you want. I just can't trust you. My instincts are telling me that you're not good for me, and I can't ignore that."

"Lily, don't you understand? I love you. I want what's good for you too. I thought you loved me too. Was that just a lie? You find out I'm not perfect and you stop loving me?"

"That's completely unfair, and you know it," I snapped. I ducked my head down. I still had three blocks to walk to my apartment, and people were starting to stare at me as I stumbled along, crying.

"Is it, Lily? Because you're punishing me for something that I did in the past. Something that I was completely honest with you about as soon as you asked me. I could've lied and told you it belonged to Thomas, you know. You'd never have known the truth," he said spitefully. "But I didn't lie because I've meant every word I've said to you. And if you give up on me for being honest and then run off and find some other drunk loser to fall for, we both know you're going to regret it."

I was stunned. I couldn't believe he'd even said that, and I had no response. He *had* told me the truth earlier, and he was right— I'd wished he hadn't. I probably would've overlooked the obvious and accepted his lie if he'd just said the drugs weren't his. And I was seemingly holding him to higher standards than other men, but I wasn't sure why.

Maybe I was scared—I knew how strong my feelings for him were already and I couldn't even fathom how devastated I'd be if things went downhill after I fell even harder for him. It all boiled down to the fact that, as always, I dove headfirst into a relation-ship, fell in love before I truly knew the man, and now was drowning in water way over my head. I needed to get out. I needed to move on, to trust my instincts.

The aching in my chest was overwhelming. I had to slow down. What if my instincts were wrong? I was already in too deep, so maybe there was no real harm in hearing Dylan out. More likely than not, I'd still decide to leave him. But maybe things would work out. Maybe I was just penalizing him for the mistakes other men had made.

"Lily?"

"Yes."

"Lily, come to London, please, baby. I miss you. Just come and see me, and if you still don't trust me or you just don't want to deal with me, I'll get you your own hotel room. Hell, I'll even hire you a tour guide. You won't even have to see me while you're here if you don't want to. But please at least come here. I'll never forgive myself if you miss out on a trip you've been dreaming of just because I'm a bloody fool."

I smiled reluctantly. "You're not a fool."

"I am. I found the most wonderful woman ever and I made her cry."

I took a deep breath. I knew he had me, and I suspected he knew as much too. "You swear it's been more than a month since you've used?"

"Yes."

"And you've never been in rehab or treatment or anything like that?"

"Correct."

"And you'll stay clean?"

"Lily, I'd do anything for you."

I sighed and winced at the sky. "It's raining."

"Here too," he said. I could practically hear the smile in his voice.

"No, it's not. You're making that up."

"I'm not. Listen." And he held the phone out to something, where I did indeed hear the distant tap tap tap of raindrops. "Are you nearly home?"

"Yes."

"I miss you."

I ducked into the apartment building. "I miss you too."

"I should let you go get dried off."

"Yeah, and it must be late in England," I realized.

"Good night," he said.

I suddenly remembered my last question. "Dylan, do you have a daughter?"

He laughed. "What?"

I decided not to bring up the picture. My inadvertent snooping had already caused more than enough problems for today. "I was just wondering if you had any other secrets."

"I don't have any children. And I don't think I have any other secrets. You could look on the internet, though," he suggested matter-of-factly. "Let me know if you discover anything else I should know about myself."

I giggled. "Maybe I will. Good night."

I hung up and went to pour myself a drink. It was definitely the drinking kind of night.

CHAPTER SEVEN

"Happy families are all alike; every unhappy family is unhappy in its own way."
Leo Tolstoy, *Anna Karenina*

*B*rothers *are an odd entity. One never speaks of "brotherhood" in a negative way, and yet, since the beginning of time, starting with Cain and Abel, history shows us this relationship is fraught with as much conflict as any other. I feel blessed to have a brother and I'm certain he'd say the same of me, though he ought not.*

Mum used to always chide us for our squabbles- "why can't you two just get along?" So we did, sometimes, and other times, we didn't. Like all brothers, I s'pose. We're alike and we're different, in just enough ways to both draw us together and tear us apart. Though she never once uttered a "why can't you be more like your brother," I know we both wonder and wish it all the same.

She'd talk of the two of us brothers growing old together, and she'd encourage us each to find a nice woman to marry. And she told us to cherish one another, because someday, we'd each be all the other had. I can't help but wonder if, by the time her words come true—which may be sooner than not—what would be left of us?

* * *

MY FLIGHT to London was thrilling. I'd always loved flying, and being on my first true international flight nearly pushed me over the edge. I was ecstatic about my impending reunion with Dylan and excited about seeing England. It didn't hurt that I was seated in first class, which was enough to get any normal girl riled up. I watched as the city grew smaller and smaller, then snuggled up with *Jude the Obscure* until we were well over the Atlantic. I was too giddy to sleep more than an hour or two on the flight, and it was still early when I arrived in London.

Dylan met me at the airport, with a driver waiting outside to take us back to his flat. He immediately apologized, again, his rich eyes hooded. I wanted to hold back, to at least pretend that I hadn't, despite all logic, somehow already forgiven him, but I couldn't. The moment he enveloped me in his strong arms, we both knew I was his.

He gave me the abbreviated tour of the area, then we had wonderful haven't-seen-each-other-in-two-weeks sex. After that, I napped. He left to do a sound check with the band while I slept, but returned just as I was waking up.

"So what's the itinerary?" I asked, eagerly nibbling on the sandwich he'd brought for me.

"Do you want to take it easy today?"

"No. I want to explore. What are you doing today?"

Dylan smiled. "We have a concert tonight, and tomorrow we're going to be filming some scenes in London for the music video. On Monday we'll head out to Ipswich."

"Can I come with you today and watch?"

"Of course. But you might have more fun exploring." He eyed

my tour book. "I'm sure you have some ideas of where you want to go."

"I do, but I can spare an hour to watch my man at work first," I insisted.

Dylan's face grew more somber. "Do you want to talk about what you found at my apartment?"

I winced. I had hoped he wouldn't bring it up, and I could tell from his expression that he didn't want to discuss it either. I slowly shook my head.

"You're sure?" he confirmed, hopefully.

"Yeah. As long as it's in the past, and you're going to throw it away when you get home and you won't keep things from me in the future, I don't see any point in discussing it anymore."

Dylan smiled and kissed me on the forehead. "You're too easy on me," he teased.

Thomas joined us then. Dylan spoke with his brother briefly, and the three of us set out together. Thomas greeted me politely, but with none of the warmth that he'd shown on the phone the other day. I wondered if he'd told Dylan that he'd spoken to me, or that he'd defended his brother so fiercely.

We stopped abruptly as a group of three teenagers asked for autographs. Both brothers obliged cheerfully, chatting with two of the girls. I noticed the third was quietly hanging in the background and assumed she just wasn't a fan, until one of the others turned and said something to her in sign language. The girl nodded and smiled.

After Dylan returned the pen to the first girl, he began to sign to the girl in the back. I'd learned to sign the alphabet as a Girl Scout once, but that was the extent of my understanding, and Dylan was clearly using more advanced signs than the alphabet. Dylan wasn't speaking aloud as he signed, but I figured he was saying something funny since two of the girls and Thomas all began to laugh simultaneously.

Then, I watched as Thomas joined in, clearly equally fluent in sign language. The smiled on the girl's face widened, and then the brothers waved goodbye to the teenagers and rejoined me.

"You know sign language," I said, perplexed.

"Yes," Dylan replied.

"You both know sign language," I repeated.

"Doesn't everyone?" Thomas asked with a smile.

"If we didn't both know sign language, how would we communicate with each other without everyone else knowing what we were saying?" Dylan asked, a mischievous grin on his face.

I shrugged. "I don't know. I struggle to follow along when you two speak aloud to each other." And it was true. I thought I'd been getting better at deciphering the English language—with the heavy British accent, that is, but now that we were in England, it seemed both Parker men had become even more British. I had no trouble understanding Dylan when he spoke to me, but when he spoke to Thomas, well, it just took me a minute to piece it all together.

Dylan smiled and hugged me close, kissing the side of my forehead. "And that's why we love you," he said.

* * *

THAT NIGHT, I waited backstage with the band before the concert, sneaking out to the front and center standing-room-only section to watch them perform. The first two songs were amazing, Sierra's performance being everything I'd remembered from the last two concerts I'd seen, and at the start of the third song, Dylan's eyes locked on mine and I realized he'd spotted me. It was a slow song, not a love ballad by any means, but it certainly felt romantic enough. By the end of the concert, I was dying to see him again.

As soon as they stopped playing, I made my way to the backstage area. I had on my VIP necklace that allowed me access, but there was already a crowd. I squeezed to the front of the crowd and started past the security, flashing my name badge, but he stopped me abruptly.

"You'll have to wait," he said in a thick British accent that somehow undermined his tough personage. "We're at capacity backstage. We'll let someone in as soon as someone else leaves."

"But the band won't stay forever," a woman behind me whined.

"I'm supposed to be back there now, though," I said, flashing my badge. "I'm with the band."

The guy rolled his eyes then returned to surveying the line.

"Hey!" I shouted, desperate to get his attention. "Can't you call someone on the walkie talkie? Ask anyone in the band."

"Lady, you'll just have to wait," he repeated.

I started to panic, then sent a quick text to Dylan, explaining the situation. I figured the chances of him actually checking his messages were slim, but at least I felt like I was doing something.

To my relief, moments later, the door opened and Dylan popped his head out. Ear-piercing shrieks from the mostly-female crowd behind me deafened me. Dylan spotted me immediately and reached for my hand. I turned to smirk at the security guard, who simply shrugged, uncaring. Then, Dylan kissed me on my lips, with a near-deafening response from the crowd.

"I'm sorry," he mumbled to his fans. "She's my girlfriend."

He pulled me backstage with him. "Did you like the concert?"

I nodded. "You guys were great, as always."

His eyes darted around the room, and then he led me by the hand to a separate room that I guessed was his changing room. He shut the door behind us. "I thought you'd watch from backstage."

"I wanted the full concert experience," I said, glancing around the room. "Hey, is this where you take all your groupies?"

Dylan laughed. "Only my favorites." He kissed my neck until I got goosebumps and then he snuck his hand up my shirt.

"Whoa there," I cautioned, already noticing that tingly feeling I got when Dylan touched me. "Don't get me all worked up when we're not going to be alone for hours."

He narrowed his eyes. "We're alone now, love." Leaving his hand in place, he started kissing my lips.

I had to admit, I'd always had a fantasy about fooling around with the lead singer from a real band at an actual concert, so it wasn't hard for him to convince me. I unzipped his jeans and slid them down before dropping to my knees. After a moment, long before I was done, Dylan pulled me back up.

"You never let me finish that," I protested.

"That's not what I want right now," he insisted, placing me on my back on the couch in the corner of the room and tugging my jeans down.

"Dylan, the door doesn't even lock."

He responded by slipping his hand into my panties and tracing his finger back and forth in a wonderful pattern that quickly had me seeing stars.

"Okay, you've made your point," I said, kicking out of my panties and shifting my hips to guide him inside of me.

Dylan smiled and kissed behind my ear. "I love you," he murmured.

We both finished quickly, but while I was ready to snuggle with Dylan for at least a half hour, the building noise outside the room suggested he might be needed sooner.

"I'm sorry to, well, you know, and run, but we're expected to socialize," he explained, quickly redressing. He hesitated by the door, clearly uncertain if he needed to wait for me.

I sighed. "Go on, I'll be out in a minute."

"Don't keep me waiting too long."

* * *

AFTER OUR LATE NIGHT PARTYING, I spent the next day as a tourist while Dylan worked. We then traveled to a few other small towns outside of London, and towards the end of the trip, or at least the end of the trip for me, we were finally in Ipswich. It was Dylan and Thomas' hometown, the place they'd lived from birth until eighteen, when they'd run off to London to start a band.

Dylan rarely spoke about his mother, so I wasn't sure what to expect when I met her. For some reason, though, I hadn't anticipated the modest cottage-style house she lived in. It oozed charm, from the ivy twining its way up the façade to the cobblestone path leading to the stone-lined door. But the house was also small, and a sharp, cozy contrast to the sterile modern apartment Dylan now inhabited.

"This is the house where I grew up," Dylan explained, seeming perplexed by my surprise.

"Your mother never moved after you both…" I stopped short of saying outright that her sons were loaded, but it was the clear implication.

"She won't leave," Thomas answered quickly. "We've offered to buy her a new place, and the best we could get her to agree to was a new car."

I smiled, trying to imagine whether my mom would let me buy her fancy things if I became rich and famous.

Their mom opened the door before we reached it, and her smile was genuine and immediately warming. She hugged Thomas and then Dylan before turning to me.

"You must be Lily. I'm Kate. Delighted to meet you."

"Thank you. I'm glad to be meeting you too. Your house is beautiful."

She glanced around it skeptically. "It has a certain charm, I suppose."

As Kate smiled, I was reminded of the photo in Dylan's drawer. I could certainly imagine Kate looking like that as a child, with her dark brown hair and sharp blue eyes. But it still seemed odd for an adult to keep a childhood photo of his mom in a drawer.

Kate offered us some tea and then we all sat and caught up. Before lunch, Kate entertained me with stories of Dylan misbehaving in high school that left me feeling quite at home. After the meal, though, I excused myself to read outside for a bit, hoping to give the guys a little more time with their mom. That evening, we all went out to dinner together.

It was late when we left her house to return to the hotel, and Dylan and Thomas were both quiet during the drive. I asked a few questions about their mom, but it was clear that neither of them wanted to speak. I was perplexed. When we returned to the hotel, a large suite with two bedrooms off of the main living area, Thomas invited the rest of the band over for a drink while Dylan and I retreated to the bedroom.

He sat on the bed, wearily, and I stepped directly in front of him. I caught his eye, then slowly began to undress. He watched me appreciatively and kissed me when I finished my striptease and crouched on his lap, my arms around his neck. Dylan continued through the motions of foreplay, but I sensed his heart wasn't in it. We made love, but even as we were as close as two people could possibly be, there was a certain distance.

"What's wrong?" I asked finally.

He kissed my forehead. "Nothing. You go on to sleep. I'm going to check in with Thomas."

I sighed as I watched him go. I was tired, though, and clearly not as accustomed to travel and time change as he was, so I obeyed and went to sleep. When Dylan rejoined me in bed, nearly two hours had passed, and he was visibly drunk. He stumbled over his shoes then crashed into the bed.

I helped him out of his clothes and he collapsed onto the bed, asleep almost as soon as his head touched the pillow. Something wasn't right, about his mood or the drinking, but I couldn't put my finger on it, and I knew there was no point in waking him to talk now. I rolled over and tried to go back to sleep, but Dylan began thrashing around under the covers.

I turned back to face him, assuming he was awake, but I quickly saw that his eyes were still closed, and his face looked flushed. Then he mumbled something. It was inaudible at first, but then he repeated it, over and over, until it was loud enough for me to hear it.

"Lucy," he groaned.

I gritted my teeth together. It was one thing for him to ditch me to get drunk with his brother, but another to come back to bed and dream about an old girlfriend.

"Lucy," he called, louder.

"Shh," I snapped.

Dylan was quiet for a moment, then flopped onto his stomach and moaned her name again, this time more frantically. Flustered, I crawled out of bed.

I pulled on a long tee shirt and panties and glanced around for my jeans. Not finding them, I tugged the shirt lower and crept out of the room hesitantly. A lamp was on, but the sitting room was quiet and empty. The rest of the band had gone to bed. I tiptoed over to the bar and filled a coffee mug with water, added a tea bag, and popped it into the microwave. I leaned back against the cool countertop and sighed, contemplating my dilemma until the beep signaled my drink was ready.

I retrieved my tea and crept over to the couch. As I passed the high-backed chair beside the lamp, I jumped, then gasped as the hot water splashed over the sides of my mug and scalded my hand.

"Thomas," I said, acknowledging his presence. He sat calmly in the chair, notepad and pen in hand. He looked tired, and I wondered if he'd been asleep when I first entered the room. That was the only explanation for how he would have remained so still that I didn't notice him, unless of course he was trying to go unnoticed.

"Sorry," he mumbled in response, his eyes focusing quickly on my bare legs before falling back to the paper.

I shook my head, now concerned that I'd interrupted his writing. "No, I'm sorry. I didn't mean to disrupt your work. I just couldn't sleep." Actually, I was so tired I probably could sleep anywhere but there, next to Dylan.

He gazed up at me, his face expressionless. "I wasn't working."

"Oh. I thought you were maybe writing."

He smiled. "I was. Dear Diary. Today was swell."

His sarcasm was almost imperceptible. I'd never met anyone so difficult to read. I looked at his notebook, decided it did resemble a journal, but figured he was joking about the content of his writings. Thomas was watching me expectantly. Not knowing what else to do, I sat on the couch.

"You really write in a journal?"

He nodded, expressionlessly.

"I bet it's pretty interesting, with everything you've done in life."

He shrugged. "Just the melancholy musings of yet another troubled musician."

I took a slow sip of my tea, trying to buy time before I had to formulate a response to that.

"Dylan's dreaming about an ex-girlfriend," I explained.

Thomas' face softened. His eyes dipped down to my thighs again, and he swallowed audibly. "He's drunk. Give him a break."

I sighed a laugh. Drunkenness didn't seem like a viable excuse for someone who succumbed to the condition daily. "I just can't sleep with the distraction. He keeps saying her name, over and over."

"You must have known you weren't his first." Now Thomas smiled.

I tested the temperature of the tea, sipping cautiously. "Yeah, but I thought I was his only woman at the moment."

"He's a rockstar, love. Be glad you're the only woman physically in his bed."

The bitterness in his tone was sharp. For brothers who seemed to get along so well, there was clearly a healthy amount of jealousy.

I swallowed another large sip, scalding the back of my throat. "He's never told me much about his past girlfriends. I assume this one must have been recent, the way he's talking about her. He keeps calling her name over and over, but in a weird way, almost like he's trying to catch up to her. Did you know her?"

There was a long pause, and Thomas' face hardened. "I knew her quite well."

I waited for him to say more. I could tell there was a history with this girl, that Thomas clearly had lots he could tell me.

"You should go back to bed," he said with finality after yet another lengthy silence. "You needn't worry about her." His eyes flitted down to his notepad, as though the conversation was over, but he didn't resume his writing.

I didn't move. I wasn't done with my tea, and Thomas' answer hadn't comforted me at all. Quite the opposite, it had intrigued me. Had Dylan been engaged to this woman? Surely he hadn't forgotten to mention a past marriage?

"He loved her?" I finally said, desperate for more information.

Thomas nodded. "Very much."

I bit my lip. Five minutes ago, I'd been pissed off that my boyfriend had the nerve to speak someone else's name in bed, even if he was asleep. Now I was oddly jealous. From the way Thomas spoke, it seemed that Dylan still loved this woman, or at least that she'd been huge in his life. I didn't know what else to say. I wanted more information, but asking directly didn't seem to be the way to get results from Thomas.

His breathing was heavy, and he was still staring back at me. His deep green eyes were filled with pain, and then, I understood.

"You loved her too," I guessed. It wasn't that crazy of a hunch, to suspect brothers so close in age fell for the same woman. And I could definitely see Thomas letting Dylan win her, even if it hurt him.

He nodded again, then shut his notepad. "You should go back to bed," he repeated, standing.

I nodded, then frowned, suddenly realizing I hadn't told him the name Dylan was saying. Despite that, Thomas had clearly known who I was talking about. None of it made sense.

"Thomas," I called before he reached his bedroom door, my voice desperate for answers. "I didn't tell you the name Dylan was saying."

He stopped, but didn't turn to face me. "You didn't have to. Dylan's talked in his sleep for years. It's always the same." He paused and exhaled loudly. "Lucy was our sister. She's dead," he said, and he locked himself in the other bedroom.

I felt my breath catch in my throat and tried to process this new fact. When I finally regained composure, I took another sip of my tea, and found it had grown cold. I crept back into the bedroom, pulled the tee shirt over my head, and slid under the sheet beside Dylan. He was sprawled on his stomach, calm and quiet, but I could see now that I'd misinterpreted the dream entirely. The covers were jumbled and twisted over him. His body glistened with sweat and his fists were still clenched. Clearly, he'd been having a nightmare.

I thought about Thomas, and his hesitance to tell me more. His pain had been evident, but not raw. Tomorrow, I'd look into it online, at least to find out what had happened and when. It could be easier to simply ask Dylan, but as I watched him sleep, I wondered if he could handle the question.

* * *

THE NEXT MORNING, I casually mentioned to Dylan that he'd been talking in his sleep.

"Sorry," he mumbled, ruffling his hair groggily.

"You were having a nightmare. You kept saying a name over and over."

The change in his expression was almost imperceptible. He stood and started toward the bathroom. "I should shower."

"Dylan, wait. How come you never told me you had a sister?"

He stopped short of the bathroom.

"I'm sorry, but you were saying her name and I couldn't sleep. Thomas was in the living room, and he told me."

"How much did he tell you?"

"Nothing. Just her name, and that she…"

"That's really all there is to tell," he said sharply, shutting the bathroom door behind him.

I realized now that his odd behavior after meeting my parents might have had something to do with this trauma. I had so many more questions for him, but I knew he didn't want to discuss it, so I tried to keep quiet. I showered when he was finished, and by the time I was dressed, breakfast had been delivered to the living room.

I sat beside him with a scone and a cup of coffee. He slowly glanced up at me from the paper he was reading and then gradually turned his eyes back down.

I watched him curiously, trying to ascertain if he was still upset over his sister.

"I can't focus with you staring," he said in a gentle voice.

"I'm sorry," I said, looking away.

He set the papers on his lap. "Lucy died when I was nine. It was a horrible accident and none of us likes to talk about it, but being here seems to remind me."

I nodded, and then I remembered the photograph. "What did she look like?"

"She had dark brown hair, a smile that seemed too big for her face, and bright blue eyes."

"You have a photo of her in your studio," I said. "I found it that day I was looking for your notebook. That photo was what made me think you might have a daughter."

He surprised me by laughing at this. "That explains it. I thought it was an unusual question."

Dylan paused. "Lily, I'm sorry if I've been sullen the past day. It's just very difficult being here and remembering her. I should've warned you beforehand."

"You don't have to apologize. I'm sorry you've been through that."

He nodded, and we finished our breakfast silently.

CHAPTER EIGHT

"I may do some good before I am dead—be a sort of success as a
frightful example of
what not to do; and so illustrate a moral story."
Thomas Hardy, *Jude the Obscure*

The last two days of my trip were uneventful. We spent one more day in Ipswich before returning to London. When the car arrived at Dylan's flat to take me to the airport, I realized I wouldn't see him for another two weeks. I hated knowing I'd miss him. Already, he'd been so ingrained into my life that I wasn't sure that I could resume my normal routine without him.

To occupy myself, I made plans with Jill. We met up at the gym, like usual.

As soon as Boot Camp Cardio was over, we hit the showers, dressed, and reconvened at the smoothie bar, where we traditionally consumed equal calories to what we'd just burned off during class. It was a splendid ritual.

"Want to see my photos?" I offered, retrieving the bulging pouch from my gym bag.

Jill laughed, but nodded. I know it's the twenty-first century and all, but I still feel like actual photo prints have a valuable place in the world. I love sliding them into the protective sleeves of floral-patterned albums and then flipping through the books on rainy days, reminiscing about my favorite adventures. I handed the whole stack of photos to her, realizing most needed little narration.

"Looks like things are going well with you guys," she said, pausing on a photo that Dylan had taken of the two of us. Our faces were off to the side, and Dylan's arm that was holding the camera was clearly visible, but we were smiling and gazing at each other lovingly.

I nodded. "He's amazing. I can't believe I almost never gave him a chance just because of his job." I paused, and remembered the more recent near-miss. "Or that I almost…"

"Almost what?" Jill looked up from the photos, clearly sensing the importance of what I wasn't saying.

I glanced around. We were basically the only ones at the smoothie bar. "I almost didn't go with him to England. We had a big fight after he left and I told him I wasn't coming.

"What happened?"

I slurped my drink. "It was weird actually. His brother called and really stood up for him, and then Dylan called and we talked and I realized I was blowing it all out of proportion."

"No, what was the fight over?"

"Oh. Well, he asked me to find something at his apartment while he was gone, and I sort of found something else that I hadn't expected."

Jill raised an eyebrow. I knew she would let up until I told her.

"It was a bag of cocaine," I whispered.

Her eyes widened.

"I know, but listen. I asked him about it and he was totally honest from the start. He admitted it was his but said it was old and that he had never been an addict or anything."

Jill grimaced. "Sweetie, I don't think that's how cocaine works. It's not like weed where someone might try it once or twice a year at a party. It's serious stuff. It can kill you and it's highly addictive."

I shrugged. "I thought that too, but I did a little research online, and apparently it is possible to use it occasionally and not get addicted. And it doesn't matter, because he doesn't do it anymore. He hasn't since we met."

Jill's face remained pained.

"Jill, I've already forgiven him. I know what you're thinking, and I reacted the same way initially. But I can't blame him for fuckups of my last boyfriends. You don't just stop loving someone because of something bad they did before they even knew you. It doesn't work that way, and it wouldn't be fair, especially since he was completely upfront with me."

"But how do you know he hasn't done it more recently? If he were an addict, you know he'd lie and hide it from you. I know how you feel about him, but Lil, I just can't stand watching you get hurt again."

"I know, I know. I really don't think you have to worry, though. He's clearly not trying to hide anything from me." I paused. "He's giving me a key to his place. He wouldn't do that if he had a secret drug habit."

Jill sighed. "Yeah, I guess you're right. You're sure he makes you happy?"

I laughed. "Did I mention he wrote me a song?"

She rolled her eyes. "How come no one ever writes me songs?"

"Because you married a lawyer."

"Oh. Right. So tell me more about the trip."

I told her about meeting Dylan's mom, about exploring

London and the English countryside, about the great sex, and even about the weird way I found out about Dylan's sister.

By the end of my talk with Jill, she was definitely on Dylan's side.

It was nearing my usual bedtime when we finally walked out together.

"Hey," Jill said suddenly. "I forgot to ask. When do I get to meet him?"

I smiled. "Soon, I hope. You're gonna love him."

* * *

WHEN DYLAN RETURNED HOME days later, it was late. I met him at his apartment where we made love, swapped stories about our last two weeks apart, and made love again before going to bed.

The next morning, I left early for work. I was still making up extra shifts at work, covering for people who'd taken my shifts at the club while I was gone, so Dylan and I had several days in a row where we saw each other only fleetingly, generally in the middle of the night.

It wasn't that I minded meeting up with him for perfect sex each night, but I really wanted something more, and I knew he did too.

"I miss you," I whimpered one afternoon as I crawled out of bed to head out to Echo. I'd gone straight from Skywards to Dylan's, and now after only two hours with him, I had to leave already.

"Really? Because I'm starting to think you're just using me for sex."

That amused me. I was by no means a prude, but I certainly couldn't compete with his appetite for sex. He was insatiable. "I don't want to go, but I have to be at work," I whined.

"I believe that's exactly what you said this morning when you were sneaking out of my bed."

I shrugged.

"Why do you have two jobs?"

"Neither is full time, and I need the money."

"Could you cut back on your hours at the travel agency?"

"No, I have to keep thirty hours a week or I lose my insurance."

"Then what about at the club?"

"I only work ten nights a month. Any less than that and they'll fire me for someone who can work more." I sighed. "It's not that bad. I get to hear lots of bands perform."

"I'll perform whenever you want. You don't need them."

"True, but I still need to pay my rent."

Dylan paused, propping his head on his hand. "What if you moved in with me?"

I had no immediate response.

"You're here all the time anyway, when you're not working," he said.

"Dylan, that's a really sweet offer, but I don't want to smother you."

"Smother me?" He laughed, sitting up. "I barely see you. I'd love the chance to be smothered!"

"You're serious?"

"Yes, Lily. Quit your night job and move in with me. Please." His big chocolate eyes were hard to reject, but I knew I couldn't answer on the spot.

"I'm going to be late, Dylan. I'll think about it. I love you!"

The more I thought about it, the more I knew what my answer would be. Of course it made sense for me to move in with him. Even if I didn't quit Echo, I'd still see more of him if we lived together, and my apartment was basically just a drain on my finances lately, since I was never there anymore.

As soon as I left work, I went straight to my apartment to talk to Carrie. Dylan was busy recording that day and wouldn't be home till late anyway.

I was relieved when Carrie came home that night, both because she was alone and looked chipper. She had just been at her Christian Women's Group, which always put her in a good mood.

She paused when she saw me, visibly surprised. "You're home!"

I nodded. "Yeah, sorry. I've been staying at Dylan's a lot lately."

She turned and began rummaging through the fridge. I knew she didn't approve of me staying at his place. She wasn't a virgin, but she definitely had saved a little more of herself for marriage than most women seemed to.

"I made brownies," I said, and she joined me at the table. I watched her as she scooped a large brownie out of the pan. She had an aura of peacefulness that I envied. We were both the same age, but her calm demeanor made her seem years younger. Maybe there was something to that religious stuff.

She gazed up at me, her bright blue eyes exuding an innocence I don't think I ever had. "You want to talk about something, don't you?"

I smiled. "Am I that transparent?"

"You never make brownies." She took a bite, then stopped mid-chew as a look of horror crossed her face. "Are you pregnant?"

"No, Carrie. Nothing like that. I actually had some good news. Dylan asked me to move in with him."

She chewed slowly. "Are you getting married?"

I shook my head. "Well, maybe someday, but not now."

She glanced at my hand, her soft blonde curls falling in front of her face. "And you're not engaged?"

"Carrie, I know that sort of thing is important to you, but I'm just not that religious."

"It's not just a religious thing."

"Okay, I'm not that traditional, then," I corrected.

"Lily, it's a practical consideration. If you both think the relationship has a future, you'd be engaged. If you don't, well, I'd say end it now. And if you're not sure whether or not it has potential yet, then keep dating, but don't move in together."

She took another bite and chewed, then stood to pour herself a glass of milk. "If you move out, I'll have to find a new roommate. And then if you and Dylan break up, you won't just be single again, you'll be homeless."

I wondered how much of this was concern for me and how much of it was her own panic at the thought of having to find a new roommate. I may not have been the perfect roommate, but I was quiet, relatively normal, and I paid my rent on time. "Carrie, I'll keep paying rent until you find a new roommate."

"Oh, I'm not worried about that. There's several girls in my Bible study who are looking to move out on their own. I was thinking about you. Don't you remember how hard it is to find an affordable apartment in this neighborhood? And this one is so close to Echo."

"I'm actually thinking of quitting that job anyway," I said.

"Was that your idea or his?"

I shrugged. "I like spending time with Dylan, and between his work and my two jobs, we hardly ever see each other."

"You always seemed to like that job. And don't you need the money?"

"Not if I'm not paying rent."

Carrie sat back down and clasped her hands in her lap. She was oddly quiet, which was never a good sign. Carrie was chatty by nature, and if she wasn't speaking, it was because she had something to say that she didn't think would be well received.

"What are you thinking?" I asked.

"I know you really like Dylan, and I can tell he has some great qualities, but sometimes I worry that he might not be the right match for you."

I laughed. She needn't have been worried about telling me that. I'd known all along that she hadn't approved of Dylan. He partook in practically everything she abhorred. "You don't like Dylan. I know that. It's not that I don't appreciate your opinion, but I really need to make relationship decisions on my own."

"You should never make important decisions alone, and you never need to. Have you tried praying over this? You'd be surprised how quickly God answers."

I stuck a fork into the brownie pan and scooped out a large bite. "That's just not my style, Carrie. I'll probably move my stuff out next week, but like I said, I'll keep paying rent till you find someone else." I stood and dropped my fork in the sink.

"Lily, wait," Carrie said. I turned and realized she seemed more concerned now. "Just hear me out, please. I'm worried about you. You spend all your time with Dylan and you never see your other friends, and now you're quitting a job you love and moving in with him. It seems like you're isolating yourself."

I took a deep soothing breath in lieu of pointing out that cohabitating was the opposite of isolating oneself. Before I could reply, she continued.

"What happens if you break up? You won't have a job or a place to live. I'm not suggesting that you stop seeing him, only that you wait before you move in with him." She paused nervously. "I think he needs counseling, or rehab. I know about the drugs."

I scrubbed off the fork, rinsed it, and moved it to the drying rack. "You don't know anything, Carrie. You think you know who Dylan is, what he's like just because you've read some things about him online or met him in passing once or twice, but you don't. And even if you did, you're hardly in a position to give other people relationship advice. You never give anyone a chance. You divide all your time between work and church and you've never had a relationship with an actual living person!"

Carrie stared back at me calmly. Her refusal to shout back made me want to smack her.

"I think I'll stay at Dylan's tonight," I said, retreating to my room to pack.

I took a cab to Dylan's, knowing he'd pay when I arrived. I called when I was close, hoping he'd come down to meet me, but he didn't answer. Luckily, cabbies took credit cards these days. The doorman keyed me onto their floor, and when the elevator doors opened, I nearly bumped into Thomas.

"Hey there," I said, confused by the startled look on his face, as though I'd caught him in some forbidden act.

"Lily," he said, glancing over at Dylan's apartment, the deer-in-headlights look still in his eyes. "Dylan's not home." He eyed my bag. "He didn't mention you coming over tonight."

"Oh. Well, I was going to stay at my place, but when I told my roommate I was planning on moving in with Dylan, she was less than supportive."

"You're moving here?"

I frowned. "You didn't know?" I thought Thomas and Dylan shared everything.

"He said he asked you, but I didn't think..."

"You didn't think I would?"

He gazed down uncomfortably. "I have a key," he said, leading me towards Dylan's apartment.

"Thanks," I said, forgetting that I had one, too. "Any idea when he'll be back? Or where he is? I tried calling, but he didn't answer."

Thomas unlocked the door and pushed it open. His level of discomfort was increasing visibly, but I still didn't know why. "He's down the hall," he finally said.

"Dylan's at your place?" I repeated, wondering why he hadn't mentioned that to start with.

He nodded.

"Weren't you on your way out when I got here, though? Are you guys working or something?"

Before he could answer, the door to his apartment opened, and a medley of loud voices and music flooded the hall.

"I bloody well did," Dylan was shouting to someone in the apartment as he started into the hall. He froze as he initially saw me. Someone hollered back at him from inside Thomas' apartment, but I didn't hear what they said.

"Lil!" Dylan exclaimed, finally coming out of his surprised stupor. "What are you doing here?"

He raced over to me and twirled me in the air in an exuberant hug that would've been appropriate if we had last seen each other weeks, not hours, earlier. His cheerfulness was contagious, and I smiled back at him. He was shirtless, reeked of smoke, and had red, bloodshot eyes.

I glanced over at Thomas, who seemed ashamed, as though he'd somehow failed me. Apparently, his awkward demeanor had stemmed from his desire to protect his brother.

Before anyone could say anything else, a tall woman with a long blonde ponytail, wearing tight-fitting jeans and a lacy black bra, stumbled out of the apartment. "Did you find it?" She asked Dylan. And then she glanced at me, Thomas, and back to Dylan.

"Shelby, this is my Lily," Dylan said, clearly oblivious to the awkwardness of the situation.

Shelby glared, gave me a once over, then turned back to Dylan. "Are you coming back?"

"We're playing a card game," he told me, in what I could only guess was his attempt at explaining their attire, or lack thereof. "Want to join us?"

I shook my head. Dylan hooked his thumbs in the belt loops of my jeans and dragged me closer for a long, slow kiss. It was the kind of kiss that nearly made me forget that he was fraternizing with what appeared to be a topless model.

"If you change your mind, you know where to find us," he said, scampering back into his brother's apartment and shutting the door.

I stood there for a moment, unsure of what to make of the situation. Out of the corner of my eye, I noticed Thomas quietly waiting next to the elevator. He seemed similarly undecided as to his next move.

"You were on your way out," I reminded him.

"Right."

"You're going to leave them in your apartment?"

"The whole band's in there. They won't miss me."

I found that reassuring. "Where were you going?"

"Just taking a stroll."

"It's cold out, you know." The weather had turned suddenly, and even though the temperature was now close to the average for this time of year, it felt bitterly cold since the last month had been unseasonably warm.

He held out his hat and gestured to his leather jacket.

I considered going into Dylan's empty apartment, alone, while he partied down the hall with strange women, and suddenly, fresh air seemed awfully appealing. "Would you mind some company?"

Thomas nodded acceptingly, and I motioned for him to wait a minute. I tossed my bag and purse into Dylan's apartment and rejoined Thomas in the hall.

We were quiet on the ride down, which wasn't surprising since Thomas had never been talkative.

"Evening Mr. Parker," the doorman greeted him, nodding politely to me. "Do you need your car?"

Thomas shook his head. "No thank you, Charles."

We set off down the street, the tall buildings adequately blocking the majority of the wind. We'd walked for about five minutes before either of us spoke.

"Does this change your mind? About the move?"

"Oh," I stammered, nervous laughter erupting from my mouth. I had to admit it was bad timing.

"You didn't tell him your answer yet."

I thought about Carrie, how self-righteously she'd react if I told her I'd changed my mind and why. "Yeah, but I didn't leave things on good terms with my roommate."

"We finished recording another song today. They were celebrating."

"You don't seem very celebratory." I glanced at him.

He smiled. "I'll celebrate when the album is done, in another week or two." Thomas tugged his hat off and pulled the hood of his sweatshirt up over his head. He handed me the hat.

"Thanks," I said. The hat was still warm from his head and smelled like men's shampoo.

"It was just marijuana," he said randomly.

"I figured," I replied, hoping it was true.

"And nothing's happening with the girls, at least not with Dylan. He doesn't even seem to notice them anymore."

"You're defending him," I pointed out. "Even though he and his rowdy friends are up trashing your apartment while you're freezing your ass off trying to avoid them."

He laughed, and I couldn't help but smile. I'd never heard Thomas laugh at himself before. He glanced at me, and his eyes were sparkling. In the dark, where the greenish hue of Thomas' eyes would've been imperceptible, Thomas' eyes looked almost exactly like Dylan's.

"He's my brother," he said. "And he really likes you."

I shivered, thrusting my bare hands further into my pockets. Moments like this, and I was ready for summer, frizzy hair days and all.

Thomas slung his arm around my waist, startling me. He must have noticed me shivering, but the gesture felt both overly familiar and incredibly wrong, all at once.

"Do you want to head back?" he asked.

I pictured Dylan and the lanky blonde again and shook my head. I could stick it out a little longer. "What was he like as a child?" I asked, changing the subject.

Thomas turned to me, smiling again. "Much like he is today."

I chuckled, although I imagined there was more truth to the statement than either of us wanted to admit.

"He was a prodigy, you know. Musically, speaking. He played the piano at three, the violin by four. Mum taught us both, but it always came more naturally for Dylan. He was an excellent performer, even in primary school, and whenever he got his hands on a new piece, he'd throw himself at it, playing it over and over again day and night until he'd mastered it."

"Really? He never mentioned that."

Thomas blew out a sigh. "Doesn't surprise me. He doesn't like to talk about his childhood much."

"Was he a happy child?" I asked. "I mean, before…"

"Who knows. He always had his moods. It was much different after Lucy, but even before he was rather melancholy from time to time. Usually on those days, he'd throw himself into his music." He paused. "Dylan was constantly reading as a teenager too, and he always had a knack for linguistics."

"What about you?" I asked him. "Were you a child musician too?"

"I played well enough, I s'pose. I performed when I had to, though my nerves were always an issue."

"Did you enjoy playing?"

He nodded. "I've always liked music. I've just never really felt it the way Dylan does. Music is part of his soul. He couldn't live without it. And when he's working on something, well, he's very driven. It possesses him until he's done, and then it's like he snaps back out of the trance."

I hesitated before asking my next question. "Was your sister a musician?"

"She played the piano quite well."

"Was she a performer?"

He slowed his pace, glanced around, then suggested we turn back. I had no idea how far we'd walked, so I agreed. I didn't expect him to answer my question, but a moment later, he continued.

"Lucy was deaf from birth," he said.

"I didn't know that. Dylan never…"

"Dylan doesn't talk about her." Thomas grew quiet and I suspected we were both thinking the same thing, that Dylan just didn't talk about her when he was awake. In his sleep, he spoke her name frequently since the trip to England. In dream, he'd speak to her and about her, but mostly he'd just call to her, like he was desperate to reach her.

"That's why you both know sign language," I concluded, remembering the day in England where they'd shown off that skill.

Thomas nodded.

"Dylan taught her to play the piano. She would sit by him for hours a day while he practiced. She was a lot like him. She could feel the music, even if she couldn't hear it." Thomas was watching his feet as we walked, but his arm was still tight around my waist.

"What happened to her? If you don't mind telling me."

"She was hit by a car." His words fell softly into the cold night. I struggled to think of a response, but then he continued.

"Mum was so protective of her, but one day Lucy was out with Dylan, and they were each carrying a big stack of sheet music. Lucy dropped hers and the wind blew it into the road. She went to pick it up. Dylan called to her, tried to get to her, but she couldn't hear the car, and the driver didn't stop in time." He sighed, and I wondered how many times he'd told that story, to be able to get through it relatively calmly.

"Before Lucy died, Dylan was Mum's favorite, and Lucy's. Mum never outright blamed him for what happened, but after that day, I was always her clear favorite. For Dylan, it was like he lost his two favorite people on the same day." He pulled his arm away quickly, as though he'd been caught in a compromising position.

I glanced up and saw we were nearing the apartment building. "I'm sorry," I said. "That's terrible."

He shrugged. "Yes, but it was a long time ago."

We made our way back into the building and up on the elevator. I returned his hat to him and he unlocked Dylan's door. "Shall I send him home before he passes out?" he asked.

"Sure," I said. "Goodnight."

Thomas smiled at me, a genuinely friendly smile. "Thank you for keeping me company tonight. Sleep well." He hesitated before turning and retreating to his own apartment. As he opened the door, I heard the same loud music and voices as earlier, and I quickly shut Dylan's apartment door.

By that time, I was tired, and it was late. I changed into pajama pants and a tank top and climbed into bed. I was asleep moments after I switched off the lamp.

CHAPTER NINE

"But his dreams were as gigantic as his surroundings were small."
Thomas Hardy, *Jude the Obscure*

When I awoke the next morning, Dylan was asleep beside me. He was wearing boxers and clearly had showered after he returned home. I tried to figure out how I'd slept through it all, but came up empty handed. I didn't have long to dwell on it anyway. It was a Friday, and I had to be at work soon.

I snuck out of the bed and went to shower. As steam flooded the room, I decided I was angry with Dylan for the previous night, so I would tell him I was still considering his cohabitation offer. I wouldn't have to tell Carrie I was maybe changing my mind, just that I was going to wait, maybe until after his album came out and he had more free time.

When I finished showering and was all ready for work, I leaned over Dylan and kissed him gently on the forehead. I had debated not waking him, but didn't want to be rude by sleeping at his place and then sneaking out. His eyes inched open slowly.

"Hey," I whispered. "I'm leaving for work now."

He frowned. "I thought you quit."

"No, that's my other job. And I didn't quit yet." I didn't bother to add that I couldn't quit at all if I wasn't moving in with him. "It's morning," I added, sensing his confusion.

"Oh." He glanced at me and smiled. "You're beautiful in the morning."

"Thanks. You had a late night last night."

"Yes. I'm sorry about that. We just had some friends that were visiting from the U.K., and I s'pose it got a bit out of hand. Why didn't you stay?"

"I was tired," I said. "And you seemed to be having fun without me."

He pouted. "Oh, Lily, everything is more fun with you." Suddenly, his face lit up. "Thomas said you're moving in. Shall I arrange for a truck for next weekend?"

I hesitated. Thomas had given me the impression that he didn't think I should move in, so it surprised me that he told Dylan. "I don't know if I can pack up that quickly."

He stuck out his lower lip and pouted. "Please, Lily."

"We'll see. I gotta go." And I headed out to work.

* * *

WITHIN A WEEK, I'd put in my notice at Echo and moved in with Dylan. Since it was the first time I'd officially lived with a boyfriend, I was hesitant to tell my parents, but, oddly enough, they were thrilled. And since Dylan knew my late nights working were drawing to a quick end, he didn't hassle me about being gone all the time. I'd managed to leave on relatively good terms with Carrie, and my mom let me store the stuff I didn't need anymore (like my giant floral bedspread) at her house, so Dylan and I didn't have to worry about too many duplicate household items.

Even the move went smoothly, with Dylan hiring people to do the heavy lifting and then staying out of my way while I arranged all of my clothes and personal stuff. He'd even cleared off an entire bookshelf in his studio for my favorite books.

On my last day of work at Echo, my boss Brad and a few coworkers surprised me with drinks at the end of my shift. I had told Dylan I'd be home shortly before two, but clearly now I was going to be later. I called him, knowing he'd worry that I'd been kidnapped or mugged if I was late. When he didn't answer, I left a message saying I was staying late to celebrate the last day of work with my coworkers. Dylan didn't call back, so I spent the next hour and a half drinking and reminiscing with my friends and coworkers.

I didn't think I'd really miss this job—the hours were terrible, and while the tips were good, it was often stressful waiting on drunks in a noisy club where the focus was on the performance and not the food or drink. But still, I'd worked there since I first came to New York, and I had lots of memories in that club. Despite the nostalgia, I was ready to move on by the time I pulled my purse out from behind the bar to leave.

Jack, the bartender, was heading out at the same time. "Come on, it's late. I'll walk with you," he offered.

"You know I moved," I reminded him as we started onto the street. "It's not much of a walk."

"You moved in with your rocker boyfriend, right?"

I nodded, and realized I hadn't chatted with Jack much lately. We used to stay late at work together a lot, and he'd always been my go-to person when I needed a male perspective on life. For some reason, though, I hadn't discussed Dylan with him. It didn't make sense, really. Jack was infinitely cooler than I was, always recognizing the best bands before they even knew themselves, and always knowing exactly which drinks to make for which ladies. So one would think I'd have bragged to him first when I finally began dating someone indisputably cool.

"You seem different lately," he observed.

"I do?" I had been rushing out of the club at the end of my shifts since I'd started seeing Dylan. "I've been really happy, though."

"That's good. I have to admit, I was a little surprised you were okay with your new boyfriend's, uh, lifestyle."

I frowned. "What do you mean?"

"Oh, you know."

"The travel and touring? The fans?"

Even in the dark, he looked flustered. "I meant the drugs. He's got a reputation for dabbling in some pretty serious stuff."

My cell phone rang before I could answer. It was Dylan. "Hey babe, I'll be home in ten minutes," I said.

"That's him, isn't it?" Jack asked.

"Who was that?" Dylan wanted to know.

"A coworker is walking me home. See you soon," I said, hanging up before he could interrogate me. I wanted to get back to the discussion with Jack before we reached home.

"Where'd you hear that?" I asked him.

He shrugged. "I don't know. It's not exactly a secret. He seems pretty open with it. I've heard he's high at most of his concerts."

I shook my head. "No, that's just a rumor. Dylan's no goody-two-shoes, but he's not a junkie either. I know he's dabbled in some stuff in the past, but alcohol's his drug of choice now. As far as the other stuff, he's been clean since we met."

"Lily." Jack said my name with such skepticism that I stopped and turned to him.

"What?"

"You never lie to me about guys." He shook his head. "I don't care. I'm not judgmental. I just pegged you as the type to settle down with a stable guy, not a partier."

"I'm not lying." I said, ignoring the rest of his statement.

His eyes narrowed and he snorted. "You really think he's not using coke?"

"He's not, Jack. I live with him. I'd know."

"Would you?" Jack was still eying me skeptically, his tone incredulous. "Moody, secretive, doesn't sleep regular hours, goes through really hyper periods…"

"You just described every guy I've ever dated," I joked. I slowed to a stop since we'd already reached the apartment.

"Red eyes, stuffy nose, jittery… You haven't noticed any of that?"

I shook my head. "I've got to go. Keep in touch."

Jack glanced up at the building. "Nice place. You be careful, and take care of yourself."

"Thanks." I hugged him, lingering longer than for a normal goodbye hug since this really was goodbye, probably not for forever, but for a while at least.

I considered what he'd said as I rode up the elevator, but quickly dismissed it. Jack and I had always flirted harmlessly. Of course it was hard for him to see me happily coupled off while he was still single.

Dylan met me in the hall as soon as I exited the elevator. "Who's your friend?"

"Jack, the bartender at Echo. You met him." I wandered into the apartment and plopped my purse down. "Sorry I'm so late. They surprised me with a little party."

The words had barely left my lips when Dylan slammed me against the wall and pressed my hands above my head. The impact startled me, but I was in no mood to protest since his lips were already on mine. I returned the kiss eagerly, welcoming his sudden assault.

I glanced into his eyes before closing my own and noticed the redness, but really, it was nearly the middle of the night. Of course his eyes would be red.

Dylan kissed me hard for another minute, his tongue

invading my mouth frantically. Then he gripped both of my wrists in one of his hands while he undid my fly. My heart was beating fast, and I could feel his doing the same through his chest.

He freed my hands, yanked off my shirt, and his mouth moved lower, nibbling on my ear, sucking on my neck, then tracing his tongue along my nipple before taking it in his mouth. A slight moan escaped my throat right before he moved to the other breast, this time nibbling and biting at me until I cried out. It hadn't hurt so much as just caught me off guard. I opened my eyes and saw him staring back at me, a wild look in his eyes.

Suddenly, Dylan lifted me away from the wall and bent me over the edge of the couch. I shrieked from the suddenness and shock of it as he entered me, but something about his desperation for me was a huge turn on. I quickly felt the tension build deep inside me as I began to move my hips in sync with his. His hands reached around to my breasts, pinching at my nipples, and his teeth grazed along my earlobe. I felt myself gasping for air, saw colors flashing before my closed eyes, and heard myself moan loudly as I came. Dylan pulled at my hair, causing me to yelp again, then he clasped his arms so tightly around me that I thought he would crush me, and then he was still.

He pulled away from me and was already in the bathroom before I had even registered any of what had happened. I stood slowly and wrapped myself in the blanket that had been draped over the couch. I wasn't quite sure what to make of the experience. Obviously, I'd enjoyed myself, although I'd never really pictured rough sex as my thing.

Dylan emerged from the bathroom and went straight to me. He lifted me up and kissed me firmly. When he set me down, he traced his finger along my neck and smiled mischievously. Before I could question him about the rationale behind the smile, he kissed my neck.

"Sorry, I left a mark," he mumbled, brushing past me into the kitchen.

I went into the bathroom to look at my neck. Sure enough, he'd left two little marks, although I wasn't sure if they classified more as bite marks or hickeys. I showered and brushed my teeth, then crawled into bed. Dylan was there waiting, thirstily drinking from a bottle of water. He eyed me hungrily as I crawled under the sheets.

His arm roped around me, sliding me close. I could feel him pressing against my back and knew he was ready for round two.

"I'm too tired," I said. "And sore."

He seemed surprised at my last comment. "Really?"

"You weren't exactly gentle."

"I thought we'd try something new. You seemed to enjoy it."

I couldn't help smiling. "That doesn't mean I want to enjoy it twice in one night."

Dylan ducked beneath the covers, covering my lower body in kisses, licking anywhere he suspected he'd made sore.

"What are you doing?"

"Apologizing for the roughness," he replied in between licks, his voice muffled from the covers.

I felt my breath quickening and knew he was doing a lot more than apologizing. "You're sneaky," I said, my voice shaking.

Dylan slowly slid back up my body, keeping my legs spread so the tip of his swollen arousal just happened to fall in place as his mouth was even with mine. "Oops," he teased. "That doesn't hurt, does it?" He shifted his hips slowly as if making a point.

I smiled and let him continue the rhythmic motion for another minute before the pressure mounted too high and I had to join in. As soon as he felt me lifting my own hips to meet his, Dylan sped up, and this time, we both came together. He slid off of me slowly, and I was asleep within minutes.

* * *

THE NEXT DAY, we'd planned a dinner with Jill and Scott. I'd had my doubts about Dylan making the stellar impression I'd hoped for, only because he clearly hadn't slept much the night before, but my concerns were totally unjustified.

The whole night couldn't have been better. He was affectionate and charming with me and friendly and calm with my friends. He was funny and seemed to be able to relate to Scott even though the two had absolutely nothing in common. Dylan even held my hand the majority of the meal.

The only thing that put a damper on the night was that stupid warning from Jack, the bartender. Dylan blew or wiped his nose at least ten times during the meal. Each time, he apologized for his allergies. While I knew that was the most logical explanation, Jack's stupid words kept creeping into my head.

After we ordered dessert, but before it arrived, Jill and I excused ourselves to the bathroom.

"Oh my God, I love him!" Jill gushed before we'd even shut the door behind us.

"Really? I'm so glad."

"I'll admit it, I had my doubts. But he really seems perfect for you. Scott even seems to like him." She paused. "Do you think he likes us?"

"Of course. You'd know if he didn't."

"I can't remember the last time Scott paid that much attention to me during dinner."

I smiled. That was one of my favorite things about Dylan, that no matter what we were doing, he always made me feel like the most important person in the room. "Oh, you know how things are early on in the relationship."

"I don't know. If you're already living together and still like each other this much, I think he's a keeper."

We returned to the table and finished the meal. When we left the restaurant and picked up the cars from the valet, Scott was thrilled by the Porsche, so we stood around and chatted some more before politely making our escape.

Dylan and I went to bed early that night, both of us needing to work the next day. Dylan was meeting with the band, putting the finishing touches on the album. I worked my normal hours, but he wasn't home until after I'd gone to bed. The morning after that, he was still asleep when I was ready for work. Apparently, we were still like two ships passing in the night even now that we lived together.

I kissed him softly on the forehead before I snuck out, not intending to wake him, but his eyes quickly fluttered open.

"Stay," he commanded.

"Can't. Work."

"But I haven't seen you for days," he whined.

"I know."

"And tonight's the big party, so I won't get to be alone with you then."

"We can spend all day tomorrow together," I promised.

"Or you could ditch work and we could hang out today." He flashed that devilish grin at me.

"I already lost one job. I should probably hold on to the other," I said, kissing him again and then heading out. It was hard, with our different hours, but I knew it would be better once the album was out. Well, at least until he started touring, and then I didn't even want to think about what we'd do.

CHAPTER TEN

"If all the world hated you, and believed you wicked, while your own conscience
approved you, and absolved you from guilt, you would not be without friends."
Charlotte Bronte, *Jane Eyre*

*T*hat night, Dylan and I went to the party celebrating the end of the recording process for Sierra's album. As soon as we walked into Echo, the noise was overwhelming. Usually, the main room was filled by live music, or at least recorded music in between live performances, but now the racket was mostly voices— hundreds of them. Dylan grinned excitedly, kissed me on the cheek, and dragged me enthusiastically into the center of the crowd.

I immediately felt like I was in high school all over again, dating the quarterback of the football team even though I wasn't head cheerleader. Not that I'd ever actually dated the quarterback, or any athlete, really, but I was just overwhelmed by the sensation that I was out of my league.

Dylan held tight to my hand as he made the rounds, introducing me to dozens of people I'd never remember, and greeting nearly every woman with a kiss on the cheek. Ari waved at me, then stole Dylan away for a moment, leaving me in a group of six grungy-looking Brits. We'd had champagne in the car on the way over, but I was suddenly feeling the need for more alcohol. I excused myself and made my way to the bar.

Brad, my boss, or rather my former boss, was at the bar next to Jack. Both men were surveying the room. I nodded hello to both of them.

"Your boyfriend sure knows a lot of people," Jack commented.

I glanced around, wondering how well Dylan knew all of them, especially some of the skankier-looking women. "Thanks for letting them have this here."

Brad shrugged. "I'm not doing anyone any favors. We're still charging for the drinks."

I nodded. I knew Ari was paying for the party, although I didn't know what the total was. Still, the club didn't often close for private events, especially not for an employee who just quit.

"What'll it be?"

"A bottle of tequila," a voice said from behind me.

I turned to see Thomas. He was wearing jeans and a black tee shirt, coordinating perfectly with the tall brunette at his side, clad in a micro-mini black leather skirt and silver halter top. "Good evening, Lily," he greeted me. "This is, uh…Heather." He already sounded drunk, even though he couldn't have arrived more than twenty minutes before us.

Jack held out a bottle of Patrón and a stack of shot glasses. Thomas filled four shot glasses then called to Dylan. By some miracle, Dylan heard his brother's voice out of the millions of other noises separating them. He quickly joined us at the bar, resting an empty beer bottle on the counter beside him. We made a sizable dent in the contents of the bottle in a matter of minutes, and then were overwhelmed with cheering as Sierra's newest single began blasting over the sound system.

The next hour was a blur of excitement. The whole band was there, tons of their friends, and I suppose some loyal fans. Dylan was happy and beyond affectionate, and we were both more than a little tipsy. I was inebriated enough to overlook the hoard of women hitting on Dylan, and, for the first time, I was starting to feel like I fit in with his crowd.

I was drunkenly chatting up Gavin and Owen, Sierra's drummer and bass guitarist, when I noticed them exchanging wary glances. I didn't think anything of it until I turned and saw a young blonde follow Dylan into the bathroom. I tried not to jump to conclusions, but it was obvious from the looks on his bandmate's faces that I wasn't overreacting.

"I'll catch up with you guys later," I said, taking off towards the bathroom. I had no idea what I was going to say or do, but heading in the direction Dylan had gone seemed like the right thing to do. I hadn't seen which bathroom they went in, but I figured I'd try the women's first. I opened the door, but there were just a few women in there, chatting and reapplying makeup.

I started towards the men's room, but as I reached for the doorknob, a hand grabbed my wrist.

"Don't," Thomas said, his voice firm.

I glanced up and saw that his date was nowhere to be seen. I jiggled the knob, but it was locked, a clear indication of Dylan's guilt. I flashed Thomas my best I-told-you-so look but then realized I had nothing to be pleased about.

I felt sick.

I contemplated pounding on the door, but for what? It was obvious what was happening, but the worst part was that I really hadn't seen it coming. Out of everyone I'd ever dated, Dylan was the last man I'd have expected to cheat on me. Especially right in front of me. He may have occasionally been reckless, but he sure wasn't stupid.

"Asshole," I murmured.

Thomas tried to pull me away from the door, probably worried I'd start kicking it and make a scene. "It's not what you think."

I let out a sick laugh. "What? You mean Dylan's not in there playing cards with some nice lady? Or maybe they're doing each other's hair. Or fixing the toilets perhaps? Because there are so many fucking possibilities for what he could be doing in there with that girl."

Thomas rolled his eyes. He looked stressed out, which seemed pointless since it didn't really affect him if his brother had issues with monogamy. "He's not cheating on you, Lily."

"Right," I said. "And you're not the pathetic big brother that covers for Dylan no matter how many people he fucks over." I turned to leave, stumbling over Thomas' foot. He grabbed my elbow to stabilize me, then pounded his fist loudly on the door.

"Dylan, it's Tom."

We heard a woman giggle, then the lock clicked and the door opened. Thomas stepped in first, then pushed the door open wider so I could see. The woman, still fully clothed, was standing by the paper towel dispenser, while Dylan, also dressed, was near the window, smoking. A second guy was in the room, by the sink.

Relief washed over me before my brain registered the full scene. Thomas was right; Dylan hadn't been cheating on me.

But since I'd been drinking, it took me a moment to realize what we'd interrupted, and why the door had been locked.

And then I saw it, the faint white residue on the black countertops beside the sink, the glossed-over redness in the woman's eyes. She gazed up at me wearily, then trudged out of the bathroom. The other guy just stood there awkwardly for a moment before following.

"Jesus, Thomas, what the fuck?" Dylan said, tossing his

cigarette out the window they'd cracked.

"She saw you go in here and thought you were cheating on her," he explained unapologetically. Then he glanced to me, expressionless, and left, no doubt heading back to his precious Heather.

Dylan laughed. "If I were going to cheat, it wouldn't be with her," he joked. "And certainly not with an audience."

"Dylan," I began.

He came closer and kissed me, his breath thick with cigarettes and alcohol. "I would never cheat on you, Lily."

I actually believed him, but found myself distracted by the residue on the counter. Dylan followed my gaze and swept his hand casually across the counter, brushing the powder into the sink. Then he wiped his nose and motioned for me to follow him out.

I waited for him to apologize, to make excuses, but he didn't. He simply led me out onto the dance floor with his hand slung low on my hip.

"What were you doing in there? Why was the door locked, Dylan?"

He leaned in closer. "It's a party, love. We're celebrating tonight. You can yell at me tomorrow, but please, let's enjoy the night."

He squeezed my hand, plastered a smile onto his face, and rejoined the party, quickly offering me another drink and taking one for himself. I drank mine, remembering to make my smile match his, and tried to ignore his red eyes, constant fidgeting, and incessant sniffling.

I glanced over at the bar, and, just as I'd feared, Jack was staring at us, a smug look of concern on his face. I smiled and waved casually at him, determined not to let him know he'd been right. At that moment, I hated Jack. I hated myself. And I definitely hated Dylan.

But Dylan was right—no good could come from making a

scene at the party.

It was after three in the morning when we got back home, and I was still drunk—drunk enough to ignore the gravity of what I'd seen that night and to be oddly flattered that Dylan wasn't cheating on me. Besides, Dylan was also all over me the second we entered the apartment. We had sex three times that night before passing out, and I was too tired to dwell on the possible connection between his insatiable sex drive and his activities from earlier in the evening.

When I woke up the next morning, Dylan was gone.

As flashes of the night before hit me, all the anger flooded back to me. I slowly crawled out of bed, my head throbbing and my stomach churning uneasily. I glanced around the room for him, then headed to the bathroom. There was Dylan, face down on the tiled floor.

"Dylan," I said, nudging him with my foot.

His eyes opened slowly, and I could tell he felt infinitely worse than I did. Good. He deserved to feel like shit.

"Fuck," he mumbled. "Where am I?"

"Your bathroom."

He sat up slowly and arched his back, stretching his neck from side to side. His skin was pale, his eyes sunken and red, and his hair was mussed. "You're angry," he realized.

I nodded. "You locked yourself in a bathroom with another woman and snorted illegal drugs at a party in a public place." I waited for him to deny it, to tell me he hadn't actually tried the drugs.

"Right," he said instead, his accent thicker than usual. "Sorry for that. It was just blow."

"What?" I couldn't help but scream. His nonchalant admission infuriated me even more.

He stood slowly, and I tried to avert my eyes, too angry to enjoy how hot he looked in his tight-fitting boxer briefs. "Well, it's not like we were shooting up heroin or meth or anything."

"Really? Are you honestly trying to tell me it's not that bad to use cocaine?"

"Whatever," he mumbled, brushing past me. He went into the kitchen and retrieved a soda from the fridge.

I followed him, unable to believe my ears. He couldn't possibly still be high, so I wasn't sure what excuse he thought he had for this behavior. I glared at him as he chugged his drink.

"Jesus, Lily, what do you want me to say? I get it, okay? You're pissed off. I'm a dick. I'm sorry. Let's move on. Now drop it."

"I'm not going to drop it. I moved in here because you swore you wouldn't do drugs again. Cocaine could kill you. Do you understand that? It's addictive and it's deadly. And very illegal."

He swung around quickly. "Fuck, Lily. I hear you, okay? But I'm not dead, I'm not an addict, and no one got caught. It was a party. My party. We were celebrating."

I opened my mouth to say something when Dylan's cell phone rang. I rolled my eyes as he checked the caller ID and then, oblivious to the stern look on my face clearly telling him to ignore the call, answered. He listened to the caller for a moment, then handed me the phone. He started to the shower.

It was my mother.

"What is wrong with your phone, Lily? I tried calling you several times."

I glanced around the room, and then realized I must have let the battery die. I couldn't remember when Dylan possibly would have given my mom his number, but he must have, since it wasn't listed anywhere.

"Sorry, Mom," I mumbled. "I need to call you later, though. This isn't a good time."

"Lily, your grandmother fell last night. She broke her pelvis and she's about to have surgery. I thought you should know, and that you might want to be here to visit her when she wakes up."

"Oh my God. Is she okay?"

"She's in a lot of pain. I'm at the hospital, so I can't talk long."

"Yeah, I'll be there as soon as I can. What's the address?"

When I hung up with my mother, Dylan was already out of the shower. Our eyes met briefly, and I finally felt like he looked apologetic.

"Take a shower and then I'll drive you," he said.

I nodded and started for the shower.

"Lily," he said, his fingers grasping mine. "I am sorry about last night. I was drunk and I wasn't thinking. It was stupid and I regret it. I swear it's not something I do regularly, I just… I don't know. Gwen and Andy were there, and they offered, and I messed up."

He sighed before continuing. "I didn't mean to hurt you and it won't happen again. I love you."

I shook free of his hand and climbed into the shower. Something told me that apology shouldn't suffice, but my focus shifted immediately back to my grandmother, and I let it drop.

* * *

DYLAN'S PHONE ran seven or eight times while he drove to the hospital in Jersey. He finally answered as we pulled into the parking lot, told Ari he couldn't come in today, then switched his phone off.

"You don't have to do that," I said. "You can just drop me off and head back. I know you're busy."

He shook his head. "I owe you, Lily. Besides, I'm not going to make you hang out at the hospital alone." He kissed my hand, and we walked into the hospital.

It was a long day, and my grandma didn't seem particularly well after surgery, but Dylan stayed with me the whole time. It was evening by the time we were driving home. We were both tired and emotionally drained, but I knew I'd forgiven him.

When we parked in front of the building, I stayed in the car, like always, since I knew Dylan would walk around and open my door for me. Before he did, though, I heard a commotion, and realized he was being photographed by the paparazzi. He leaned in the car, lingering for a moment.

"I guess the press is picking up over the new album, love," he whispered. "Do you still want to come in with me now, or would you rather wait?"

I considered this, then held my hand out to him. I probably didn't look my greatest, but then again, no one would be looking at me as long as Dylan was at my side.

He held my hand tightly as he handed the keys to the doorman then waved at the photographers. He smiled politely, but ignored their requests for details on the album.

As we rode up in the elevator, he kissed me. "Sorry about that. I'm not too accustomed to being stalked. Ari warned us but said it's a good thing. I suppose we shall see."

"Dylan, that girl from last night, Gwen, have you ever slept with her?"

He appeared to consider this for a moment, then shook his head. "No. I don't believe I have."

His response puzzled me, but seemed honest, and I decided not to bring up anything from the night before ever again.

* * *

THE NEXT FEW days were busy for Dylan. Even though the band had finished recording, it was already time to plot out the tour and other publicity. On top of that, they held near-constant practice. I grew accustomed to dropping by the studio after work to listen to them rehearse for a while each day, but I never stayed long. When Sierra played, it was wonderful. But in between each song—or sometimes several times during a song—they'd stop and yell at each other for various slip-ups or artistic differences. It was not a relaxing way to spend an evening.

On a couple occasions, the girl Thomas had brought to the

party, Heather, was there too. In theory it should have been nice to have some female company while we watched the guys rehearse, but seeing her just reminded me of the night of the party and Dylan's foray into narcotics.

I could tell just from looking at Heather that I had nothing in common with her. The first day, she'd worn faded jeans with holes, her black bra showed clearly from underneath her too-tight white tee shirt, and her shirt hardly came even close to covering her belly button piercing. She had a pack of cigarettes wedged in her back pocket and long acrylic nails that were painted black.

She wasn't a big conversationalist and when she did talk, she didn't seem to have much of substance to say. I supposed she was nice enough, but she certainly wasn't the brightest bulb in the pack. I just didn't know what Thomas saw in Heather. He couldn't possibly have anything in common with her, but he was all over her whenever there was a break in between songs.

When Dylan and I were alone, he'd play the guitar for me, massage my shoulders, and read Shakespearian sonnets while I curled up in his lap. But when he was away, which was often, he seemed irritable and unpredictable. He worked all night several nights a week, greeting me in the morning with bloodshot eyes, and then waking for his day when I returned from work. His allergies seemed to be worsening too, but then again, that could have something to do with the sleep.

I had no reason to suspect anything was awry, but that didn't stop me from worrying. I kept replaying Jack's warnings in my head and I couldn't shake the feeling that something was wrong.

The next week, Dylan had to be in Vegas on Monday morning. He had some sort of interview that day, then something else Tuesday, so he wouldn't return until Wednesday. It would've been the perfect opportunity to catch up with Jill, since I'd been so busy with Dylan since our double date that I hadn't really seen her, but she and Scott were on vacation. I also hadn't gone to my parents since my grandma's fall, so I decided to spend the day with them on Sunday.

I caught the late train that night, but by the time I caught a cab to drive me back to the apartment, I regretted dining with my parents. My stomach was flip-flopping and I started to sweat. I clutched my midsection as I searched in vain for Tums in my purse, and prayed the cabbie drove fast.

I barely made it in the door of the apartment before vomiting. After, I felt a little better, but only long enough to clean up the mess and curl up on the couch.

It was the longest night of my life, and I ended up spending the vast majority of it on the bathroom floor. I finally fell asleep at some point, but my phone awoke me before much time had passed. It was Dylan, so I answered despite the overwhelming weakness that made me question my ability to lift even something as light as my cell phone.

"Hi Dylan," I mumbled.

"Lily, you sound terrible. What's wrong?"

"I think I have food poisoning or maybe a stomach virus." I had called my parents earlier to check on them, and they too were sick, so it had to either be something we'd all eaten, or some contagion we'd all been exposed to.

"Oh no, that's terrible. I wish I could be there to take care of you."

"Me too," I mumbled. "I've never felt this horrible before." Then I heard the dreaded gurgling in my stomach. "I better go. Good luck today."

"Thanks love," he said casually, clicking off the phone just before I turned to the toilet again.

By evening, the vomiting had stopped, but my heart was still racing and I felt feverish. The weakness had spread, and I was so dehydrated that I had to sit down in the shower to keep from collapsing.

Dylan texted when his interview was over and asked how I

was feeling. I'd typed a simple "like I'm dying" in response, but it honestly didn't feel like an exaggeration. I crawled towards the kitchen in the late afternoon, praying I'd find a Gatorade or soda cracker or even a seltzer water, but to no avail. The fridge held a variety of beer and an opened bottle of chardonnay, along with some salad greens and other veggies I'd bought at a farmer's market that weekend. The pantry had loads of tea and some granola, but nothing that looked suitable for my stomach's current state.

Irritated, I texted Dylan, demanding to know why he never went to the store. Within minutes, he called.

"I thought you were too sick to eat," he said.

"Well now I'm too weak to move. I just want a piece of toast or something. Soup, maybe crackers, I don't know. But you don't have any real food in your fucking apartment." I felt moderately bad about my tone, since I knew I wasn't really mad at Dylan, but it was hard to monitor my attitude when I felt like I was dying.

"You could go to the store sometime. You live there too," he replied dryly.

"Gee thanks, that's super helpful now." I grimaced as I heard several female voices in the background.

"What do you want me to say, Lily? I'm on the opposite side of the bloody country and you call to yell at me about my shopping habits."

"A little sympathy would be nice."

He sighed. "I'm sorry. Why don't you call Jill or your parents or another friend?

"My parents are sick too, and Jill is out of town." And I didn't really have any other friends since I'd started spending every waking moment with my boyfriend.

"Order some food then. I've got to go Lily. Feel better."

Then, he actually hung up. I was so angry that I nearly chucked the phone across the room. Instead, I made myself a hot cup of tea and nibbled on an apple and crawled back into bed.

When I awoke the next morning, I was ravenous. I sat up quickly, then winced at the throbbing pain in my head. I reached for the cup on my bedside table, only to discover that it was empty.

I was debating whether I could shower without fainting when I realized there was a knocking at the door. Since a key was needed to reach the floor, I knew it wasn't some random salesman. It was probably the doorman, bringing up food that Dylan had ordered for me after our talk. Or maybe it was Dylan, and he'd just forgotten his key.

I made my way as quickly to the door as possible in my current condition and peered through the peephole. But it wasn't Dylan or some wonderful surprise he'd orchestrated as an apology. It was Thomas.

I glanced down to make sure I wasn't indecent and then opened the door. The surprise on his face when he saw me was palpable.

"Wow, Lily you look terrible!"

"Gee thanks," I mumbled, shuffling to the couch. I plopped a pillow on my lap and curled over it.

"Sorry, I didn't mean…"

"Yes you did. But I know. I feel terrible too."

I turned to see what the rustling sound was. Thomas was unpacking a bag of groceries.

"I thought you were in Vegas with Dylan," I said.

"I was. I took the red-eye and got in earlier this morning."

I swiveled to face him. "Is Dylan back too?"

"No, he couldn't leave yet."

"Couldn't or didn't want to?"

Thomas handed me a plate with toast on it.

"Thank you," I said politely. "I can't believe you brought groceries."

He went back to the kitchen and returned with a small bottle of Gatorade. "This beverage is blue," he said warily. "Are you sure it's intended for human consumption? I could brew some tea instead."

I wrinkled my nose. "I'm sick of tea." I snatched the Gatorade from his hand. He watched me curiously as I sipped it.

Within minutes of eating and drinking, I started to feel moderately better.

"I also brought some lemon-lime soda, gelatin, soda crackers, applesauce, bananas, soup, and seltzer. Can I get you anything else?"

"No, this is great. Really, thank you Thomas. I'm already starting to feel better."

He sat on the armrest of the couch opposite me. "Your color is improving."

I smiled. "So how come you needed to rush home? The red-eye can't be very pleasant." Thomas handled more of the business side of the band. It wasn't unheard of for him to handle meetings that Dylan managed to skip.

Thomas frowned. "No reason."

I washed down my last piece of toast with a large sip of Gatorade before realizing what he was saying. "Wait, you flew overnight to bring me groceries and Dylan couldn't even bother calling this morning to check on me?"

He hesitated. "Dylan needed to stay another day and I didn't. He asked me to check on you and bring you some groceries." He paused. "Although I'm sure he would've come himself if he knew you were this badly off."

"I doubt that," I mumbled. "He sounded like he was enjoying himself. He could barely tear himself away from those girls long enough to yell at me over the grocery shopping."

"Dylan loves you, Lily. He just doesn't always know how to show it."

"What did he have in Vegas today that was so important?"

"I don't know, but honestly you don't need to worry about him. Ari is there too."

"I'm not dating Ari."

Thomas stood. "I'm going to warm up the soup. You need to eat more."

"Why are you always defending Dylan?"

"He's my brother," Thomas said. "And he's a good man. I see the effect you have on him and how much you mean to him and, I don't know. I just can't stand watching him fuck it up."

"Do you think he'd do this for you? Fly all night to bring soup to your sick girlfriend so you could stay in Vegas and party?"

"In a heartbeat. But really, it's not like that. It's just been so long since Dylan's had a functional relationship that he doesn't know how it works."

He brought a bowl of soup to me and sat down again.

"You shouldn't get too close to me. I might be contagious. And besides, I probably stink."

"You smell like oranges and vanilla, as always," he replied.

I smiled at the unexpected compliment and then wrinkled my nose, knowing that no matter how I smelled, I still looked nightmarish. "I guess I should be relieved that Dylan isn't seeing me looking like this."

"You look beautiful," Thomas said, not missing a beat.

"I appreciate the British charm, Thomas, but you already said I look terrible."

"You looked like you felt terrible. But you could never really look terrible. And actually I think it suits you to go without so much makeup."

"Are you saying I wear too much makeup?"

"I'm only saying that you look pretty without it," he replied. Shaking his head, he added, "Sheesh, I see what Dylan means now. You're exasperating. You know, British women know how to take a compliment."

"Heather isn't British," I reminded him.

"Heather isn't a lot of things."

My phone buzzed just then and we both glanced down. It was Dylan.

"Don't tell him I'm here," Thomas said quickly, standing. "I'll come by later to check on you."

I nodded, but found it odd that he wouldn't want Dylan to know, since he said Dylan asked him to come. "Thank you," I mouthed as he let himself out.

* * *

DYLAN RETURNED HOME the next afternoon. He brought flowers and a gorgeous chocolate brown suede purse. He apologized for his short fuse on the phone and gave me an hour-long massage without even nagging me for sex. We took a long bubble bath later, and then he offered to go to the store so he could make me dinner.

"You don't cook," I reminded him.

He glanced around the kitchen. "And I see you already went to the store."

"Oh, no, that's just the stuff Thomas brought over."

Dylan raised an eyebrow. "My brother Thomas? When was he here?"

"He came by yesterday, after he got back in town," I replied, understanding now why Thomas hadn't wanted me to mention his visit to Dylan.

"How thoughtful," he mumbled, leaning in to kiss me.

I pulled away. "Dylan, I might still be contagious. We never figured out if it was food poisoning or a virus."

"I'll take my chances. No stomach virus could be worse than the pain of not being able to kiss you another day." And he pulled me close for a slow, delicious kiss. When he finally released me, the weakness had returned, but in a good way.

"Let's just order in dinner," he murmured, guiding me over to the couch.

CHAPTER ELEVEN

"These violent delights have violent ends
And in their triumph die, like fire and powder, Which as they kiss
consume."
William Shakespeare, *Romeo and Juliet*

*A*fter taking a couple sick days that week, I was in an amazing mood when I left for work the following Monday morning. Dylan had been practicing with the rest of the band late the night before, but as soon as he'd gotten home, he'd awakened me for the best sex we'd had to date. It was the kind of sex that had me still smiling hours later, despite the obnoxious buzzing of the alarm clock.

I had snuck out to avoid waking him, grabbing coffee and a scone on the way to work. By the time I got to work, I was whistling.

Bridget frowned as I walked into the office. "Why are you so chipper?"

I grinned and shrugged, hoping it wasn't that obvious. "New

boots," I finally said. And that was true. Dylan had bought me boots over the weekend. They were smooth black leather with a sassy pointed toe and a delicate heel, accented with soft beige faux-fur around the top and inside, making them every bit as comfy as they were stylish. I'd had my eye on them for some time now, and they went perfectly with my purple paisley skirt and cable knit sweater.

Bridget nodded approvingly at the boots. "You always have the best accessories," she said. "Seriously, where did you get the purse? And that necklace?"

I smiled. "Dylan," I admitted. There was no way I could afford a Prada bag or any sort of jewelry that didn't turn my skin green. I had to hand it to him—he definitely had taste. He knew how to spoil a girl. Of course, I was sure the sex was more responsible for my current smiles than the gifts, but they didn't hurt either.

"I better get to work," I told her, and I skipped off to my desk.

Dylan sent me a text on his way to meet with the rest of the band. They were supposed to finalize the schedule for their tour and approve the promotional materials. I didn't know what that encompassed, but I figured it couldn't possibly take all day, so I tried to finish up early so I could sneak out of the office right at five.

I called Dylan at five, but he didn't answer, so I met up with Jill at the gym. We sweated it out during a boot camp torture session and then gossiped in the locker rooms as we showered and dressed. I did my makeup, then decided not to dry my hair. It was cold enough outside that hopefully I could avoid turning into a frizzy mess, but not so cold that I'd get icicles forming on my strands. Jill eyed me warily.

"You're in a hurry to get somewhere," she guessed.

I bit my lip. "I'm hoping I might get a repeat performance of last night."

She grinned, having gotten a general overview of my past

twelve hours already. "I'm so jealous. I can't remember the last time Scott and I had sex in the middle of the night."

I shut my locker. "I'm sure if you woke him up, he wouldn't protest."

Jill laughed. "True, but the thing is, I'd rather be sleeping most nights."

I cringed. "Then I think you guys must not be doing it right," I joked.

"Yeah, yeah. We'll see if you're still glowing like that after you and Dylan have been together for this long. Things start to get boring after the five year mark."

I laughed and headed out. I tried to imagine Dylan in five years and couldn't get a clear picture. It wasn't that I didn't think we'd still be together—but more that I just always imagined us continuing exactly as we were today. There'd still be lots of flirting, lots of romance, and lots of sex, of course. Maybe we'd even be married in five years.

As I hopped off the elevator and started into the building, I realized I was whistling again. The apartment was dark, leading me to think maybe Dylan still wasn't home. "Hello?" I called quietly, setting my purse on the counter.

Dylan emerged from his studio. His eyes looked red and tired, but his gait was energetic and quick. "Where were you?" he asked.

Before I could answer, he reached out and touched my hair. "Why is your hair wet?" He paused for only a nanosecond. "I called and called and you didn't answer." His voice was panicked and urgent.

I rummaged around in my purse until I found my phone. Dylan snatched it out of my hand.

"See?" he said, pointing to the missed calls. Then he started scrolling through it.

"I must not have checked it after class," I realized. "What are you doing?"

"Trying to see where you were," he said, still furiously tapping at the phone.

I reached for the phone, but he swiveled away. "My phone won't tell you where I was, but I could. I went to work today and then…"

"You didn't shower at work," he cut in.

"If you'd stop interrupting me, Dylan, then I could tell you that I met Jill at the gym and we went to a class. I hadn't seen her since our double date so we wanted to hang out. And then I showered at the gym, but I didn't dry my hair because I wanted to hurry home to you. Of course, if I'd known you were in a shitty mood, I might have stayed longer."

He sighed, clearly even more irritated now, and dropped my phone onto the counter. "I'm sorry that I can't always be giddy like you," he mumbled. "Why were you so happy anyway?"

I laughed. "Ironically, because of you. I was excited to see you." I went to the fridge to see if we had any leftovers for dinner. Judging by Dylan's mood, I didn't think we should go out to eat.

"If you were excited to see me, why didn't you come home earlier?"

"I called you after work and you didn't answer."

"I called you three times and you didn't answer," he replied.

I closed the fridge, seeing it held nothing promising. I knew I needed to stop engaging him. He was grumpy and this argument wasn't leading anywhere productive. "Do you want to order something for dinner?"

He shrugged. "I'm not hungry."

Now he looked pouty and sullen. I stepped closer to him. "Dylan, what's wrong?"

He stormed into the living room and sat on the couch. I followed. "You're wearing the boots," he noticed.

I nodded. "I got complimented on them too."

His eyes widened. "By whom?" he asked, as though I'd just said I'd been groped.

"Calm down. Just Bridget and Jill." I frowned. This paranoia was totally out of character for Dylan. He usually oozed confidence. "Dylan, you didn't really think I was cheating on you, did you?"

"I don't know what to think when you don't answer your phone or call me. And you just snuck out this morning."

"I just didn't want to wake you." I reached out and touched his hand. He felt jittery.

"Big coffee day?" I asked.

He shrugged.

"Seriously, Dylan. You're acting strange. Are you feeling okay?"

"I'm fine," he said defensively.

"How'd the meeting with the band go? Did you guys get everything done?"

"I don't want to talk about it."

I went back to the kitchen and made myself a peanut butter sandwich. Not exactly a gourmet meal, but it would do the trick. Dylan retreated to his studio, so I flipped through a magazine while I ate and then went to dry my hair. When my hair was done, I saw Dylan seated at the piano. He was intently focused on a sheet of music in front of him, but his hands were tapping furiously on the bench at his sides in lieu of playing.

I stepped behind him and placed a hand on his shoulder.

Startled, he jumped up suddenly, his hand smacking into the side of my cheek and knocking me backwards. I stumbled then tripped over the guitar case on the ground. I saw Dylan lunge for me right as I fell, my head cracking against the corner of the piano bench.

"Shit, Lily, you scared me!" Dylan said, dropping to his knees beside me. "Are you okay?"

My head was throbbing and my eye felt like it was on fire. I pressed my hand into the side of my face and tried to focus on my breath. Dylan reached for me again.

"Don't touch me," I snapped.

"Jesus, Lily, calm down. It was an accident. I'm sorry. I didn't expect you to sneak up on me."

"I hardly snuck up on you." I shifted my hand away from my eye to wipe away a tear. I figured I probably looked like a total wimp, but I couldn't help crying. It hurt.

"Fuck, Lily, you're bleeding," Dylan said. He lifted up his shirt and held it against my head. "Shit, I'm sorry. This looks bad."

I swallowed and leaned on his arm for support as I stood up. Then I shook free of his hand and made my way to the bathroom. I was dizzy and lightheaded, and the fluorescent lighting was blinding.

I leaned close to the mirror and winced. There was a gash right along my eyebrow, and possibly another one under my hair line. I couldn't see the cut on my scalp, but something was bleeding. I hated blood.

"We have to go to a doctor," Dylan said. "You might need stitches."

I hated hospitals, and my health insurance sucked. Plus I knew I'd waste my entire night waiting to see the actual doctor, and I'd probably wind up catching hepatitis from the waiting room. "No, it'll be fine," I insisted.

Then, the room went dark.

When I came to, I was seeing double. Dylan was crouched over me, peering at my head, but there was another Dylan pacing nervously in circles around where I lay.

I blinked several times, then realized the face closer to mine belonged to Thomas, not Dylan.

"Good," Thomas sighed. "She's up," he said to Dylan.

There was a cold cloth on my head, but the pain was still alarming.

"Can you walk? We need to get you to the hospital," Thomas said.

This time, I didn't have the energy to fight the suggestion. I slowly stood, with Dylan supporting one arm and Thomas supporting the other. Dylan grabbed my purse on the way out, and helped me back into my boots, and then we made our way downstairs. They must've called the doorman in advance, because the Porsche was already there, waiting. Dylan helped me into the passenger seat and Thomas climbed behind the wheel.

"Dylan?" I said, confused.

"I'll call you if we're going to be very long," Thomas said to his brother, pulling away from the curb. He glanced at me wearily. "Are you okay? Are you still dizzy?"

"No, I'm okay. It just hurts."

"You must have hit your head really hard. Dylan came over to get me and you were out cold."

"No," I said, "It's just the blood. I can't stand the sight of blood."

He chuckled at this. "Well, you still need a doctor to look at it. The cut by your eyebrow is going to need stitches."

I winced.

"You're not going to be sick, are you?" he asked, clearly worried. Then he laughed. "Actually, go for it. It would serve the prick right, having you puke in his car."

"I'm not going to be sick." I frowned. "Why isn't Dylan coming?"

Thomas glanced quickly from me to the road then back to me. "Are you serious?"

"Is he still mad at me?"

"Why would he be mad at you?"

"I don't know. He's been angry with me since I got home today. He was just acting paranoid, like he thought I was cheating on him or something, and then I guess I startled him when he was working," I explained, adding, "I'm not cheating on him."

I felt the need to continue to fill the silence in the car, so I said, "I don't even know why we were fighting really. I should've kept my phone with me or checked it when he called."

Thomas remained quiet, his eyes focused on the road. His fingers clenched the steering wheel so tightly that his knuckles turned white.

"So that's why he asked you to take me, because he's still mad?" I felt myself starting to cry again. Even if he was angry with me, Dylan still should be the one to come with me. I wanted him to hold my hand when I got stitches, not his stupid brother.

"Lily, Dylan can't drive you because he's high as a fucking kite. He could never walk into a hospital without getting arrested now, let alone drive a car," he shook his head. "Actually, I'm surprised he was sober enough to even realize he couldn't drive you himself."

"He's what?" I'd heard what Thomas had said, but it didn't make sense. I was with Dylan, and he hadn't been doing any drugs. Not to mention the fact that he said he was done with all that, now that they'd finished the album.

Thomas turned to me again, confused. "Lily, you had to have noticed. That wasn't Dylan, that was…" A guttural growl escaped his throat. "He's coked out beyond belief. He could've killed you."

I ignored his last comment and sighed. At least that explained why he wasn't acting like himself. So he wasn't really a paranoid jerk, it was just the drugs.

"Lily, I'm serious. It could've been much worse. You've got to move out."

"It was an accident," I said.

"What exactly happened? How did you fall?"

"I don't know. I just tripped over the guitar case."

Thomas's eyebrows narrowed. "They're probably going to ask you that at the hospital. They're going to want to know exactly what happened, and whether anyone hit you or pushed you."

"Well I don't see why it's relevant, and that's all I remember anyway. I tripped and fell. It was just a stupid accident."

Thomas swore under his breath, then silence ensued.

Neither of us spoke the rest of the drive to the hospital.

Thomas pulled up to the entrance of the emergency room and helped me in, before going to park the car. I had already checked in when he returned, and he sat silently next to me in a stained blue chair. He appeared to be catching up on emails on his phone, and I considered doing the same, but decided I'd rather just rest my eyes. It wasn't like I had anything important waiting in my inbox anyway.

After a while, I sensed someone was watching me. I slid my eyes open and turned to Thomas.

"You're still conscious, right?" he asked with a smile.

I nodded. "I told you. It was the blood that made me pass out. I'm squeamish."

Thomas didn't speak, but he was still watching me.

"Thank you for driving me," I said. "I'm sure you must have something better to do tonight. Tell Heather I'm sorry if you guys had plans."

"I'm not seeing her anymore," Thomas said. "She wasn't exactly what I was looking for."

I bit my lip to keep from saying how not surprising that was.

"Did you like her?" he asked.

"She was a little scary," I admitted.

Thomas laughed, and then he was quiet. Slowly, my eyelids drooped closed again.

"Oh my God," a girl's voice shrieked, causing my eyes to snap open. There was a twenty-something girl in front of us.

"You're that guy from Sierra. You're Thomas Parker!" the girl shouted.

I glanced at Thomas, who smiled politely.

"I am a huge fan. I just got your new album and it is totally awesome. Are you guys touring soon?"

"Thank you. That's very kind of you to say." He flashed the Parker grin again. "We haven't worked out the schedule for the tour yet, but it should be finalized soon. Check our website for details."

The girl went on to ask for an autograph, but just then, I heard a nurse call my name.

"Do you want me to come with you?" Thomas offered. I shook my head. He helped me up anyway, but then stayed near his fan while I went into the exam room.

One hour and three stitches later, we were on our way home. Thomas helped me to the door, then retreated to his apartment. As soon as I went into the apartment, Dylan rushed to me.

"Lily, I'm so sorry. Are you okay?"

I nodded. "I had to get three stitches, but the cut was along my eyebrow, so they don't expect any visible scar."

He winced. I could tell he felt guilty, and I was glad. He should've been the one to take me to the hospital. High or not, he should've figured out a way to be there with me. I stared at him longer, and noticed that he was no longer jittery and his pupils seemed normal.

"I'm tired. I'm just going to go to bed."

Dylan sighed. "Can I make you some tea?"

"Sure."

I was undressed and in bed by the time he returned with the tea. He picked up the copy of *Jane Eyre* that was sitting on my nightstand and scooted onto the bed beside me. "Why don't I read to you?"

"No, Dylan."

"You're mad."

I rolled my eyes. "Of course I'm mad.

"I'm so sorry, Lily. You have every right to be upset with me. I swear it was an accident, though."

"I know that. But I needed stitches and you couldn't even take me to the hospital because you were high. You told me you were done with that." I paused. "Was it coke?"

He hesitated, then nodded again. "It was stupid, Lily, and it was the last time. I swear. I just was really stressed out from the meeting, and then I couldn't get a hold of you, and I figured I just had a tiny bit left over."

"You're not yourself when you take that," I told him. "And you should've been there when I got stitches."

"I know. You're right." He paused. "What if you called in sick to work tomorrow so I could spend the day making it up to you? We could go out for lunch, maybe do some shopping, a little ice skating."

"Ice skating?" I repeated with a smile. I couldn't picture Dylan skating, but I'd sure like to see him try.

He shrugged. "It could be fun."

"Yeah, but I just got caught up after missing work from that stomach bug."

"That doesn't make this absence any less legit. Lily, you were in the hospital."

He gently kissed my forehead by the bandage and then started reading aloud. I was too tired to analyze our situation further. I settled against his chest, closed my eyes, and drifted off to his melodious voice reciting the familiar words of Charlotte Bronte.

* * *

DYLAN FOLLOWED through with his promise to take me skating the next day, which was every bit as amusing as I'd envisioned. Then we went to lunch, and back to the apartment. I decided to take a nap, still weary from having spent the better part of the prior night in the hospital, and when I awoke, there were flowers by the bedside.

Dylan was in the kitchen unpacking a bag when I walked out.

"You went to the store," I guessed.

"Did you like the flowers?"

I nodded.

"I got you something else," he said. "In case you didn't like the flowers."

I anxiously peered into the bag he was holding. I pulled out two beautiful, if not a little slutty, bras, and four very slutty looking thongs. "Is this for me or you?" I teased.

He shrugged, then held out his other hand. In it he held a beautiful emerald ring. He slid it onto my finger and kissed my hand while I smiled, admiring it.

"Wow, I should get stitches more often," I mumbled.

He grinned, then glanced down. "I forgot I had a prior commitment this afternoon. I need to leave in a bit, but I won't be gone long."

I thrust my bottom lip and pouted. "It was your idea that we both stay home today. I called in sick to work. You can't ditch me!"

Dylan hugged me tightly, then kissed my forehead. "I'm so sorry love. I didn't have this on my calendar because I didn't want Ari to know, and then I simply forgot until Thomas reminded me just now."

"Thomas is going too? What are you guys doing?"

"A quick performance at the deaf school. Very short, I promise. I'll be back in a couple of hours. Sooner if you need me."

I frowned. "The deaf school?"

Dylan nodded. "Thomas and I were going to do just a couple songs, then sign some autographs. It was my idea, so I can't well back out now."

I nodded and forced a smile. "So you're off to make thousands of children happy and I'm giving you a hard time about it?"

"Hundreds, not thousands, Lily. It's not that big of a school," he replied with a wink.

"I love you," I mumbled.

He kissed me in response, then began packing up a bag and placed a guitar on the counter by the door.

"What, you're not bringing all five?"

He shook his head, smiling.

"Wait, you can't wear that," I said, realizing he intended to leave in his current state.

"What's wrong with this?" he protested, glancing down at his jeans and plain black tee shirt.

"You can't go to a school wearing your undershirt," I began, heading to the closet. "And besides, the girls will love this." I handed him a thin, fitted v-neck sweater that always made my heart race when he wore it.

He kissed me on the forehead again, then opened the door to leave right as Thomas arrived, his own guitar in hand.

"Have fun guys," I said.

They waved and left.

I puttered around the apartment, bored during their absence. I was tired of reading and relaxing, but didn't want to get out of the house badly enough to risk Jill or anyone else seeing my face and demanding an explanation. Dylan texted me a few pictures from the school, and I felt immediately better about my situation, comforted by the fact that the man I loved was such a good, if not faultless, person.

When he returned home, Dylan spent the rest of the night nursing me back to health, even going to far as to cook dinner for me. I could tell he felt bad about not being able to drive me the night before, and I believed him when he said he wouldn't use again. Or, rather, I believed that he meant it when he said it, that he sincerely didn't intend to use again.

Maybe I didn't expect him to stay clean at that point, but I did at least hope he'd hide it from me better. If he needed it to work and sobered up before he came home, who was I to judge?

CHAPTER TWELVE

"She would have laid down her life for 'ee. I could do no more."
Thomas Hardy, *Tess of the d'Urbervilles*

The next week, the band was working nonstop. By Thursday, I was accustomed to falling asleep alone in the bed. I was out cold when there was a pounding at the door. I groaned, and after confirming Dylan's side of the bed was still empty, I realized he must have lost his key. I shivered as I crawled out from under the covers, wishing I'd worn pants to bed instead of just a tank top and lacy panties.

I was almost to the door when I heard the key in the lock. I rolled my eyes and started back to the bedroom as the door opened.

"Lily!"

I turned and saw that it was Thomas, not Dylan. He looked panicked, but distracted. As I watched him avert his eyes—after lingering a moment longer than appropriate—I remembered I wasn't fully dressed.

"Dylan's been arrested," he said.

"Oh my God. Is he okay? What happened?"

"He was parked illegally or something and they found drugs in the car." He glanced over at me again briefly, clearly distracted by my attire. "He just called me."

"We've got to get over there. Where is he?" I hurried into the bedroom and pulled a pair of jeans on and then located my bra. I fastened it and then shimmied it up under my tank top.

"I called Ari. He's going over to the station with a lawyer. I can't go there. It'd bring even more attention to the situation, which we don't want."

"I'll go then. I'll call for a car." I started towards the kitchen when Thomas stopped me.

"There's nothing you can do there," he said, placing his hand on my arm.

I pressed my fingers to my chest, feeling my frantic heartbeat through my top. Honestly, I was stunned. In all my worries about Dylan lately, him getting caught had never been a primary concern. I suppose I'd known it was a possibility, but he somehow seemed exempt from the rules.

Thomas released my arm. "Listen, Lily. I need you to tell me where he keeps his stash here. We've got to get rid of it in case they get a warrant to search here."

"Can they do that?"

"I don't know. Maybe. Ari just said to make sure there was nothing else they could find on him anywhere. It's his first offense here, so the lawyer thought he could get him off, but sometimes the cops like to make an example out of people like Dylan." He shook his head angrily. "We don't need any bad publicity now, not with the album coming out."

"I'll check in the bedroom," I finally said. "You might look in the studio."

Thomas nodded and went off on his search. I sleepily stumbled into the bedroom and began digging through Dylan's nightstand. I wasn't sure we'd find anything. Dylan never used anything in front of me, and if he kept it in the apartment, well, he hadn't told me where. I found a few loose cigarettes, but nothing else of interest. Thomas came in a moment later. He lifted up the mattress.

"I don't think he'd put anything there," I said, just as Thomas reached his hand in and retrieved a small plastic zipper bag. "Oh. Jesus."

Thomas sat on the edge of the bed, peering at the bag. I imagine he was focused on the same thing I was—the sheer quantity of white powder in the baggie. It was astounding. He sighed. "This is good. We knew he had it somewhere, so this probably means it wasn't in the car. The less they found, the better."

"Do you think there's more somewhere?"

"I don't know." He glanced around the room. "Are there any other parts of the apartment you never really look? He wouldn't hide it anyplace where you'd find it. Or the cleaning lady."

"I don't use the kitchen much," I finally said.

Thomas laughed at this. I don't know if it just amused him that I don't cook, or if he just thought it was funny to think one would hide drugs in the kitchen.

"Shit," he finally said.

I sat beside him and we were quiet for a few minutes.

"Are you going to flush it?" I finally asked.

He stared at the bag then shook his head slowly. "I'll probably just take it back to my place and hide it somewhere."

"What? Why?"

Thomas shrugged. "I don't know, Lily. I don't want to risk pissing him off and I don't really want him going out to get more. I imagine it's worse if he gets caught buying it than if he just has it on him."

His phone buzzed suddenly, and we both jumped.

"Yeah?" he answered, clearly knowing the caller. "Uh huh." He paused and listened. "Yes, I'm here now. I told her." He glanced down at the bag. "No, we looked everywhere and didn't find any. I don't think he has more anywhere."

I eyed Thomas warily. Whoever he was talking with clearly knew the situation, and yet Thomas still felt compelled to lie about what he'd found.

"Are you sure?" he asked the caller. "Okay, yes, that's good." He listened again for another minute, then hung up. He exhaled loudly, and I felt my heart race.

"That was Ari," he explained.

"Is Dylan okay? What happened?"

"He said the lawyer talked to the cops and they already weighed what they found. It was less than 500 milligrams, so the most they can stick him with is a misdemeanor charge."

"Oh," I sighed. "That's good, right?"

He nodded. "And I guess he was just sitting in his car and not driving at the time the cop saw him, so they didn't have implied consent to test him for the drug in his system, but they still could test him later. Ari said the lawyer acted like they'd probably test him by morning."

"How long would it stay in his system?"

Thomas shrugged. "A few days, maybe."

I considered this. "I don't think he's used any since I was at the hospital."

Thomas rolled his eyes. "Lily, he was probably using tonight. They had to have seen something that made them arrest him."

He sighed again and shook his head. "You should get some sleep. I don't think we'll hear anything else until tomorrow. Ari said they'll let him out on bail, and we can go from there."

Thomas wedged the baggie into his pocket and stood. "I don't think anyone will search here, but I'll take this just to be safe. I need to get back to my place, though."

He paused uncomfortably before adding, "I have company."

I raised an eyebrow. "Heather?"

Thomas shuddered. "No. Hailey."

I suddenly felt very lonely, and then a wave of guilt washed over me. Dylan had to be feeling much more scared and isolated than I was. I smoothed the duvet covering the bed where I was seated. Dylan usually slept in that spot.

"Thomas, he won't go to jail, will he?"

"I don't know. Ari said he could get up to a year for the misdemeanor. If they don't find any in his system, the lawyer thought Dylan could get away with a fine. But Dylan might lose his driver's license too. I just don't know."

I took a deep breath, but couldn't hold back the tears. Dylan couldn't go to jail. I would never last a year without him. And what would happen to the band? I wiped my eyes and noticed Thomas watching me with a pained expression. He crouched down in front of me.

"Try not to worry about him, Lil. He's got Ari there looking out for him, not to mention the best attorney money can buy."

I nodded. Thomas patted my thigh and stood.

When he left, I quickly left a message for my boss telling her I was sick and wouldn't be in for a day or two. I knew I'd already missed more days than I was allotted for sickness, and all of it within the same month, but I didn't know what else to do. I couldn't possibly concentrate on work with Dylan maybe going to jail. I stripped back to my panties and tank top and crawled under the covers, knowing I'd never fall back asleep.

I called Thomas the next morning, and he said Dylan would be home soon. I showered, made a pot of coffee, and slipped into a pair of long black leggings and a purple scoop-neck tee shirt. I read some, watched TV for a while, and then went online to check my email. As soon as I saw the internet browser, I winced.

One of the top gossip headlines read "Lead singer for Sierra, Dylan Parker, spends night in jail."

I held my breath and, against my better judgment, clicked on the link. The article lacked pertinent details, saying only that he was being detained on "suspected narcotics charges" and included a quote from Ari that the whole ordeal was a misunderstanding.

There was a noise at the door and I popped up.

The door crept open and my heart pounded anxiously.

Dylan was home. Relief flooded my system.

He looked terrible. His hair was matted and he had huge bags under his eyes. I rushed to him and immediately pulled him into a hug.

"I was so worried about you. Are you okay?"

He kissed the top of my head and then pulled away. "Yes. I need a shower though. Thomas and Ari are on the way over."

I nodded and watched him head back towards the shower just as Thomas came in with Ari. They both plopped onto the couch without acknowledging my presence. I stood in the corner, awkwardly uncertain of whether I should join them or retreat to the bedroom near Dylan.

"Ed should get back to us later in the day with the details on the deal. He seemed optimistic, though," Ari was telling Thomas.

"Who's Ed?" I asked.

"The lawyer," Thomas answered. Ari gazed up, startled, as though he hadn't noticed me standing there. He turned quickly back to Thomas.

"Once we hear back from Ed, we can start managing press better. I'll make sure no one asks about it at any of your scheduled interviews, and I'll confirm that no one is canceling your appearances."

Thomas nodded. "Okay."

"In the meantime, Dylan needs to stay out of trouble." Ari's voice was sharp. He turned to me. "How long has he been using?"

I stared back at Ari, unsure of how to respond.

"Was this a fluke or is it serious?"

"I don't, um," I stammered. I had no idea what Dylan would want me to say to his manager and I was too tired and stressed out to even formulate a response. Just listening to Ari and Thomas talk was making me start to tear up again.

"It's recreational, not serious," Thomas said authoritatively. "But nothing new either."

Ari sighed impatiently and addressed me again, his tone filled with condescension and annoyance. "Just make sure he stays clean for now, okay? Can you do that, Lily? He's not to use anything illegal here at the apartment, and he's not to leave the apartment unless he's going to practice or some scheduled appearance. Got it?"

I froze, unable to agree to the prospect of babysitting my wayward boyfriend.

"Lily, do you understand?"

I understood completely but still had no response.

"Ari, come on," Thomas said. "Lily can't do that."

"Why not? You said she's clean. She needs to keep him in check then."

Thomas glanced over at me. "Ari, she can't physically stop him if he tries to use and she's not going to want to monitor his whereabouts either."

Ari stared pointedly at Thomas. "Well too bad, she's going to have to. We can't take more of this crap, not now with the album coming out."

"Ari, you're not hearing me," Thomas said, his voice louder. "You can't put that on her. She can't control him."

"We don't have any other options. He needs a babysitter," Ari barked.

"Ari, no," Thomas snapped back. "That's not going to work. Jesus, look at her. Look at her eye."

Ari turned and gazed at me. I instinctively raised my hand to my face and covered the cut, which was now mostly healed.

Ari turned back to Thomas. "What do you mean? What the fuck do you mean? Did Dylan do that?"

Thomas looked at me, then dropped his head down. "It was an accident," he said uncomfortably.

"Damnit!" Ari said, standing up and pacing in a circle. "So now he's beating women and doing drugs? That'll make even better fucking headlines."

I bit my lip, desperate to hold back tears, but just when I knew I couldn't resist any longer, I felt a hand on my back. I turned into Dylan.

"Why don't you go relax for a few minutes?" he whispered, his arms enveloping me then quickly receding. "I need to talk to them and then I'll send them along, okay?" He kissed my cheek as I nodded and thankfully scurried out of the room.

I closed the bedroom door behind me but could still hear their angered voices. Dylan insisted they leave me out of it, saying he could take care of himself. Ari and Thomas both said that he couldn't, apparently, and they left it that Thomas was going to keep an eye on him. I heard footsteps, the door shutting and clicking locked, and then silence.

Dylan appeared in the bedroom a moment later. He looked serious and apologetic. He sat beside me on the bed. "I can't even imagine how bad your night was," he said.

I tried to smile. "Probably not as bad as yours."

He propped his head on his hands. "I've really muddled things up this time. I'm so sorry, Lily. I'm sorry I put you through all that, and I'm sorry for Ari and Thomas' behavior. They're just trying to fix my mess."

I nodded.

He squeezed my hand. "Can you forgive me?"

I wasn't even sure what precisely he was seeking forgiveness for this time. "You've been asking me that a lot lately," I finally said.

Dylan gently touched my forehead, his fingers barely brushing across the thinning scar. "I know. And I hate that, I really do."

I did believe him, but part of me still thought he deserved to feel guilty. Over the last two weeks, our lives had been a mess, and it was all his fault. And now, I was that girl, cowering in a bedroom, ashamed to have the world know that the person I loved hit me, whether by accident or not.

That wasn't me, and I knew it. But what I didn't know was how I got there, or what to do next.

Dylan sighed. "You have to know I'm trying, Lily. Believe me, I don't like that I'm constantly disappointing you. I want more than anything to be the type of man you deserve. I want to make you happy. I don't know what's wrong with me lately. I didn't used to be such a fuckup."

He slid onto the ground in front of me, kneeling in between my legs and pressing his chest into my stomach as he pulled me closer. "I needed this to snap me back into shape. I've let this go too far, and I see that now. I don't want to ever hurt you again, and I don't want to leave you worrying about me all night either."

He sighed. "I wish I could just be perfect like you."

I laughed softly. "I'm hardly perfect."

He placed his hand on my chin, guiding my face upwards until our eyes met. "You're perfect to me, Lily. And I'm going to be a better man from now on. For you." He kissed me, and I knew he meant it.

* * *

THE NEXT WEEK WAS TENSE, but at least Dylan was home more. And sober. Thomas spent an inordinate amount of time with us, probably because of his promise to Ari. He was polite enough to me, as usual, but he averted his eyes whenever Dylan kissed or touched me. It seemed almost like he didn't want to even talk to me or look at me. He clearly didn't think I was good for his brother, but I had too many other things to worry about to dwell on Thomas' behavior.

The band went ahead with a charity concert they'd planned before the arrest, and it went wonderfully, a fact which reassured me since I knew Dylan was drug-free during the concert. I had panicked, thinking maybe he needed the drugs to perform, but at least now I knew that wasn't the case. He hadn't been writing at all lately, though, so maybe he had been relying on the drugs just for that.

Dylan's lawyer came through for him, getting everything settled for a large fine with no jail time, and I found I was able to sleep much more easily after that. With the threat of jail looming over us, I'd been extra clingy with Dylan, and I'd been more tolerant of his moody reactions to the demands of his job than I otherwise would've been.

Still, Ari was clear that none of us was to discuss the arrest with anyone. The official story was that he'd been arrested for possession, but that it had been a misunderstanding and the charges had been dropped. I assumed if the news of the arrest hadn't already been spread so widely, we'd be instructed to deny that too. I supposed it all made sense, though. The band had upcoming appearances on two different network morning shows and one daytime talk show, so they didn't want to risk tarnishing their reputation.

It wouldn't have been a big deal if I wasn't such a terrible liar. As it was, though, I was afraid to talk with Jill or my parents because they'd ask me how I was doing, and what could I say? I couldn't tell them that I was going crazy—that my boyfriend seemed to have some degree of problem with an illegal drug and that he'd been arrested and that we were now constantly babysitting him.

So instead I just avoided them as long as possible.

At the end of the second week, though, Jill called, and I knew I had to face reality.

"Wow, you're actually answering? I thought you were avoiding me," Jill said as soon as I answered.

"Why would I be avoiding you?"

"I don't know. I just haven't been able to reach you lately. I even tried dropping by your office the other day, but you weren't there."

"Oh, yeah. It's been crazy lately. Dylan's been doing a lot of interviews and stuff promoting their new album, and then they're trying to plan out the tour and everything. So when he's actually here, I've been trying to spend as much time as possible with him."

Jill paused. "So things are good with you guys?"

"Yeah. And we're actually going back to England in two weeks, so that should be nice."

"How's Dylan doing with all of it?"

"With all of what? The publicity? Oh, you know. That's not his favorite part, but he pulls it off." I laughed. "Neither he or Thomas has any real public speaking skills to speak of, but those sexy little accents seem to distract people enough that they always get the audience excited."

Jill sighed loudly. She sounded stressed. "I read that he was arrested."

That confirmed my suspicions as to why she'd been calling me so much lately. "Oh," I replied.

"For cocaine possession, was it?"

I hesitated. Jill was my best friend. I never lied to her. But Ari had been clear—no one was to say anything about the incident.

"Yeah, but it was all just a big misunderstanding," I finally said.

"What do you mean?"

"He's fine, Jill. You don't need to worry."

"I wasn't worried about *him*."

"Well you certainly don't have to worry about me. I'm not the one whose reputation is getting dragged through the mud."

"I haven't seen you lately, Lily. You're always with Dylan. And when I read that about him getting arrested, well, I just kept thinking about what you told me you found a while back. If there's something going on, you can talk to me about it. You know that, right Lily?"

"Of course. And I really am fine, but we should still meet up at the gym sometime or get coffee. I miss you."

"Okay, when?"

"How about next week? We could go to that spinning class that plays the eighties music."

"Yeah, okay."

I asked her about her day and then quickly made up an excuse to get off the phone. If Jill had heard about the arrest, that meant my parents would find out soon enough. And if they were going to hear it from someone, it should be me. I took a deep breath, and called my mom.

We spent the first few minutes going through the typical pleasantries and it was clear she hadn't yet heard about Dylan. Still, I knew it was only a matter of time.

"Sorry Dylan and I haven't been by for dinner lately," I said, gradually leading in to the topic.

"Oh, it's alright. I know he's been real busy with that new CD of his coming out. Oh, I saw him on that morning news show. He sure is a good performer. You watched it, right? We recorded it if you want to borrow the tape sometime."

"I saw it, Mom, thanks. And you know I don't have a VCR." *Nor does anyone else*, I thought.

"Now that other one that sings, you said that's his older brother?"

"Yes, Thomas."

"They sure do look alike."

I started to point out that in person, they weren't that similar —that everything about them was different, from their eyes and the way their stubble grew in to their personalities and demeanor, but really that would just get me further from my goal in calling.

"Yeah, you know it's been really hard on Dylan with the

promotions they've been doing lately, and some of the competition has been trying to give them some bad publicity lately."

"What do you mean?"

I took a deep breath. "Well, there was some big misunderstanding and Dylan got arrested. I mean, everything is fine now. They got it all straightened out, but it was just such a mess, and we all felt so bad for him."

"Arrested?"

"Yes, but like I said, it was just a misunderstanding. He didn't do anything, of course."

"Of course," she repeated, her voice uncertain. "What did they accuse him of?"

"Um, just a misdemeanor drug possession thing."

"Drugs? What drugs?"

"Oh, who knows."

"But Dylan doesn't do drugs?"

"No, Mom, of course not. I think I'd know if he did drugs. I live here with him, you know."

She was quiet for a moment. I interpreted her silence as skepticism.

"Anyway, we're leaving for England in a couple weeks, remember? Dylan and I are going up the weekend before the rest of the band so we can do some sightseeing in Paris."

"That's exciting," my mother said. "We'd love to see you both before you leave."

I considered this. I knew if my mom saw Dylan that she'd be reassured, but with his busy schedule, I just wasn't sure when we could fit in a visit to Jersey.

"Hey, I know," I said. "Why don't you and Dad come here sometime? I can check Dylan's schedule, but I'm sure he could squeeze in a dinner. We could go to a Manhattan restaurant."

"Well, I'll mention it to your father. How is work going?"

I sighed with relief, then told her about my most recent trip sales and commissions. By the time we hung up, I knew I'd succeeded on my mission of preemptively assuaging her concerns about the arrest rumors.

I didn't have to wait long to ask Dylan. He and Thomas walked in right as I was hanging up. I'd been hoping for him alone, but that never seemed to happen lately.

"Hey sweetie," I greeted him.

He kissed me in response. It was a friendly kiss, with lots of tongue and heavy petting, not the kind you typically do in front of an audience. Uncomfortable, I nudged Dylan away after a moment, gesturing in his brother's direction. Dylan simply grinned.

"My parents want to meet us at a restaurant sometime for dinner before we leave town."

"I'm pretty busy. Why don't you go alone?"

"Dylan, they want to see that you're okay before I leave the country with you. I told them you were too busy to go there, so they're coming to Manhattan."

"Sounds reasonable," Thomas said.

Dylan chucked a shoe at him.

"Fine. You pick the day and I'll be there." He picked me up and carried me towards the bedroom, then paused and turned to Thomas. "Now if you'll excuse me, I need to talk to Lily in private for a few minutes." He kicked the bedroom door shut behind us and dropped me on the bed, eliciting loud giggles from me. Shortly after, I heard the front door shut and lock.

* * *

WE JOINED my parents for dinner on Monday of the next week. Dylan had been particularly edgy and weird that morning, but the dinner went great. He showed absolutely no sign of having used any drug ever, and he was graceful and calm when my parents questioned him about the arrest. He ultimately gave them no more info than I had, but somehow they seemed more reassured hearing it from him.

By the end of the meal, I came to a realization.

I had been wrong to panic and think Dylan had a drug problem. Dylan had told me he wouldn't use again, and he'd kept his word. Obviously, if he could just stop on his own accord, he wasn't an addict. I had completely overreacted. And it was equally clear that he loved me, enough to give up something he apparently really liked.

We made love in the kitchen that night, right on top of the dishwasher, and as I stared into Dylan's eyes as we finished, I knew we were going to be okay. "I love you," I whispered.

"I love you more," he replied.

For the rest of the week, we both lingered in that happy place, calm, relaxed, and just glad to be together. Since we were leaving for Paris at the end of the week before meeting up with the rest of the band in London, I felt even better about it all.

CHAPTER THIRTEEN

"If all else perished, and he remained, I should still continue to be;
and if all else remained, and he were annihilated, the universe
would turn to a mighty stranger: I should not seem a part of it."
Emily Bronte, *Wuthering Heights*

*O*ur flight to Paris was magical. Not so much in the mysterious or romantic sense of the word, but in that I managed to sleep the majority of the trip. Okay, and maybe that wasn't so much magic as the sleeping pill that Dylan offered me on takeoff. Now I understood his secret for always arriving at his destination sans jet lag.

Regardless, I was appreciative. It was early Saturday, local time, when we arrived, and we planned to spend the entire day touring the city. I needed my energy.

After we collected our bags, Dylan chatted with a flight attendant, a perky Parisian woman who seemed more than willing to answer his every question about the city. When he returned to me, I must have eyed him skeptically.

"I wasn't flirting," he immediately said, nervously.

I laughed. I was certain he had been, but in an innocent way. Anyway, that hadn't been why I'd looked at him so quizzically. "You speak French," I said.

He seemed relieved. "Oh, oui, mais juste un peu."

I rolled my eyes. "Dylan, you're fluent, aren't you?"

He shrugged. "France was so close by growing up."

"I don't understand it. I'm the one with the college degree, but you're fluent in French and probably better read than me."

"Shit, then I should probably not mention I have a knack for German too."

I giggled, and he wrapped his arm around me as we started our tour. The day couldn't have been more perfect. We toured the Musée D'Orsay, dined at a romantic café for an early dinner, then went up the Eiffel Tower at sunset. We returned to our hotel early, made love, and fell asleep snuggled together. The next morning, Dylan dragged me out of bed early, bribing me with chocolate-filled croissants and hot coffee.

We went to a street in Montmartre that he said I just had to see in the early morning light, L'Allée des Brouillards. "The Alley of Mists," he translated, leaning close and snapping a photo of the two of us.

"Wow," I murmured, glancing around me. It was breathtaking, calling to mind key scenes from almost every one of my favorite books.

"Gérard de Nerval used to write here," Dylan explained. "I visited here once a few years ago, and as soon as I caught you reading *Wuthering Heights*, I knew I'd have to show you this someday."

"But that's not set in France," I said.

"I know, but can't you just feel it here?"

I nodded. We sat together on a stone wall and watched the mist rise off the street, speechless but happy.

"Everyone always says how romantic the Eiffel Tower is," Dylan began.

"That was pretty romantic."

"Yes, but if I were going to do some big romantic gesture, like proposing, I'd come someplace like here. It just has... hey, I saw that!"

"Saw what?"

"Your pupils dilated when I mentioned proposing." He paused. "See, there, you're doing it again. You're scared shitless."

I squeezed my eyes shut and turned my head. I didn't know how I looked, but honestly, I felt a little dizzy.

"Geez, Lily, I'm not going to propose. I just said *if* I was going to, this would be a good spot."

I inhaled deeply, letting the soothing atmosphere permeate me until I felt calm, and I smiled at him. His deep chocolatey eyes were sparkling back at me and the mist seemed to be rising right off him.

He kissed me, then laughed. "I thought women were supposed to think constantly about marriage. I've never seen someone so terrified at the prospect. I should be offended."

I settled into the space beneath his arm. I could tell already it was going to be a beautiful day, but at present, it was still chilly. "I thought rockstars don't get married. You just surprised me."

"So if I brought you back here in a few months, you wouldn't panic?"

"A few months? You don't think that would be a little soon? We haven't even known each other a year."

"Too soon?" He chuckled. "Lily, I feel like I've been waiting for you for nearly thirty years. Now that I've met you, time could just stand still as far as I'm concerned."

I sighed. "That's a good line. You should add that to your proposal playbook."

"A character in a Gérard de Nerval novel would never respond that way to a romantic gesture."

I turned and kissed him fervently. "Is that response better?" I asked.

He nodded solemnly, his eyes pleading with me like those of a lost puppy.

"I love you," I whispered.

We walked hand in hand back to the hotel for a quick romantic interlude before finishing our tour of the city.

We left for London the next morning, and the idyllic trip continued. When Dylan wasn't busy with the band, he showed me around the town. On two of the nights, the band performed, and I got to see again how magical he could be in his element. We spent a few days in the English countryside, the band dividing their time between work on the music videos and publicity for their tour, and then we were slated to spend the final week in Ipswich, Dylan and Thomas' hometown.

As we approached the Parker's childhood home, I knew the increase in my heart rate was not nervousness about seeing their mother again but concern about what this visit might do to Dylan. The way that Dylan had fitfully cried out for his deceased sister after our last visit to Ipswich was still too fresh in my mind.

Drinking and nightmares were one thing—drugs were an entirely different league. I reassured myself with the knowledge that Dylan hadn't brought any illegal substance with him—no way was he stupid enough to try that on an airplane, particularly when he was on probation, but I couldn't deny that he probably had connections in his hometown.

Kate greeted me warmly, and I started to relax as she conversed easily with her sons, catching up on their more recent adventures. She inquired about my parents and my work, then hounded Thomas for details of his newest relationship. When she turned to Dylan, her face tightened.

"Thomas," she said sweetly, still eying Dylan, "Would you mind escorting Lily on a stroll around the neighborhood for a few minutes? I was hoping for a moment alone with your brother."

Thomas snickered, but Dylan nodded for me to go, so I did. It was a breezy but sunny day outside, and the fresh air awakened all of my senses.

We started along a gravel path away from the house. Thomas glanced at his phone, then stuffed it back into his pocket.

"You don't have to keep me company if you have things to do," I told him. "I won't get lost walking alone."

Thomas shook his head dismissively.

"Why do you think she wanted to talk with Dylan?"

He turned to me. "Why do you think?"

The first thing that came to me was Dylan's mention of marriage that morning in Paris. Maybe he wanted to discuss me with his mother.

Thomas' voice cut into my thoughts. "Her son was arrested, Lily. She wants to know if he's okay."

"Oh," I murmured, feeling silly for having forgotten that. Of course that was what they were discussing. "Do you think he is?"

"Okay? Dylan? Yes." Thomas nodded fervently as he walked. "We probably shouldn't leave him alone with mum for too long, though. She doesn't go easy on him lately."

"Won't that be bad for him?"

"Nah. Dylan wants to please her more than anything in the world. He's felt like he's been letting her down since the accident. Maybe a swift kick in the arse from her is exactly what he needs to snap out of it."

"I hope so."

We paused in the center of a meadow. Thomas pointed out a tree he and Dylan used to climb when they were younger, identified a few flowers by name, then steadied my elbow as we shuffled down a steep embankment to a stream.

It was a shallow stream, but the water was moving quickly,

making a gentle trickling noise as it flowed over rocks. We sat along the rocky edge.

"This is peaceful," I said.

Thomas nodded. "I used to go here to think when I was a child."

"I see why. It's beautiful. Everything about your hometown feels much more magical than New Jersey."

I turned to him just as the smile left his face. He inhaled slowly through his nose, then closed his eyes for a moment.

"I'm sorry. I didn't mean to…" I wasn't sure how to finish the sentence. Clearly I'd hit a nerve about his sister with all this talk about his childhood.

"I think I'd rather raise my kids in New Jersey," he finally said. "Or better yet, New York."

I smiled at the thought of Thomas with children. I actually could see that about him. He'd be a great dad. He was responsible and a natural care-taker, but he still knew how to have fun. But I couldn't imagine choosing the hustle and bustle of New York over this serene setting.

"Bad things happen there too," I said.

"Not to me," Thomas said, a hint of finality in his voice. He stood and brushed the dust from the rocks off his jeans. "We should probably head back now."

When we returned to the house, Dylan and Kate were calmly talking, clearly having already concluded the lecture portion of the evening. We took a car to a restaurant for dinner, and while Thomas rode home with their mother before returning to the hotel, Dylan and I chose to walk.

The evening was just as serene and beautiful as the day had been, making for a perfect walk. Dylan was quiet as we walked back to the hotel after dinner. I asked him a few innocuous questions, then took the hint and left him alone. He walked up to the hotel room with me and then hesitated by the door. "I need to run out for a minute," he said, averting my gaze.

I started to ask where he was going, if he wanted me to come, or even when he'd be back, but he was already gone. I sighed, then sunk onto the couch with a book.

Nearly two hours had passed and he still wasn't back. I tried his cell phone, but he didn't answer. It occurred to me that he might have gone to Thomas' room, so I zipped my boots back up and made my way to the door right as it clicked open.

Dylan stared at me with wide eyes. "Where were you going?"

"To look for you. I thought maybe you were in Thomas' room."

"You were going to my brother's hotel room, dressed like that?"

I glanced at my outfit. I'd chosen a knee length, clingy grey skirt and a plum colored button down sweater. It was cute, I thought, but hardly provocative. "This is what I've had on all day."

His hands were fidgeting in his pockets, and that was the sign that initially tipped me off. This time, I knew what to look for. I looked into his eyes again and spotted it immediately—the dilated pupils and the reddish hue surrounding them.

"You put on lipstick," Dylan said, stepping closer and letting the door slam shut behind him. He rubbed his thumb across my lips, hard.

I shook my head and backed away. "You're high." I said, surprised at how strange it felt to say it aloud.

"At least I'm not a whore," he retorted.

I rolled my eyes. "You're an asshole. You're the one who just disappeared for two hours. You know damn well I'm not cheating on you. God knows what you've been up to since I last saw you."

He laughed. "I'm certainly not cheating on you. Come here, I'll prove it."

I didn't move, so he came closer. He kissed me, the stench of cigarettes filling my mouth. I turned my head. "You smell like smoke."

Dylan kissed me again, then thrust his hand up my shirt. He groped my breasts for a moment, then moved his hand to the outside of the sweater. I thought he was going to attempt to unbutton it, a task which I didn't anticipate him doing easily while his hands were shaking so violently, but instead he just tugged on it. Two of the buttons popped off and the others slid open easily.

"Jesus, Dylan, you just broke my fucking sweater."

"I'll buy you a new one," he murmured, kissing my neck and lifting my breasts out of my bra.

I nudged him backwards. "I'm not having sex with you now."

Dylan gazed up at me, a sad look in his eyes. "Why not?"

"Because you're being a jerk."

"But you love me. And you always want me."

"I don't even know who you are right now."

His eyes narrowed. "Who is it then? Who were you going to see?"

I shook my head. "Dylan, I don't even know anyone here. I'm not cheating on you."

He started undressing. "Then show me," he said. He slipped my underpants down and pushed me backwards onto the chaise in the corner of the room.

"Dylan, no. I don't…" I started, but I didn't know what else to say. He lifted my skirt and pushed into me.

"Ouch, Dylan, you're hurting me."

He didn't respond, but he slowed down a little. He was rougher than usual with me, but I didn't even care. At least he wasn't yelling at me anymore.

I tried to think, while he was distracted, but I couldn't come up with anything. I was angry and hurt, and I was really worried. I'd just spent the best two weeks of my entire life with this man who was now a completely different person and apparently didn't even realize it. I knew I needed to do something, but had no idea what.

The worst part was that I'd seen it coming. From the moment that we pulled up to Kate's house, I'd known that he was going to react badly to the visit. When I'd passed the time during his talk with her walking with Thomas, I'd done anything I could to keep my mind off of tonight, when what I should have done was figure out a way to help Dylan, to keep him from resorting to this.

Dylan groaned suddenly and I realized he was finally done. He relaxed on top of me, but was quiet for only a minute.

Then he lifted his head. "You didn't come." He said it like an accusation.

I considered lying, but didn't have it in me. "What do you expect?"

He climbed off of me. "You always come at least once."

"I told you I wasn't in the mood. Something about you disappearing mysteriously and then coming back and yelling at me."

He frowned, and I almost thought he was going to apologize. Instead, he laughed.

"What?"

He didn't answer.

"I'm going to bed." I stood up and started to walk away when he grabbed my hand and pulled me back onto the chaise.

"Maybe we should try again," he said.

I rolled my eyes. "No. I guarantee you won't have any better luck this time."

"I'm willing to try," he said. He pressed his hand into the back of my head, pushing me towards his groin. He was already hard again and I was still stinging from our last encounter.

No part of me was in the mood for oral sex. I pushed him out of my face and shook free of his hand, but his fingers got stuck in my hair. "Ouch!" I shrieked, jumping backwards.

"What the hell, Lily?"

"Don't touch me, you fucking prick!"

I saw him flinch, and then he slapped me. I screamed again, and my hand reflexively rose to my cheek where he'd hit me.

Without thinking, I pressed both hands into his chest and shoved him backwards. He stumbled, then stopped and glared at me.

He raised his arm again and swung at the desk, flinging a large ceramic vase across the room where it shattered into pieces. I screamed.

We were both quiet for a moment, and then I shouted. "Stop it!"

"What the fuck is wrong with you?" Dylan's eyes were wild with anger and his hands were still shaky. There was a trace of blood on his palm, presumably from the broken vase, but he didn't even seem to notice.

I bit my lip. "You need to leave," I told him as calmly as I could.

Dylan stared back at me, his eyes cold and unforgiving, and then he moved towards me.

I cringed, anticipating the blow, but he just bent down for his jeans that were by my feet. He pulled them on, without his boxers, and then pulled his tee shirt on and grabbed his coat.

"I'm flying home tomorrow," I said as he reached the door, feeling more empowered after he seemingly agreed to my last demand.

He laughed. "No you aren't."

"Yes I am."

"I have your ticket, and I'm not changing it."

I should've shut up, but I didn't. "I'll do it myself," I said.

Dylan glared at me again, then shoved his hand into my purse, sitting on the table beside the door. He held up my wallet, grinned, then shoved it into his jacket and left, slamming the door behind him.

I picked up a nearby book and threw it at the door with a scream, then sank to the floor and cried. As soon as I calmed down enough to catch my breath, I pulled out my phone. I clicked to open an airline app, but nothing would load. I tried going through my normal internet browser, but my phone showed no internet connection. I dropped the phone beside me and thrust my head into my hands.

Minutes later, I froze, mid-sob, as someone pounded at the door. Housekeeping had already come for the day, and if it was Dylan, the fact that he wasn't using his key must mean he didn't have one. I waited for whoever it was to go away. But they didn't. The pounding repeated, and I grimaced.

"Lily, open up. It's Thomas."

I wiped my nose on my arm and rose to my feet. I peered out the peephole to confirm it was in fact Thomas before unlocking the door. I took a deep breath, pulled the sides of my sweater together, and did my best to look calm as I opened the door.

Thomas invited himself in, his eyes wide and his fists clenched. He pushed past me and shut the door before looking at me. As he stared at me, he winced, his eyes revealing pain and embarrassment.

"He left?" Thomas asked. "Are you alright?"

I tried to nod, but instead my shoulders shook and my face crumpled into tears. Thomas reached for me, grabbing me in his arms just as I felt my entire body about to wilt into the floor. He helped me to the couch.

"What happened?"

I shook my head. He was Dylan's brother. His best friend. His bandmate. Nothing good could possibly come from confiding in him. At least if I kept my mouth shut, I knew Dylan would come down sooner or later and would be his normal self again. If I blabbed to Thomas and Dylan found out, there was no saying how he'd react the next time he was high.

"Lily, I heard him yelling. I heard you scream."

I realized his hair was wet and his clothes were rumpled and damp. "You were in the shower," I guessed.

He nodded. "I'm sorry. I came over here as fast as I could." He offered me a tissue and brushed my hair out of my face.

I saw him glance down at my sweater, which hardly covered

much now that the two key buttons were gone. Thomas winced again, and I prayed he didn't notice my underpants on the floor across the room. He stood, collected a blanket from the armoire across the room, and handed it to me.

I covered myself then took a moment to catch my breath and collect my thoughts. "I can't figure out the internet here," I finally said. "My phone keeps saying there's no service and I need a wi-fi connection."

He narrowed his eyes. "Why do you need internet?"

"I wanted to look for return flights. I'd like to go home."

"I see."

"I told Dylan I thought I should just go home and he said I was on my own for the ticket." I paused to control my crying. "I probably can't afford it anyway, but I can't even get online to check. I'm a fucking travel agent. I should be able to figure this out."

Thomas reached out and rubbed my back. "What did he do?"

"Nothing. He just said he wouldn't switch my ticket and he left."

"No, before. What did he do to make you want to go home?"

"Nothing," I repeated. "We just had a fight."

I blew my nose. Thomas handed me another tissue. Then he stood up to make me tea. I nearly smiled, those Brits and their tea. I waited silently for him to return.

He handed me the tea a few minutes later and stared expectantly. When I still didn't speak, he crossed the room and bolted the door before sitting beside me again. "He's not here now. I doubt he'll be back for a while. You can tell me what happened."

"You're his brother."

He frowned. "I'm not going to tell him, Lily. What did he do?"

I swallowed, but had no intention of answering.

"It's just going to keep escalating, Lily." Thomas shook his head. "I tried to warn you about him."

I nearly laughed at that, remembering all the times he'd

defended Dylan, apologized for him, or covered for him. "No, you didn't."

"I did so. When I first met you."

I tried to think back, but only one possibility came to mind. "That day, in the recording studio?"

"Yes."

"I didn't know that was a warning. You never explained it. I thought you were telling me not to hurt him." I paused. "And you take his side on everything. You knew he was on the edge and you were the one who convinced me to stay with him."

"I didn't do that for him," he said without explanation.

"He was high. More cocaine?" I asked.

Thomas nodded.

"Is he an addict?"

"I don't know. He's always dabbled with weed and blow. It seems to help him write. Much of the time he's on nothing at all." He paused. "It's hard for him being here, and seeing Mum. He and Lucy were so close."

"Stop making excuses for him," I said. The irritation was bubbling up in me now, threatening to overflow at the slightest motion. "You should go before he comes back. I need to clean up anyway."

He glanced around the room. I did the same, although I'd been talking about myself when I said I needed to clean up. Aside from a broken vase, the hotel room didn't look too bad. I was a different story altogether.

"Lily, you need to tell me. Did he hurt you?"

I pondered the logic behind this question. Obviously Dylan had hurt me. Any idiot could probably guess what had happened. My shirt was torn, my panties were loose across the room, and my cheek had to be swelling already from the slap. But I knew there was absolutely nothing Thomas could do to make me feel better, so I shook my head.

"I'll be fine," I said.

"What are you going to do?"

"Take a shower, get dressed, and call housekeeping to tell them I accidentally bumped into that vase."

He seemed to consider this, then nodded.

"It's only five more days," I said.

Thomas grimaced when I said this.

"Do you think he'll come back tonight?" I asked. Usually, I worried about Dylan when he was gone, but I knew I needed time away from him now.

"Probably not. My guess would be early tomorrow morning. Maybe five or six."

That made sense to me. He'd wait until it left his system and then he'd come back to sleep. I probably had a full day before I'd need to actually say whatever I wanted to say to him. I thought about getting a different hotel room, just so I could get some sleep tonight. I wasn't afraid of Dylan, but I wasn't likely to fall asleep worrying about when, and in what state, he'd come back to me.

"This isn't the first time he's hit you," Thomas said suddenly.

I avoided his gaze and drank my tea. I wondered if my cheek was bruised from where he'd hit me or if Thomas was just remembering my trip to the ER for stitches.

"You should go home," he said. "Book the first flight tomorrow morning. Move out of the apartment before he gets back."

"I can't. He took my wallet."

"Call the airline. They can just change your original ticket."

"They were nonrefundable."

He chuckled at this. "Lily, I'll pay for it, but you need to go."

I forced a smile. "That's really nice Thomas, but I can't take your money, and I wouldn't be able to pay you back anytime soon."

"It's not a big deal."

"It won't work. I can't exactly spend the night at the airport here tonight, and I don't want to sneak out on Dylan to get to the airport."

Thomas rubbed his forehead, then stood. "I'll be back. Chain the door and go take a shower."

I did as I was told and he returned less than fifteen minutes later.

"I got you a seat on a flight out of London tomorrow at noon. There's a train leaving here for London at eight. It'll get you there in plenty of time. And I checked about getting you a separate room tonight, but the hotel is booked. You could go to a different hotel, but there aren't many in the area."

He paused. "I think you should stay in my room tonight. I'll sleep on the couch."

I suddenly felt like crying all over again. Here I was, a total disaster, and he was being so nice to me. "Thomas, I really appreciate that all, but I can't ask you to do that. This whole mess is my fault, I'll fix it."

He grabbed my hand. "None of this is your fault, Lily."

I shook him off. "Yeah, it is. I knew he was having a hard time and I kept pushing him. I shouldn't have let him go in the first place. I could tell he was upset when we got back from dinner and I just let him leave."

I knew Dylan was a jerk, that he'd behaved badly, but he was high. What did I expect? And even after I'd known he was high, I had to keep arguing with him. Why couldn't I just shut up?

Thomas pressed his hands on either side of my face. "It is not your fault. Jesus, Lily, do you hear yourself?"

I nudged his hands down and turned away. "I don't think it'll help anything if Dylan comes back and I'm in your room. Then he'll hate both of us instead of just me." There wasn't a doubt in my mind that Dylan would assume the worst about Thomas and I if I went to his room either, but I didn't want to share that with Thomas.

"I'm going to worry about you if you stay here."

I smiled. "Don't. I'm a big girl. I can take care of myself."

He sighed and handed me a sheet of paper he'd wedged in his pocket. "Your flight itinerary," he explained. "And I wrote the train schedule and location on the back. Once you reach London, just take a taxi to the airport. Do you need any money?"

I shook my head. "Thanks," I said, relieved that I'd kept my passport and some local currency in a separate change purse. I leaned forward and kissed Thomas on the cheek. I'd intended to pull away quickly, but he held me tightly in a hug.

"I'm sorry about all this," I added, realizing he probably had enough on his plate without the added stress of his brother's relationship problems.

When Thomas left, I rummaged through Dylan's bag until I found a bottle of sleeping pills. I quickly packed up my stuff, then took one of the pills and curled up in the bed. I hadn't expected it to work, but I had apparently fallen into a deep sleep.

CHAPTER FOURTEEN

"I'd cut up my heart for you to wear if you wanted it."
Margaret Mitchell, *Gone with the Wind*

When I awoke, Dylan was kneeling on the floor beside the bed, gently running his fingers along my hair.

I could tell instantly from Dylan's touch that he was back—the real Dylan, and that he was himself and sober. I opened my eyes slowly, but didn't say anything. The room was dark, aside from the soft glow of a light that he'd left on in the bathroom. I saw that Dylan's lips were moving, but I couldn't hear what he was saying. I watched closely, and realized he was saying my name, over and over, almost like a meditation.

He had showered and changed, all without waking me. I was usually a light sleeper, and I didn't know if it was the pill or the utter exhaustion that had let me sleep through it all.

Suddenly, Dylan pulled his hand back.

"I'm so sorry, Lily," he said, his voice still quiet, but audible now.

I had no response. He should be sorry. And I couldn't tell him it was okay, because it wasn't. None of it was okay.

"You packed," he said.

"Yes," I whispered. I hadn't planned to tell him I already had a ticket, but since he was back, I couldn't lie about my plans.

"I wish you'd stay."

"I don't think that's a good idea."

He licked his lips and took a deep breath. "Okay. I'll take you to London in the morning. I'm sure there's a flight then."

"I'll just take a train."

Dylan bit his lip now and I realized his eyes were red. Only this time, it wasn't from drugs. His eyes and cheekbones were damp with tears. He squeezed them shut for a moment, then gently traced his fingers across my bruised cheek.

"I'm so sorry, Lily."

"I know."

He winced. "No, you don't. I really am this time. I don't know what happened."

"You were high," I told him. "Do you remember?"

"Lily, I remember everything. I remember every cruel thing I said to you and every fucking thing I did. And I'm so sorry." He rested his head on my stomach. "I never meant to hurt you. I hate that I did that to you. I don't understand how I could even do that."

"I'll be fine," I finally said, unable to handle his tearful apology any longer. He was obviously in pain, and every bit as appalled by his behavior from the prior night as I was.

He shook his head. "No, Lily. You don't understand. You are the most important person to me. I love you more than I even knew was possible, and it kills me to know what I've done to you, how I've hurt you. I can't live with that. I don't deserve to live after that."

I propped my head on my elbow and slowly rose to a seated position. Dylan scooted closer, his head still in my lap. My fingers roamed absentmindedly through his soft hair. "Dylan, that wasn't you last night. You weren't yourself. It was the drugs."

"I don't know when I got like this. I didn't used to... it makes me anxious now."

"Paranoid," I said, remembering his accusations.

He lifted his head up. "I didn't mean any of that, Lily. I know you'd never be unfaithful." Dylan plopped his head back down. "Not that I'd blame you if you were. I deserve that. I deserve much worse. I don't deserve any part of you."

"Dylan," I began, but then I paused, unsure of what I wanted to say. When I'd gone to bed, I'd planned to leave in the morning, move my things out of his apartment, and break up with him by phone before he even returned to New York.

Now, none of that would work, and besides, it didn't seem right. Sure, he'd fucked up. I wasn't discounting that. But he was sincere in his apology, and I wasn't certain that ending an otherwise perfect relationship over something so trivial was the right step. I loved Dylan, and I was happy with him, happier than I'd ever been. I knew he wasn't perfect, but he wasn't a bad person either. He only did bad things when he was on drugs, and he didn't seem to be able to help that by himself.

"You need help," I finally said. "You can't keep using."

He nodded. "I know."

"I'm serious, Dylan. You can't use cocaine ever, at all, not even a little, not even only once in a while."

"I know. You're right." He paused. "I can't lose you, Lily. You're all I have."

I felt myself smiling. Dylan had apartments in two countries, a hundred-thousand-dollar car, a thriving career, and cash to spare. How I was so valuable to him, I'd never understand.

"You don't have to lose me," I said.

"I'll do whatever it takes, Lily. I promise. I don't ever want to be like that again."

I motioned for him to join me on the bed. He crawled up and wrapped his arms around me. I lay back onto his chest and realized I was crying too.

I couldn't believe I had planned to leave him. If I could just block out the last six hours, everything was perfect. The feeling of his body holding tight to mine, his breath falling evenly on my forehead, his hands slowly tracing up and down my arm, that was heaven to me. I could stay like that forever.

"Why can't you just stop?" I asked suddenly. "Just never touch it again."

"I can," he said. "I will. I'll do anything for you, Lily."

I shook my head. "You've said that before. And then you do great for a while, and then something happens and you use again." I paused. "What was it yesterday? What happened that made you leave me here?"

I felt his body tense up beneath me.

"Nothing. Nothing happened."

"Dylan, you owe me an explanation. Something must have changed. You were so happy, and then... You knew exactly what you were going to do when you left, and you had to have known what would happen, and you did it anyway."

He kissed my head. "Lily, I'm so sorry. I swear to you if I had known how it would affect me, I never would have touched the stuff yesterday." He sighed. "It's being back here, this fucking town. I can't stop thinking about her."

"Lucy?"

He twitched at the sound of her name. "Yes. And I can't stop replaying that day in my mind and trying to fix it, trying not to fuck up. If I'd just turned a little sooner... If I'd just yelled a little louder at the driver, then Lucy would still be here and everything would be okay. Mom, Thomas, everyone would be happy. If I could just go back and do it all over... but I can't, and it's my fault."

His shoulders shook, but he continued, breathlessly. "Lucy had so much potential. She was so kind and so talented and she would've done so much with her life, more than Thomas or I could ever do. And she's dead, and that's never going to change. Every time I come back here, I'm older, and she's still just a memory of a child. She's never going to change."

"Dylan that wasn't your fault. It was an accident. You can't blame yourself for that."

"Why not? My mother does. She always has."

I'd noticed a reservation on the part of his mom when she'd interacted with him, but I hadn't pinpointed a cause. I'd assumed it was because she hadn't seen him in so long, or just that they were British and that was how families acted there. She'd been kind and polite, but far from warm.

"No, she doesn't, Dylan. That wouldn't make any sense. She knows it wasn't your fault."

"She hates me, Lily. She tries to hide it, but she can't." He paused. "If you knew her before, if you'd seen any of us before then, you'd see the difference."

"I'm sorry Dylan. I can't imagine how hard it is living with all that guilt, but you have to know on some level that it wasn't your fault."

"It doesn't matter if it was or not. It's done." He sighed. "You know, I wasn't a fuck up when Lucy was still alive. I was the good son."

I smiled. "You're not a fuck up now."

He laughed. "Now you're just lying to me, Lily."

"You need to go to counseling. As soon as we get back. And no more drugs."

"We?"

I didn't immediately realize what he was asking, but as soon as I did, I found myself nodding. "Yeah."

"So you'll stay?"

"I'll stay as long as you're you. If you so much as look at cocaine, I'm gone."

"I won't. I swear."

I kissed his chest and closed my eyes.

"You're my angel, Lily."

"I thought I was your flower."

"You're my everything," he replied.

I fell back asleep as he caressed my arm.

* * *

LATE THE NEXT MORNING, the band was supposed to travel to Cambridge for a concert that night. It wasn't far, so we were going to stay at the same hotel. I didn't want to be alone in the hotel all day and didn't feel like exploring Dylan's hometown alone, so I went with them.

Dylan wasn't looking great that morning—his eyes were swollen and the lids were dark and sunken. I suspected he hadn't slept at all. And while I appeared better rested, the top of my cheekbone was red and puffy where he'd hit me. It likely wasn't noticeable to anyone who didn't know what they were looking for, but every time Dylan glanced at me, the pain in his eyes was evident.

He grabbed a wide, dark pair of sunglasses for himself. I took his lead and did the same, pleased to see my glasses mostly covered the bruise. Dylan kissed my cheek gently.

"I'm so sorry," he said, for what had to be the millionth time. Then he shook his head. "We're a pathetic match today."

I smiled and leaned into him. We walked down to the lobby, Dylan's arm wrapped so tightly around me that I couldn't have moved away if I'd wanted to. When we reached the lobby, he wrapped his other arm around me too, pulling me in for a hug.

"Good morning," Ari said, startling me.

"Morning," Dylan replied, not releasing me from the hug. Since he was normally so physical and affectionate, I didn't think Ari would find anything suspicious about his behavior.

But then I heard an alarmed voice say "Lily."

I glanced up to see Thomas, a confused expression on his face.

"And Dylan," he added, recovering from his surprise. "Rough night?" he asked, motioning to the sunglasses we both wore despite being inside.

Dylan kissed the top of my head then released me, turning to speak to Ari.

Thomas was staring at me pointedly. I shrugged, then broke eye contact. I didn't know if he was mad I'd wasted his ticket, or what, but I could tell he was disappointed. I stepped closer to Dylan and reached for his hand, desperate to avoid Thomas' demanding gaze.

The rest of the trip was uneventful.

As promised, Dylan stayed clean, and as expected, he stayed right at my side. He'd never been more loving, more attentive, or more affectionate than he was the last five days of our trip. We were happy, we were in love, and I could've easily forgotten the entire incident if not for Thomas and the condescending glances he shot me every few minutes.

When we returned home, Dylan found a counselor without any prompting from me. He didn't tell me what he discussed with her or how much he confessed, but he went to see her two to three times a week, and he stayed clean. I could tell a difference immediately. He slept more, seemed calmer—more even-keeled, and he even started exercising more.

I'd been successful at avoiding Thomas for more than a week when he finally cornered me in the lobby of the building. We were both headed upstairs, and I had no plausible excuse not to share an elevator with him.

As soon as the elevator doors closed, offering us a semblance of privacy, I spoke. "I put the ticket in your mailbox," I told him.

"But I know you probably can't get a refund or anything, so I will repay you. It's just going to take me a while."

"Don't bother," he said. "I don't need the money."

I sighed. I already knew he didn't *need* the money; he was rich, after all. But he was clearly mad about something. "Then why do you keep looking at me like that?"

His mouth twitched. I suspected he was considering denying it. "It's not about the money, Lily. I'm worried about you. You should've left him that night."

"Thomas, I couldn't. He came back earlier than I'd expected, and he was so sorry."

"I bet he was." Thomas laughed. "Nice necklace."

I self-consciously clutched the necklace Dylan had bought me at a jewelry store in London before we flew home. I caught Thomas' implication, but he was wrong. Dylan always bought me nice things, not just when he felt guilty. "He was sorry, Thomas. He's clean now, and he's been going to counseling."

If this surprised Thomas, he hid it well.

I continued without pause. "You've seen him since then. He's been great."

The elevator stopped and the doors slid open. Thomas placed his hand on the door to let me exit first. "It's only a matter of time, Lily, and you know that. He'll slip again. He always does." And he went into his apartment.

I went into Dylan's apartment and called Jill, desperate to vent to my best friend. She answered immediately, but she had her own problems. Her husband wanted to start a family; she wanted to wait longer. Apparently, they'd always agreed on three kids, starting this year, but now that the time had arrived, Jill wanted another year or two.

"Everything's been going so well with my career lately," she explained, "And I'm finally at my goal weight. It's taken me two years."

"Jill, if you don't want a baby now, just tell him. You're the one who'd have to be pregnant. It's more your decision than his," I told her.

"That's not how marriage works, Lily. If I say no and he's unhappy, then I'm going to be miserable too. It's just a mess."

I didn't have any response for that.

Jill sighed. "So what's up with you? I haven't heard about the rest of your trip yet."

I paused, debating whether to tell her anything at all. "Well, it was mostly good."

"Mostly?"

"I don't know. Dylan just, well, he parties too much sometimes. And when he's sober, he's perfect, but… it's nothing, I guess. I'm just worried."

"You think he's an alcoholic?"

"No," I said, and it was the truth. Dylan drank, sure, but that never seemed to be the issue. "I'm just overreacting," I said.

Jill was quiet for a moment. "Lily, I think sometimes you blame Dylan for some of the stuff your exes did. I know he's in the same profession as them, but he's different. He's so good to you, and I've seen how happy you are with him. I just don't want you to sabotage it."

I sighed, knowing she'd never understand any of it if I told her everything that had happened. In fact, as much as she was trying to convince me to stay with him now, she'd do a complete about-face if she had any idea what went on in England.

I was happy that Jill was on Dylan's side now, but I missed the days when I could be completely honest with her, or actually, with anyone other than Dylan. Lately I spent so much of my time trying to placate Dylan or massage the truth so as to prevent someone else—my mom, Thomas, or even Jill—from forming a negative opinion about Dylan. It was exhausting.

I heard a key in the door then and told Jill I'd call her another day right as Dylan came in.

He kissed me cheerfully. "How was your day?" he asked.

I shrugged. "Work sucked, and I just got off the phone with Jill and she was a little depressing."

He raised an eyebrow.

"Just some stuff going on with her and Scott," I explained. "How was counseling?"

"Good." He sat beside me. "I wanted to talk with you about something," he said. I waited for him to explain. "You know how we're going on tour soon," he began.

I nodded.

"We're going to be gone for a long time."

I nodded again. He said they were doing three month stretches at a time, totaling about nine months of travel over the course of the year, spanning the U.S. and several other countries.

"I want you to come with us," he said.

"I was planning on it." We'd already discussed this. I'd fly out and meet them most weekends, giving me plenty of time to get in the hours I needed at work but still plenty of time to see Dylan. And that way, I could take care of the apartment while he was gone.

He shook his head. "No, Lily, the whole time. I was talking about it with Sharon today at our session, and she doesn't think it'll be good for me to be apart from you so long."

I smiled. "I'll miss you too, but if I see you every weekend…"

"That's not enough, Lily. I'll be performing, and then you'll never have time to explore any of the places we go. If you come with us the whole time, you can see the whole world. That's why you told me you took this job to start with, so you could travel and see the world. Now you can."

"Dylan, you know I'd love to come with you. But I can't miss that much work. They can't hold my job that long for me. They've really been accommodating so far in letting me miss so much work."

"Why do you need a job? You don't enjoy it anyway."

I shrugged. My job was fine, but I'd rather spend my days

reading and traveling the world with my hot boyfriend, of course. "Health insurance," I replied.

"So if I get you health insurance, you'll quit?"

"Dylan, it's not just that. I need some source of income."

"Why? I can support you. I'll give you whatever you need, whatever you want."

"That's a really sweet offer, Dylan, but I can't let you do that for me."

He squeezed both of my hands and then traced his finger along my collarbone. "It's not really for you, Lily. I'd do anything for the chance to spend more time with you." He kissed me. "We've been so happy lately, and I've been doing so well. I just don't want to jeopardize anything by trying a long-distance relationship while I'm also under the stress of touring."

I considered this. I didn't doubt for a minute that he could afford to support me, or that he'd do it without resenting me. And I didn't need my job so badly that I was willing to risk causing him to relapse.

On the other hand, I'd always had at least one job. I'd worked after school in high school, worked my way through college, and then worked two jobs since then. I'd always planned on continuing to work, even if I ever married and had kids. And it certainly had never been in my long term plan to quit before doing either of those hypothetical things.

I didn't love my job, but I didn't hate it either. It was really the only thing, lately anyway, that was just mine, the only place where I could relax and just be myself as an individual and not merely as a piece of this complicated couple. Then again, I was part of a couple. Why did I constantly feel like I needed to carve out something separate from that? Dylan wanted me to be a part of every aspect of his life. I owed him the same.

I nodded slowly. "Okay."

His face lit up. "Really? Yes?"

I nodded again. "I'll put in my notice a few weeks before the tour."

"Why wait? Couldn't you tell them tomorrow? Then you'd have some extra time to help me get ready for the tour." He lifted me up and swung me around. "And I sort of wanted to surprise you with a little trip just the two of us before we leave."

"What kind of trip?"

He raised his eyebrows provocatively. "You'll just have to put in your notice sooner and find out."

I wrapped my legs around his waist and kissed him. We toppled over onto the couch, giggling. Just thinking about not having to get up for work or deal with one more whiny traveler made me feel giddy and free.

CHAPTER FIFTEEN

"One fairer than my love? The all-seeing sun
Ne'er saw her match since first the world begun."
William Shakespeare, *Romeo and Juliet*

I gave my notice at work the very next day but waited a week to tell my mother. She'd been extremely happy when I'd quit my other job, but I suspected she wouldn't approve of this decision.

I was right.

"That's ridiculous, Lily. You can't just quit your job without another one lined up." she said without pause.

"Mom, I quit so I could go with Dylan on the band's tour. I can't exactly get a new job lined up while I'm traveling around the country, but I will as soon as I'm back."

"What about health insurance?"

"I bought an individual policy."

"How will you afford the premiums? And the deductible?"

I hesitated, and she answered her own question.

"Lily, you can't live off him."

"It was his idea, Mom. It's not like I'm using him for his money."

Now my mother sighed. "Lily, even if you're married, I don't think it's a good idea to be entirely dependent on a man. Especially when you're not even engaged, it's a terrible idea. What will you do if you break up? You'll be unemployed and homeless."

Been there, done that, I thought, recalling the summer after graduating college. Somehow, I didn't think that would comfort my mother, though. "If we broke up, which we won't, I hardly think Dylan will kick me out of his unoccupied apartment while I'm looking for a job and my own place."

She snorted. "Yes, because your breakups always go so well."

I ignored the snide comment. "Mom, you know I've always dreamed of traveling. This is my chance. Have I even told you everywhere we're going? How else will I ever be able to visit all these countries and cities we'll go to on the tour?"

"You could keep working and save the money to go," she replied tartly.

"Mom, the band is going to be gone for most of the next year. If I don't go with Dylan, I'll hardly ever see him. I can't be away from him that long."

"Then marry him so I don't worry as much," she said. "I've got to go flip the burgers. Your father is off chatting with the Rosens." She hung up before I could protest.

* * *

THERE WAS a cake in the office on my last day of work. The combination of sugar and excitement made the day fly past. Before I knew it, I was saying my final goodbyes to my coworkers and climbing into Dylan's Porsche. I'd packed my bags the night before, knowing we were heading out on our surprise weekend trip right away.

Dylan leaned over and gave me a long, drawn out kiss before we pulled away from the curb, and then he asked me about my day. As we got further and further from the city, we relaxed even more. Dylan was able to show me a little more of the speed the car was capable of, and we blasted the music and sang along together.

When we arrived at our destination in the Hamptons, I smiled. It was a small, but expensively outfitted cottage right along the beach. Dylan carried our bags in while I looked around.

"Is it okay?" he asked.

"It's perfect." I brushed my lips across his, and he dropped the bags and pulled me in to him, deepening the kiss.

"I thought we could use some time all alone together before the trip," he said, as I tried to collect my bearings after the kiss.

"You mean since we won't be together much during the tour," I teased.

"We won't be alone much," he replied. "Shall we go for a walk on the beach before dinner?"

I went into the bedroom to change while he made a call. We strolled hand in hand along the beach for close to a half hour, our bare feet leaving side by side imprints in the damp sand. When we returned to the cottage, candles lit the dining room, and a feast was set out on the table. My eyes widened with delight. Dylan had always been one for big, romantic gestures, but this caught me completely off guard.

"You like lobster, right?" he asked, pouring me a glass of wine.

I nodded, still speechless.

Dylan pulled out my chair for me. I sat, still eying the beautiful table.

"Where did all this come from?" I finally asked.

"I arranged for a restaurant to set it up. That's who I called while you were changing. I needed to let them know the timing."

"You're amazing." I said. "Really, Dylan, you've outdone yourself this time."

He shook his head. "Lily, it's only Friday. I haven't even begun to charm you yet."

I giggled, and we toasted over the wine, drank, and ate. After dinner, we moved all the dishes into the kitchen, changed into our swimsuits and went outside to enjoy the hot tub. Another bottle of wine magically appeared, but before I'd even finished my first glass, I was out of my swimsuit and on Dylan's lap. I've never been one to play hard to get, especially when walks on the beach, fancy candlelit dinners, and wine was involved.

The air was chilly when we finally emerged from the hot tub, but Dylan carried me into the house and plopped me onto the bed. I slept soundly, despite the excess of food and wine, and awoke feeling refreshed and giddy. Dylan was just starting to stir too, so we snuggled in bed for a while then made love before heading to the kitchen where fresh coffee and pastries awaited us.

"I suppose I shouldn't be surprised that you arranged for the breakfast fairy to visit too," I mused.

When we finished eating, Dylan insisted he needed to make a few calls. He suggested I get dressed, then head to the cozy front porch to read in one of the oversized rocking chairs or the wooden swing bench. I eagerly complied. He set out to walk along the beach while he talked on the phone.

Nearly an hour had passed when Dylan returned and anxiously suggested we walk along the beach again. After the previous night's lobster dinner and a breakfast of croissants, I welcomed the chance for some exercise. He led me by the hand towards the beach, smiling.

"You shaved," I noticed, trying to decipher his quizzical grin.

He nodded, then pointed at something in the sand.

It was a message that someone had drawn with a stick. It read, "I love you Lily."

I squeezed his hand. "Phone calls, huh?" I teased, realizing he must have been out drawing in the sand while I was reading. "You are too sweet," I said. We kissed, then kept walking.

A few minutes later, Dylan stopped again. This message was easy to read, and it said, "Lilies are my favorite flower."

I knew I was blushing, but this was too charming, even for Dylan. "There aren't more, are there?" I asked him as we walked on.

He shrugged.

"Seriously, what do I do to deserve you?"

He pointed at the sand again. "Your laugh is my favorite melody," read this message.

A few minutes later, we passed one reading, "You're the most beautiful woman on earth," and another saying, "I cherish ever moment I'm with you and miss you when we're apart."

The next one claimed my eyes "sparkled brighter than the stars," and the one after that said my kisses were "sweeter than cotton candy."

"Like we had on our first date," he explained.

I stopped and kissed him. Of course I'd understood the reference. It was the best date I'd ever been on, and I'd never forget it.

He ended the kiss before I was ready. I pouted, but he shook his head.

"There's two more," he said, and I willingly followed.

The next one was longer. I imagined his wrist cramping up as he traced each letter in the sand. It said, "Without you, I am nothing. Your happiness gives meaning to my life."

"Oh, Dylan," I said. "You should save these lines for a song." I knew I'd cry if there were any more. I'd never done anything this romantic for him. How did I deserve this?

"One more?" I asked, unsure if that one had counted as two since it was technically two sentences.

Dylan nodded and pointed further up the beach. He motioned for me to go ahead, so I released his hand and walked on. When I got to the message I froze. I think even my heart stopped.

This message wasn't drawn in the sand, but was actually written out with sticks. It was shorter than the last one, but more poignant.

All it said was two words: "Marry me?"

I blinked repeatedly as tears blurred my vision. I hated taking my eyes away from the message for fear it would disappear. "Oh my God," I whispered, so softly I could barely hear myself.

I wondered how I hadn't seen this coming, but then again, it simply wasn't so out of character for Dylan to do romantic things for me. He was constantly showering me with praise, flowers, and the sort of fancy dinners that might signal an impending proposal to other, less fortunate women. Besides, we'd only been together for six months.

I realized Dylan wasn't at my side and I turned to find him.

He was a few feet behind me, his deep brown eyes planted on me hopefully, holding a small box in his hand. I bit my lip and slowly walked towards him, hoping I didn't ruin the moment by fainting. When I reached him, he held my hands in his and smiled.

"I know it isn't Paris," he began, "And I sorta told you I'd wait longer, but I don't see the point of waiting. Never in my life have I been so certain about what I want. I can't imagine a life without you, and I don't want to. I don't want to rush you into anything. We can wait until after the tour to even start planning anything, and by then I'll have proven to you that I've changed, that we can do this together. I'll do anything I can to make you smile every day for the rest of your life, Lily. I just need to know if you feel the same."

And then he dropped to his knee. "Will you marry me?"

Thousands of thoughts popped into my head at once and all blurred together. There were visions of our first few dates, of the day I first met Dylan, and of our first fight. I saw us making love in every room of the apartment, and I saw the look in his eyes the first time I knew he was high.

In a single moment, I was reminded of all the reasons I loved him, and all the reasons we needed to move slowly.

Then, when the moment had passed, I looked straight into Dylan's eyes and knew nothing else mattered, that I wanted—no needed—to be with him as much as he did me. So, I said yes.

Dylan immediately leapt up and picked me off my feet, kissing me passionately. When my feet reached the ground again, he pulled the ring out of the box and I nearly fainted a second time. It was a beautiful, clear, round cut diamond, with two equally stunning smaller stones on either side, all mounted on a perfect platinum band. "It's gorgeous," I murmured.

"So are you," he replied. And then he pulled out his phone and snapped a picture of his stick-message. "For your photo albums," he explained, and I smiled. Of course I couldn't omit this memory from my scrapbooks.

We retraced our steps, photographing each message as we passed by, then hurried back to the cottage for our first sex as a betrothed couple.

For the rest of the weekend, we barely made it out of the bed, and that was just fine by me.

CHAPTER SIXTEEN

"It is a curious subject of observation and inquiry, whether
hatred and love be not
the same thing at bottom. Each, in its utmost development,
supposes a high
degree of intimacy and heart-knowledge; each renders one
individual dependent for the
food of his affections and spiritual life upon another; each leaves
the passionate lover,
or the no less passionate hater, forlorn and desolate by the
withdrawal of his object."
Nathaniel Hawthorne, *The Scarlet Letter*

Some say betrayal is the worst kind of evil, but I don't see it that way. Most often, betrayal stems from love, because without love, you can't have a true betrayal. It seems inexplicable at first, and yet, as long as love and pain are intertwined, the paradoxes will continue. In my case, I didn't set out to hurt the ones I loved. My heart was pure, and I wasn't focused on myself. But I suppose it is what

I initially did for love that paved the road for my subsequent act of betrayal.

They say love is patient, love is kind, and love is not resentful. Perhaps so, but I think unrequited love is quite impatient, full of resentment, and oft times cruel rather than kind. Who's to say I'm wrong? Who can honestly say any human is capable of that first kind of love?

And the rest? I've seen a love that bears all things, believes all things, hopes all things, and endures all things—and I knew if that love didn't end, it would kill her, the only innocent one of us all. That couldn't be right. Her only crime was love, the pure, selfless kind, and for that she'd already been punished too much.

As for me, I've paid my debt for my crimes. As if the guilt weren't enough, the three years without them—without one that I loved and one that I hadn't even known to love but did—surely was. But alas, here I am whining about my past again, and that's not the point of my journaling. No need to plead my case to myself.

* * *

I WAS STILL WALKING on clouds by the next week. I'd shared the good news with my grandma, mom, and Jill, and even called my old roommate Carrie to gloat. Everyone was thrilled for me, and everything in my life was perfect. Dylan was diligently attending each of his therapy sessions, deftly balancing that with rehearsals and music video development, and spending every minute of his free time doting on me.

In my spare time, when I wasn't busy bragging to my friends and family about my perfect fiancé, I was shopping for a new wardrobe for the tour. By Friday, I was exhausted, and decided to spend the afternoon in the apartment. Dylan wasn't working with the band that day, but after moping around the apartment for a while in the morning, he'd left to go run errands.

It was late afternoon when someone knocked on the door.

Even though the floor was only accessible by key, rendering

our visitors few and far between, I was still in the habit of checking who was knocking before answering the door. Not surprisingly, it was Thomas. I unlocked the door, then hurried to scoot the whistling tea kettle off the stove as he walked in.

"Dylan isn't here," I said, pouring the hot liquid over the bag in my mug. I glanced up and saw Thomas was gaping at me. "Tea?" I offered.

Thomas stepped closer and reached for my hand. "Jesus, Lily," he muttered.

I frowned, then realized he was focused on my ring. I couldn't help but smile when the sparkly diamond caught my eye. "He didn't tell you? I figured you'd know before me. It's been almost a week."

He shook his head, still seeming dazed. "I certainly didn't know he was planning that. If Dylan had told me beforehand, I would've..."

I poured him some tea, even though he'd never replied to my offer. "You would've what, talked him out of it? Gee thanks."

Thomas reluctantly took the mug and nudged the door shut behind him. He swallowed loudly, shaking his head.

"Thomas, what's wrong?"

"Lily, you can't marry him."

His words were so unexpected that I nearly choked on my tea. "I think what you're supposed to say is congratulations."

"Lily, you can't. He's not getting any better. He's just going to drag you down with him." He paused. "This is just too much for him right now."

"Thomas, I know you're worried about him, and trust me, I am too. I'm not going to add any more stress to his load. I promise I won't become one of those Bridezilla types."

"Did he talk to his therapist about this?"

I laughed. "I have no idea what they talk about. It doesn't matter, though. He proposed, and you know it wouldn't make him any better for me to say no. Besides, you're wrong. Dylan is fine now."

"But what about you, Lily? Wouldn't it be better for you to say no? At least wait until he's been clean for a while."

"We are waiting. We're waiting until after the tour, after he's done with counseling, everything. We're not rushing into anything."

I sipped my tea and then glanced up. Thomas looked sick. He was massaging his forehead and breathing heavily. He slammed his mug onto the kitchen counter, sloshing some tea over the sides.

"Are you okay?" I asked him.

"No," he mumbled, avoiding eye contact. "This is all my fault."

"What is? You're not making any sense."

"This," he repeated, shaking my left hand. "Jesus, all the times I had to bloody interfere. Why did I convince you to come to England with him? You were right to want to stay away and I made you come because..."

Thomas ran his fingers through his hair. "And then when he asked you to move in, I should've talked you out of it. I should've told you Dylan was using again, but I didn't. Instead I told him you'd already agreed to move in because I knew you wouldn't say no to him after his hopes were up."

I offered my best reassuring smile. "You're his brother. You're supposed to be loyal to him. And it all worked out for the best anyway."

"That's just it!" He was shouting now. "I'm not bloody loyal. I didn't do it for him. I just," he exhaled loudly, shaking his head. "You really don't know, Lily?"

"Know what?"

"I wanted you to stay with him because I knew if you broke up, I'd never see you again. I couldn't stand the thought of not having you in my life." He laughed bitterly. "And now I've possibly ruined your life."

I frowned. None of this made any sense. Thomas hardly ever spoke to me except to defend his brother and always seemed uncomfortable when we were together.

"You don't even like me," I finally said.

"Lily, you know that isn't true," he replied, his eyes frozen on mine. "You have to know how I feel."

I set my tea on the counter, certain my hand couldn't support the weight of the mug any longer. As I registered the full meaning of his words, I simply stood there, mouth agape, staring at Thomas for God knows how long.

Thomas finally spoke again. "Lily, I'm sorry to put all this on you now. But you can't marry him. Please. Just don't."

I was crying now, although I don't even know why. I was overwhelmed and confused and starting to be a little angry.

Dylan and I were engaged. Thomas was supposed to be happy for us, not upset, and certainly not worried or, worse yet, jealous.

Thomas stepped closer.

"Don't touch me," I said certain any comforting gestures on his part would only confuse me more. "You should go."

He hesitated, and then we both turned as we heard a noise. Dylan was standing just inside the door.

"What the fuck are you doing?" he snarled at Thomas.

The second I set eyes on Dylan, I knew that he hadn't been running an errand. He was high, and now he'd walked in on me crying and telling his brother not to touch me. I clenched my fingers together nervously.

"Dylan, it's fine. He was just leaving," I said, praying Thomas would keep his mouth shut and leave.

Thomas rolled his eyes. "I'm not leaving you alone with him, Lily. Look at him. He's higher than a fucking kite." He shook his head. "I told you he wasn't better."

His words stung. I knew Thomas was wrong, that Dylan had been better. This was his first time, and it had to be Thomas' fault. Something must have happened to make him…

"Why are you here? What did you do to her?" Dylan asked, stepping closer to Thomas.

"Nothing, Dylan," I said, answering for Thomas. "He came by to talk to you and I told him the good news. And now he's leaving." I shot Thomas a pleading stare.

"You can't marry her," Thomas said instead of leaving. "You're a bloody mess. You're going to ruin her fucking life and you know it."

Dylan swung his arm out and nailed Thomas in the cheek. By the time I realized what had happened, Thomas was already staggering back to his feet and lunging at Dylan.

I snapped into action and leapt in between them. Thomas stepped backwards as soon as I reached Dylan. I pressed my hand into Dylan's stomach. His body relaxed at my touch, and he didn't resist me as I nudged him backwards. Thomas raised his hand to his cheek and winced at the blood.

"You should go," I told him. "Now."

Thomas looked flustered. "I'm not leaving you alone with him when he's like this."

I glanced at Dylan. He was still glaring at his brother but seemed otherwise calm.

"He's not going to hurt me. Right Dylan? Thomas, please leave."

I turned to Dylan and wrapped my hands around his waist, resting my head on his shoulder. After a moment, I heard the door click shut and Dylan folded his arms around me. He was shaking, but I didn't know if it was from the drugs or the adrenaline. I supposed it didn't matter. I just needed to calm him down.

I kissed him softly on the cheek. "Where were you?" I asked.

"Out," he replied, his eyes blank and cold.

He'd been "out" for nearly four hours. I considered the possibilities for that span of time. Clearly, it had been at least a couple of hours since he'd snorted, since he was no longer in the happy, manic phase that seemed to precede the paranoid, angry stage. I breathed deeply in through my nose, still pressed close to his jacket, trying to detect any smell of another woman. Nothing seemed out of the ordinary, but still, I knew my earlier instincts had some merit.

I glanced up and saw that he was eying me suspiciously. Suddenly, I felt guilty. Here I was, the one who'd just been caught in a somewhat compromising position with his brother, and I was contemplating his loyalty. For all I knew, he'd done nothing wrong since I'd seen him that morning, and I was acting like he was the town whore.

"I'm so sorry," I gushed, eager to keep him calm to avoid a situation like we'd had in England. "It just caught me off guard that your brother didn't know about the engagement. I thought you would've told him beforehand, and, well, he didn't exactly react the way I thought he would."

Dylan frowned, apparently not having expected me to say this.

"He's worried that the wedding planning will be stressful, that it'll make things harder for you. He didn't want it to interfere with your tour." I intentionally omitted the part about Thomas admitting he'd wanted to spend more time with me.

"And that's why you were crying?"

I nodded.

"He didn't touch you?"

"No, of course not."

Dylan leaned in and kissed me. It was the kind of kiss I knew would lead to more. And despite how frazzled my brain felt, my body reacted accordingly. I let him slip my shirt over my head, felt my own fingers unbuttoning his pants. He guided me towards the couch, where we finished undressing each other as the kisses grew stronger.

"Dylan," I whispered, as his hand, already swelling from having hit Thomas' face, reached my breast. "Is your hand okay?"

He glanced down at it, clearly oblivious to the physical pain he should've been feeling, and nodded.

"Promise me you won't hit Thomas ever again."

"I promise," he said, pulling my body closer to his.

As we made love, I prayed that Thomas wasn't right. I prayed this was just a slight setback. I prayed that Dylan really was better.

* * *

THE NEXT MORNING, I left before Dylan was awake. I went out to get breakfast to take to Thomas as an apology for what Dylan had done. However, since I wasn't sure what Thomas liked, I ended up buying enough to feed practically the whole apartment building. I stuck with just the two coffees, though, guessing Dylan wasn't likely to awaken while it was still hot. Besides, I could barely carry two cups of coffee with the food, let alone three.

I made it all the way to the apartment building and up the stairs without spilling. When I reached our floor, I hesitated by Thomas' door. It was nearly 10 AM, so I figured he was awake, but I had no idea if he was alone. When I'd mapped out the plan to bring him breakfast, I'd intended for it to be a nice gesture, not something to interrupt his morning.

As I debated calling, Thomas' door swung open. I hadn't expected that, and I jumped, dumping scalding coffee all over myself.

"Ow! Oh shit!" I screeched. It was incomprehensible how the coffee was still this hot, after a five minute walk and at least another minute frozen outside his door.

Thomas grabbed the other coffee and the food from me and set it just inside his apartment. He glanced around, presumably looking for something to help me wipe up the coffee on my skin, and finding nothing, he tugged off his own shirt and sopped the scalding liquid off my arms. I winced and continued blotting at the coffee stains, but my shirt was sticking to my chest like hot glue.

Panicked, I pulled my own shirt off, desperate to get the coffee off of me.

Thomas pulled me into the apartment and shut the door, disappearing for a moment and returning with a damp towel. I held it to my chest and sighed.

"Thank you," I said after a moment.

He nodded, and then after making a series of odd faces, burst into laughter. I joined in after a moment. It was fairly amusing, in a depressing sort of way—both of us shirtless and covered in coffee.

I shifted the towel more towards my stomach, where the coffee had also scalded me, and then suddenly became self-conscious. I remembered what Thomas had said to me the prior day, and I was acutely aware that I was now inside his apartment wearing one of the new trampy bras Dylan had bought me.

Thomas must have picked up on my discomfort, because he averted his eyes.

"Could I trouble you for a shirt?" I asked. "I'll wash it and bring it back when I return this one," I said, holding up the coffee-stained shirt.

"Course." He returned quickly with a Sierra tee shirt. I wondered if he'd chosen that just because he had so many, or if it was so that Dylan wouldn't suspect I was wearing his brother's shirt.

I slipped into it then turned to back to him. As soon as I took a good look at his face, I cringed and remembered why I was there. It was quite a sight—his normally smooth, olive complexion was now marked with a massive bluish black bruise, covering the better part of his cheekbone and eye.

"I'm really sorry to barge in here, Thomas. I actually came by to bring you coffee and breakfast to apologize for Dylan yesterday." I glanced at the coffee. "And now I've ruined that, and possibly two of your shirts and a towel. So, I'm sorry for that too. All of it."

He handed me one of the coffees and sat beside me. At this point, both cups were about half full. I shook my head. "I don't think I can handle any more coffee today. You take both."

Thomas smiled, an expression which looked painful.

I glanced around the apartment. "Are you alone?"

Thomas shook his head, chuckling.

"Why is that funny? I just didn't want to interrupt anything."

"I'm not seeing Hailey anymore, if that's what you're asking."

"Good," I blurted out. As soon as I realized I'd spoken aloud, I slapped my hands over my mouth. "I'm sorry, Thomas. I didn't mean that. I'm sure she was a really nice girl." I felt my cheeks reddening. I couldn't believe I'd just insulted his girlfriend, ex or not, when I was trying to apologize.

He laughed again, and then winced, clearly bothered by his injuries. "No, she wasn't. She was shallow and immature." He paused. "But quite attractive."

I nodded in agreement. "I didn't mean to say that. I guess she just doesn't sound like the type of girl I'd picture you with."

"Oh? Tell me, Lily, what is my type?"

I shrugged awkwardly.

"You don't seem to like anyone I've dated. Why is that?"

"I just think you could do better," I finally admitted.

"How ironic for you to say that," he replied.

I frowned. That shouldn't have surprised me. I already knew he didn't think I should marry Dylan. What I wasn't sure of was why I did care who Thomas did and didn't date. It really wasn't any of my business, even if I was going to be his sister-in-law. So why was I so repulsed by each of the women I'd seen him with lately? I needed to change the subject.

"Are you sure nothing's broken?" I asked.

"Yes. It's really not as bad as it looks. Hardly hurts unless I move."

I reached out and touched his bruised skin softly with my fingers. I wasn't sure what I'd expected it to feel like, but his skin was actually still very smooth and warm. "I'm so sorry. This is all my fault."

He winced and I yanked my hand away.

"Sorry. I didn't mean to hurt you," I said.

"You didn't."

"You should have just left when I told you to. I could've dealt with him on my own."

"Lily." The doubt in his eyes mimicked his tone.

"He was fine after you left," I said softly.

"Good. I was worried."

"I don't want you to feel like you have to worry about me."

"Then leave him. Every night you're alone with him, I'll worry."

I retrieved the box of scones, muffins, and donuts I'd brought and placed it on the table like an offering. Thomas selected a lemon poppy seed muffin. I took a donut. It was already shaping up to be a donut type of day.

"Do you worry about Dylan?" I asked.

He shrugged, a gesture I interpreted as a no.

I wanted to ask him why, but I realized that was none of my business. I'd already intruded on his morning enough. I stood.

"I'll get out of your hair," I said. "I just wanted to bring that by and say I was sorry."

"You're not the one who owes me an apology."

"Thomas, he's sorry. You know he is."

"He always is," he mumbled, opening the door for me.

I sighed as his apartment door shut. I reached Dylan's door before I realized I'd left my shirt in Thomas' apartment, but I decided not to bother him for it. I'd just get it another time. I reached for the door right as it opened.

Dylan stood there, and I instantly knew he was high. Again.

I froze, uncertain of what to say or do. Finally, I just shook my head. The sugar from the donut was already coursing through my veins, giving me the strength I needed to actually speak my mind to Dylan without being distracted by his charm.

"Dylan, less than twelve hours ago, you promised me you would never use again. I can't deal with your lies anymore." I brushed past him to go pack my things. I needed to get away from him for a day or two.

"My lies?" he repeated. He was furious now, but I wasn't sure why.

Dylan spun me around, his fingers pinching into my arm just above the elbow. "How can you even say that to me? I saw you, Lily. I saw you with my brother. Is that your normal routine when you sneak out of my bed in the morning, take some breakfast to Thomas and have a morning fuck?"

"I am not sleeping with your brother. I have never touched him and there is nothing going on between us. I brought him breakfast this morning to apologize for your behavior last night."

He squeezed my arm harder and the breath caught in my throat.

"Ouch. You're hurting me," I squealed.

He released my arm, inadvertently knocking me back several feet as he did. "I saw you. I heard the elevator and went to greet you but as soon as I looked out the door, I saw you go to his apartment instead of ours." He shook his head disdainfully, his eyes full of hurt and disgust. "You had your top off before you even got in the bloody apartment."

"I spilled coffee on my shirt."

Dylan's gaze darted towards the door. "Oh look, and here's Thomas, our knight in shining armor. Come to return my fiancée's blouse, have you? Splendid. Now tell me, how do you think she is in bed? I personally think she could…"

"Shut up," Thomas said forcefully, stepping closer to Dylan. "If you say one more fucking word, I'll give you a nice black eye to match mine."

I panicked. I couldn't stand the thought of them fighting any more, but I wasn't sure I could restrain either of them if I had to. They weren't huge guys, but they were both strong. Thomas would probably have the upper hand in a fair fight, but Dylan had no sense of pain when he was high, and that seemed to give him a distinct advantage.

I quickly picked up the phone and called down to the lobby. "Yes, I need some help carrying some bags down from Dylan Parker's apartment." I paused. "If you could hurry that would be great."

I hung up and glanced up at both of them, who bore equally perplexed looks. I knew they wouldn't kill each other in front of Charles, the doorman, and I hoped if they started fighting before then, he could help break it up. But instead, neither of them moved for a moment.

Finally, Dylan spoke. "What bags? Are you going somewhere?"

His voice sounded so concerned. I started closer, but noticed Thomas shaking his head at me and I stayed put.

"I think it would be better if I gave you a little space, Dylan," I began, straining to force the words out instead of just running into the bedroom and pretending the morning hadn't begun yet. "I can't live like this, constantly wondering when you're going to be high or how you'll react to me. I know the real Dylan realizes I would never cheat, especially with your brother, but you're crazy when you're high. I can't even talk to you."

"You're leaving?" Dylan asked, starting to look like he was hyperventilating. "Where will you go?"

That was a good question. I couldn't very well go to Jill's, since she thought my relationship was so damn perfect, but that left my parents are the only other option. I decided that was a safe enough bet. "My parents' house. That way I'll be able to spend more time with my grandma."

"Are you coming back?"

I noticed Charles hovering in the doorway. I motioned for him to come on in, and then I cleared my throat. "I'm actually not quite ready, so if you could give us just a few minutes…"

He nodded. "Sure, I'll come back in a few."

"No!" Thomas and I both spoke simultaneously.

"If you could wait in here, that would be great," I said, trying to ignore the confused look in Charles' eyes.

By the way Thomas and Dylan were standing, he'd have to be an idiot not to know why I'd called him. Both brothers were staring angrily at each other, their legs in a perfect fighting stance just over shoulder-width apart, with their hands curled into matching fists at their sides.

Thomas glanced at me, then back to Charles. "I was just leaving," he said. "You should wait here until she's ready to go. Don't leave without her," he repeated.

Charles nodded nervously. Thomas slowly backed out of the apartment.

Dylan looked at me, and I almost thought he was going to cry. "You didn't answer my question," he said, apparently not concerned about the doorman overhearing our private conversation.

"Help me with my bags," I suggested calmly. "Be right back in a jiff," I told Charles. "Thanks again for waiting."

In the bedroom, I began frantically throwing my clothes into a bag. I grabbed a few novels too, then moved on to the bathroom.

"Stay," Dylan said. "I know I'm a bloody mess. I need to try harder. I'll go see the counselor more. Don't go."

"Dylan, I have to. If I don't leave, you're never going to change. You need to get help not just for me, but for you. You have to get clean, Dylan. I can't stay here with you and be worried all the time."

"You said you loved me."

I wiped a tear off my cheek and bit my lip to keep from retorting with all the things he'd told me which didn't seem true at the moment. "I do, Dylan. But you're not you right now. You're not the Dylan I love." I paused and zipped up the suitcase before turning back to him.

It was an inexplicable feeling I had, where I wanted to slap him and hug him all at the same time. I'd never felt so conflicted in my life, but I knew I needed to go.

I realized I still hadn't answered his question. "If you can get clean, for real, and you still want me, I'll come back."

"I will always want you, Lily," he said.

I wiped away another tear and kissed him fleetingly on the lips. I started out of the bedroom, dragging my suitcase behind me, then paused and lowered my voice. "You know I was telling the truth about Thomas, right?"

He nodded, but his eyes told a different story.

"Well, I was. And if you touch your brother in any way, I swear you'll never see me again. He's your best friend in this world and you can't fuck that up. If you're going to get help, you'll need him."

Dylan didn't reply, so I went on to Charles.

Charles frowned and eyed the single suitcase, which I was effortlessly dragging on my own. I grabbed my purse and handed him the suitcase.

"Just the one bag then?" he asked.

I nodded. "My grandma is in the hospital, so I'm going to stay with my parents to be closer to her for a bit. Hopefully, if all goes well, I'll be back real soon." I turned pointedly to Dylan.

Dylan stepped forward and gave Charles a fifty dollar bill. I knew nothing about tipping, but it seemed that amount was paying Charles for his discretion more than his assistance with a single bag.

"I'll call you a car," Dylan said, turning his back.

I nodded, and we left.

CHAPTER SEVENTEEN

"You are very good. But it strikes me that there is a want of
harmony
between your present mood of self-sacrifice and your past mood
of self-preservation."
Thomas Hardy, *Tess of the d'Urbervilles*

I had plenty of time to think up a lie for my parents during the ride to Jersey, but by the time I arrived, I was a sobbing mess of blurred mascara and knew I couldn't hide the general truth.

As soon as my mother opened the door, I blurted out, "Dylan and I had a fight. Can I stay here?"

My mother, of course, said yes, and helped me up to my childhood room which was currently serving as both a guest room and sewing room. Moments later, she returned with a massive bowl of ice cream.

By that evening, a bouquet of flowers had arrived from Dylan. The next morning, another came, along several custom organic chocolate bars and a fruit bouquet, which was a cross between a fruit basket and a floral arrangement.

In addition to the deliveries, Dylan called several times, but I didn't answer. I couldn't even bring myself to listen to the voicemail. Instead, I sent a text to Thomas asking if he was okay. Thomas quickly replied that they both were fine. He said Dylan seemed to be keeping clean, although he was mostly hibernating in the apartment. He added that he thought I was doing the right thing by giving Dylan some space.

On my second full day at my parents' house, a package arrived, carrying a box of designer shoes. They were beautiful, completely my style, and my precise size, of course.

I was practically drooling over the shoes when my mother came up behind me.

"He must have cheated on you," she said matter-of-factly.

I frowned. "No. He would never cheat on me."

"Well, I can't think of anything else a man could do to warrant this extravagant of an apology gift."

Since I'd arrived, my mother hadn't once pressured me to tell her what the fight was about, but I could tell from the tone in her voice that that was about to change.

"He's just rich, mom. He can afford shoes like other men afford flowers."

My phone rang again, and I'm sure my mom read the caller ID before I rejected the call and slid my phone out of sight. She sighed pointedly. "Lily, you're not sixteen. You can't get mad at someone and just give them the silent treatment. He's your fiancé, and you need to talk with him."

"Not yet," I said. "It's only been two days. He needs longer to think."

"And what, dear? Feel guilty?"

"Yes!" I shouted, possibly a little too loudly.

She rolled her eyes, but then seemed to calm down. "Lily, what's your plan here? If you aren't going to forgive him, you need to be out looking for a job and an apartment, like yesterday. If you are, you need to get your butt back to New York and do it already. Men don't like to wait forever, and they certainly don't like childish women. And ignoring him is just immature."

I retreated to my room. Listening to my mother's lecture was infuriating. I had to keep reminding myself that it was my own fault she felt this way—I had built Dylan up to be this perfect man in her mind, constantly defending or hiding his every wrongdoing. If she knew the truth—if she had any clue about the drugs, what he'd done to me in England, how he treated his own brother…well, she'd be singing a different tune.

I went to bed early that night, waking early to head over to the hospital to sit with Grandma. My mother, who'd been going every morning, was ecstatic to have that burden lifted for the day. I found it relieving to talk with someone who didn't know anything about Dylan or our fight, even if it was only because she was having a bad morning in terms of her dementia.

When I returned to the house, I felt refreshed and my mother was whistling, which had to be a good sign. I met her in the kitchen, where she handed me a glass of sweetened iced tea. "Thanks," I said. "Do you need help with that?" She was cooking something, although it seemed awfully early for dinner preparations. "Are we having company tonight?"

"We are. Here, you can peel the potatoes."

"Who's coming?"

"Dylan."

I nearly sliced off my finger with the potato peeler. "I assume you're joking," I finally said.

She shook her head.

"Absolutely not, Mom. You cannot butt into my life like this. You have no idea what even happened between us."

"As a matter of fact, I do."

I waited for her to explain.

"Dylan stopped by while you were at the hospital. He was

here to see you, but I invited him in since he looked so depressed. I mean really, Lily, I've never seen a man look so devastated." She paused and scooted a small box across the counter to me. I knew without opening it that it was jewelry.

"He brought this for you," she continued. "Anyway, I told him you were still pretty upset but that you wouldn't tell me anything, and he came out with the whole story."

"The whole story," I repeated. "And what exactly did he say?"

"Well, he said that you two had been having some troubles lately on account of him working so much and at all hours of the night, but that the final straw had been that day you came here. He said he saw you heading into his brother's apartment early in the morning and that it just made him crazy. He said he accused you of having an affair with his brother and that he and his brother nearly got in a fight and you packed up and left."

I inhaled sharply, surprised that Dylan had shared that much.

"Now look, Lily, I understand you're angry, but he said he's sorry and he believes you, so it's time to make up and go home. I invited him to dinner and then you can head home with him."

I shook my head. "I can't go with him. And I can't see him tonight either."

If I saw Dylan, I'd forgive him.

I knew I would.

I'd go with him, he'd beg my forgiveness, and we'd make love. He'd be super affectionate and romantic, and then within a week, he'd get high again and do something else he'd regret.

"So he was right then?"

"About what?"

"The affair?"

"No, of course not!" I was now truly offended. "I can't even believe you'd ask that. Is that how you think you raised me?"

"Why else wouldn't you go back?"

"Because he didn't tell you the whole story. That's not all that happened." I paused. "And I can't tell you the rest, but I also can't see him tonight. I won't."

My mother turned sharply. "That's your choice, but you need to tell him that yourself, and you need to find somewhere else to stay. You can't just lay around here and grovel all day. I told you not to quit your job, and you insisted I was wrong. I've watched you mess up your life with plenty of losers and now that you've finally found a good man, I'm not going to sit by and watch you ruin that."

I couldn't believe my ears. "You're taking his side?"

"Lily, if you'd tell me your side of the story, maybe I'd feel differently, but all you've given me to go from is what Dylan told me, which you're not even disputing. You can stay the night if you want."

The potato slid out of my hand and rolled across the counter. I grabbed the stupid present from Dylan and stormed up the stairs. I sent Dylan a text telling him not to come to dinner, and then I packed my things in lieu of responding to Dylan's next call. When my things were packed, I called for a cab to take me to the train station.

My cab arrived at the same time as my father returned home from work. I hugged him on my way past. "Ask Mom," I said when he eyed my luggage.

I had just missed the 5:30 train when I arrived at the station, so I had a little wait. I tried calling Jill, knowing she was my only chance for a free room for the night, but I got her voicemail. Flustered, I sat down with my book.

It was long past dinnertime when I arrived in the city, but I still hadn't heard from Jill, so I grabbed a sandwich from a shop at Grand Central Station and plopped down in a chair while I ate. My cell phone was now registering fifteen new voice mails, and I figured I was probably close to the maximum capacity. It was time to either delete them or listen to them, and I chose the latter.

They were all from Dylan, of course. The first were loud and questioning, and the next several were apologetic and depressed. In some of them he sang to me, in others he recited love poems. In one, he just breathed. I noticed Jill was calling me back, finally, but I couldn't tear myself away from the recordings of Dylan's voice, instead letting her call go to voicemail too.

He sounded so sad, and sincere. I could feel how sorry he was just from the tenor of his voice. He promised to stay clean, to go to rehab if I wanted. He offered to quit the band, to run away with me to a small town where we could start over.

He was hurting, and it was my fault.

Sure, he'd been horrible to me on occasion, but what was I doing to him, abandoning him instead of getting him the help he needed?

Dylan's voice changed by the second to last message. He had already met with my mother, and while he was disappointed not to see me, he was excited about dinner. He promised he'd stayed clean since I'd seen him last, told me he'd come up with a full detox plan and that he would submit to random drug testing to help keep him on track. He said he missed me so badly and wanted me to come back so much that he'd stay in a hotel if I wasn't ready to share the apartment with him.

I wiped my eyes and hailed one of the cabs waiting outside the station. I gave the driver Dylan's address and then listened to the final message. It was left shortly after I sent the text, canceling dinner. I had to turn up the volume because his voice was so soft. The message overall was more cryptic, and I could hardly make out his full sentences. It was clear he was upset, that my text had devastated him, but he wasn't making a whole lot of sense.

I listened to the message again, focusing harder on the last part. "Thomas is right," he said, followed by something about Lucy and me ending up like her if he stuck around. "I'd rather just lose you this way," he finished off, breathing into the phone for a good twenty seconds before hanging up.

"Oh my God," I murmured, panicked by the ominous message. "Can you hurry please?" I begged the driver.

He shrugged. "There's speed limits, lady. And other cars."

I quickly dialed Dylan, but he didn't answer. Next I tried Thomas, praying for him to answer. He didn't.

I hated leaving him such a terrible voicemail, but I'd rather be safe than sorry. "Thomas please go check on Dylan right away when you get this. He left me a weird voice mail and I'm worried he's going to do something. I'm on my way, but if you get this, please check on him."

We were in the neighborhood, but traffic was tight as we neared the building and my nerves were quickly getting the best of me. I rummaged through my wallet and found two fifties and a twenty, clearly leftover from when I was still staying with Dylan. I held it all out to the driver, then dropped the twenty for him.

"It's an emergency, and I need to run the rest of the way so I can get there faster. I'm leaving the hundred dollars with the doorman though and he'll give it to you when you drop off my suitcase." I glanced at his ID card, then addressed him by name so he knew I'd track him down if he drove off with my stuff.

"Thanks," I mumbled, flying out of the car while we were stopped in traffic in the middle lane.

I practically threw the money at Charles, telling him to give it all to the cabbie who would bring my luggage in a few minutes, then sprinted to the elevator. I unlocked our apartment and burst in, calling Dylan's name.

The apartment was quiet and suspiciously clean. Dylan wasn't by any means a slob, and his cleaning lady did a fair job at covering up for him when he was, but he always left empty bottles out on the counter. Tonight, the kitchen was clear. I glanced in the studio and bedroom, and saw no sign of Dylan. I was about to relax, assuming he wasn't home, when I heard a whimper from the bathroom.

I rushed in, and sighed with relief. Dylan was perched on the edge of the tub, hunched over. He didn't look too good, but he hadn't shot himself or anything, so that was good.

"You came back," he said, his words so slurred I could barely understand him. He glanced up briefly, and I could see that his shirt was soaked through with sweat and had remnants of vomit on it.

I winced from the smell of it just as Dylan slumped forward onto the floor. He made no attempt to break his fall and there was a loud sickening thud as his head smacked into the tile.

"Dylan!" I dropped to the floor beside him, not even caring about the mess I was kneeling in, and I lifted his head slowly. His eyes were open and struggled to focus, but couldn't. They were red, swollen, and watery.

"I'm okay," he mumbled, and then he vomited again. I turned his head to the side, then stood quickly to get a cool washcloth for him. He was shaking and covered in goosebumps, but his skin felt like fire and he was sweating profusely. I'd never seen him like this before.

I suspected it wasn't a normal reaction, but I didn't know what to do.

I wiped his mouth with a paper towel and held the washcloth against the back of his neck. "Dylan, you're scaring me. I love you and I came back to be with you, but I'm scared right now and you have to tell me what to do. What did you take? Is this cocaine?"

His head fell into my hands, and I realized he was now unconscious, which scared me even more. Before I could decide whether to take his pulse or call 911, I heard a noise at the door.

"Lily?" Thomas called. "Are you alright? I just got home and Charles gave me your suitcase to bring up."

"In the bathroom," I replied. I'd tried to shout, but my voice came out weak. It didn't matter. Thomas was at my side in an instant.

"What happened?"

"I don't know. I just got here and he was vomiting and then he passed out."

I could tell Thomas was trying to look calm, but the look on his face betrayed his efforts. He pressed his hand to Dylan's throat to gauge his pulse. Feeling useless, I rewetted the wash cloth and dampened Dylan's forehead.

"Shit," Thomas mumbled. "His heart's racing and he's burning up. Take his shirt off." He started the faucet and held a larger towel under it.

I complied, then crouched beside him, pulling his head onto my lap. I tried turning him over and Thomas stopped me. "Leave him face down," he said. I had the eerie sensation he'd been through this before, but I didn't have a chance to ask him because Dylan began convulsing.

At first, I thought he was simply coming to, but then I could tell by the way his body was violently thrashing into me that this wasn't normal.

"Thomas!" I cried.

He turned quickly, then pulled out his phone. I heard him call for an ambulance for a drug overdose and give the address, then he hung up and called someone else.

"What do I do?" I shrieked. I felt like the shaking had gone on for ages. It just wouldn't stop.

"Nothing. Just stay with him," he barked. And then he spoke into his phone. "This is Thomas Parker. We've got an ambulance coming for Dylan and I need all your guys working security. Get the lobby closed off if you can and clear the street around the entrance. We don't want anyone seeing anything, understood? And make sure no one gets any fucking photos."

He hung up then rejoined me on the floor just as Dylan stopped convulsing. I was sobbing by this point and shaking considerably myself, but I couldn't seem to make it stop. Thomas draped the towel over his brother, rubbed my back quickly in what I assume was supposed to be a comforting manner, and then stood.

I watched as he examined the bathroom counter. There was the white powder, which we'd both expected. Thomas scraped that into his hand, then dumped it into the toilet. He then lifted up another ziplock bag. It also contained a white residue. Thomas sniffed it, then frowned. He stuck his finger in and tasted it.

"Thomas!" I hardly needed a second brother high.

"They'll need to know what he took, Lily, and I don't want them to find any on him." He paused and took another small sample. "Check his pockets."

I stuck my hands into Dylan's pockets, wishing I was getting this close to him under different circumstances. "Empty." I had my hand on Dylan's head, so I could still feel his pulse, but I leaned closer to confirm he was breathing.

Thomas nodded. "Ecstasy," he said. He took both bags and rinsed them in the sink, then wedged them into the bottom of the trash can. There was a noise at the door and I was instantly relieved.

"Lily, listen to me. I can't go outside with you guys, it'll attract too much attention. You go with Dylan in the ambulance and I'll meet you at the hospital soon."

I didn't have time to protest—the paramedics had arrived. I scooted out of the way to allow them some space while they checked his vital signs or whatever they were doing, and Thomas wrapped his arm around me.

"We think it was cocaine, ecstasy and whiskey," Thomas was saying. "I don't know how much or how long ago. He was conscious twenty minutes ago and had a seizure about ten minutes ago or whenever when we called."

Dylan was already loaded onto the gurney. They'd covered

him with a blanket. Thomas followed us out to the lobby. "Please cover his face when you get off the elevator. Please," he repeated.

I couldn't tell if the paramedics heard him or not. They seemed all business, and I was too panicked to notice much else.

"Are you family?" the female one asked.

"I'm his fiancée. That guy in the room was his only real family in the U.S. He's going to meet us at the hospital and said for me to stay with Dylan."

One of the male paramedics looked up. "You must be Lily," he said, a peculiar grin on his face.

I nodded, not bothering to ask how he knew.

"From the song," he said by way of explanation.

"Why won't anyone write a song about me?" the female was whining.

I tuned them out. In a way, I suppose the senseless chatter should have relaxed me. Surely they wouldn't be so casual if Dylan were dying. But it really didn't help. All I knew was that Dylan might be leaving me, and I was responsible.

Not only that, but I'd wasted our last three days together making him miserable over a stupid fight. My mother was right. I was immature and childish.

I felt my tears growing out of control again, but I'd remembered what Thomas had said as we started into the lobby. I grabbed the sheet and tugged it up over his face. The third paramedic, the less chatty of the trio, frowned and started to uncover it, then stopped.

"Just till we get in the bus," said the paramedic who'd guessed my name.

I passed the night doorman, the nighttime building manager, a security guard, and several other random building employees who all seemed to be doing their best to follow Thomas' instructions. They all stared at me unabashedly, but I didn't care. I couldn't stop crying.

The time I spent in that ambulance were the longest minutes

of my life. They uncovered Dylan and placed several ice packs on his chest as soon as he was fastened into the ambulance. Someone buckled me in to a seat where I could see Dylan, but couldn't quite reach to touch him.

Our entire time together flashed before my eyes like stamps on a passport. I saw Coney Island, London, Paris, and the Hamptons. I remembered the feel of his slippery skin against mine as we read together in the bubble bath. I could still hear his voice the day he first told me he loved me.

"Wake up, Dylan," I said aloud.

I bit my lip, realizing the two paramedics in back were both eying me warily.

The female offered me a tissue, then checked his pulse and temperature again. "It's probably better for him to be unconscious," she said. "He'll recover faster that way, and he's not going to feel good when he's awake."

"Can't you make him feel better?"

"We're lowering his body temperature, giving him IV fluids to keep him hydrated, and we've given him a low dose of a medication to slow his heart rate and control his blood pressure. We're trying to stop the seizures and prevent any heart or respiratory distress. I'm not really concerned with whether he still feels nauseous from the illegal drugs he ingested."

"I wasn't with him when he did it," I said regretfully, by way of explanation and apology. "I should've been there."

The man shook his head. "He's a habitual user, right? This would've happened sooner or later no matter what you did. He needs rehab."

They asked me all sorts of questions about his medical background, his height and weight, his allergies, and so forth. I suppose I answered what I could, but I didn't recall specifics. When we finally arrived at the hospital, Dylan was rushed into a room, and I was forced to stay outside, answering the same questions for a nurse while Dylan was all alone being poked and prodded by the doctors.

The nurse had left, and I was on my own again, crying silently at the window outside Dylan's room, when I felt an arm wrap around me. I immediately turned into the arm, burying my head in Thomas' chest and sobbing. He held me silently, until the doctor came out to speak with us.

"Are you family?" he asked.

Thomas nodded quickly, answering for both of us.

"He's stable," he began. "Dylan tested positive for cocaine, ecstasy and alcohol. The amount of cocaine in his bloodstream wasn't an amount we typically qualify as an overdose. Is he a habitual user?"

I turned to Thomas. His face remained cold and unchanging.

"Well, without knowing that for sure," the doctor continued, clearly realizing we weren't going to respond. "I'd guess that he is, and that he's developed what we consider a sensitivity, where the body just begins to react more strongly to a dose it's accustomed to, possibly because of excess buildup already in the system."

"What about the ecstasy?" I asked. I'd never known Dylan to take that before, but I realized I couldn't be sure of anything now.

"That more likely caused the overheating. The combination of the two, especially with the alcohol, isn't safe or healthy by any means, but I don't think it was a lethal quantity."

"You mean he wasn't trying to kill himself?" I asked hopefully.

Thomas glared at me.

"Correct. Unless you have reason to believe otherwise, I'd say this was an accidental overdose."

"Will there be any longterm effects?" Thomas asked.

I frowned at the double standard—he could ask questions, but I apparently couldn't.

"I don't believe so, no. We're monitoring him closely

overnight, and we'll probably keep him tomorrow, but then he could go home after that."

"Could you transfer him to a private rehab facility instead?" I asked, this time wisely avoiding Thomas.

This seemed to surprise the doctor. "Yes. I could recommend that if you'd like."

"No thank you," Thomas said. "We'll handle that privately."

The doctor frowned. "It's all confidential. I understand your concerns about privacy given your brother's particular situation, but his uh…"

"Fiancée," I supplied.

"Your brother's fiancée has identified the one thing that might prevent you from finding yourselves in this exact situation again."

"Cocaine isn't addictive," Thomas said.

"Most would agree that it isn't physiologically addictive the same way a drug like heroin is, but I'd still wager that your brother's behavior is characteristic of an addict. A habitual user may crave the high whether or not his body physically needs it. And his body is building up both a tolerance and a sensitivity, meaning that it'll take more and more of the drug to get him high but less and less of the drug to potentially kill him."

The doctor paused. "I'll check on him in a little while and then talk with you again if his condition changes."

"Thank you," Thomas said.

"When can we see him?" I asked.

"He's still unconscious. Wait until he's awake."

I sighed. Thomas pulled me over to a chair, but it felt too far away, so I returned to the window. He followed, and again wrapped an arm around me for support.

I wasn't sure how long had passed when I heard another familiar voice. It was Ari. He asked about Dylan first, and Thomas caught him up to date. Then he offered me some coffee. I shook my head.

Thomas slowly loosened his grip on me and I turned abruptly. "We'll be back in five minutes," he said. "I'd feel better if you sat down."

I shook my head, and they left.

They returned shortly after, and after forcing a cup of coffee on me, Thomas stood with me for the most part. He and Ari disappeared about once an hour to discuss something, but I stayed glued to the window.

It was hours later when Dylan finally awoke, during one such period where I was alone. As soon as I saw his eyes open, I rushed into the room and sat at his side. He groaned, wincing from the light. I fidgeted with his bedside remote to dim the lights.

"How are you feeling?" I asked.

"Terrible."

"Do you remember what happened?"

"Where am I?" he asked in response. I took that as a no.

"You're in a hospital. When I got back to the apartment yesterday, you had just mixed ecstasy, cocaine and whiskey. You were..."

"You came back to the apartment?" he asked, perking up.

I nodded.

"Jesus, if I had known that, I wouldn't have... I was clean the whole time you were gone, until yesterday. When you canceled dinner and you wouldn't talk to me, though, I figured there was no point. I thought you were gone for good."

"I'm sorry Dylan. I shouldn't have done that. I was angry and impulsive."

He shook his head, then winced from the pain. "This isn't your fault. I'm sorry."

I stretched out beside him on the tiny hospital bed, careful not to interfere with his IVs. "You scared me."

"I'm sorry," he said again.

"You're going to rehab before the tour," I said.

"Okay."

I had prepared a rebuttal, not expecting him to agree so readily. His response threw me, so I tossed out the script. "I missed you."

"Me too."

"I love you," I said.

"I love you more," he answered.

I was so tired that I probably could've fallen asleep right there, on that tiny uncomfortable bed. I struggled to keep my eyes open, even after I saw that Dylan's had closed again, and then I noticed Thomas standing outside the window. He was smiling, and when he saw me look up at him, he nodded slightly, acknowledging me. Then he stepped barely into the room, pulled the blinds shut, and walked out silently.

CHAPTER EIGHTEEN

"Longing hearts could only stand so much longing."
Margaret Mitchell, *Gone with the Wind*

*T*he next morning, I learned that Thomas had arranged for Dylan to be transferred to a private rehab facility. It was equipped to handle detox patients, which meant it had enough medical capabilities to allow the hospital to safely discharge Dylan that day. I didn't understand the details of his stay there. The length and exact goals were unclear to me, but Dylan had a private room, and I was allowed to visit at will. That, combined with the knowledge that he would be safe and sober in the new facility was enough to thrill me.

I remained with Dylan through the transfer, until a nurse suggested I leave for the day. Dylan nodded agreeably, so I went. I hadn't slept for more than a few brief stretches since his overdose, and even before that, my sleep had been patchy thanks to my distress over our fight.

When I got back to the apartment, I was pleasantly surprised that the bathroom had already been cleaned. It was odd being in the apartment without Dylan, but at least it looked as though nothing bad had happened.

I went to bed early that first night alone, waking in a panic around midnight. I called the rehab facility and they assured me that Dylan was doing fine and sleeping, but the anxious feeling remained.

Still unable to sleep, I began thoroughly searching the entire apartment. When I was done, I took what I assumed to be two additional doses of ecstasy and three baggies presumably containing cocaine and I flushed it all down the toilet. Convinced I'd accomplished something important, I was then able to fall back asleep.

I awoke at nine and went to see Dylan. He was glad to see me, but clearly didn't feel well. He said his head hurt and he was nauseous. Whatever the cause, he was also cranky. I left when he had an appointment with his counselor, but I returned in the afternoon. By that time, Dylan was a new man.

He was sweet and flirty, clearly the Dylan I'd fallen in love with. When he tried to seduce me, I knew he was feeling better. I resisted at first, as much because of his medical condition as the fact that we were in an unlocked room that a nurse could enter at any time.

"Come on, don't you miss me?" he goaded.

"More than anything," I confessed. Makeup sex with Dylan was never disappointing. Not that any kind of sex with him ever was, but he was a particularly attentive lover when he felt guilty about something and was trying to repay his debt.

"I think it'll make us both feel better."

"I feel fine."

"No," he said. "You're clearly stressed. Your shoulders are all tense."

"I suppose I could use a massage," I teased.

He wrapped his legs around me and began rubbing my shoulders. The rhythmic motion was soothing and apparently disarming, because by the time he started kissing my neck and nibbling on my earlobe, I had lost all interest in saying no.

We made love under the covers in his tiny rehab room with the door unlocked. I'd like to say it was as satisfying as normal makeup sex with Dylan, but we were fairly limited. Neither of us was willing to make any noise, and the bed was just too small for some of his more impressive moves. Besides, I was terrified by the possibility of someone walking in on us.

Still, I felt better after that visit. We still didn't know exactly how long Dylan would stay there, although it was clear that he planned to check out prior to the band's scheduled tour. I visited every day over the next week, and each day, it was a gamble. Some days, he was my perfect Dylan, and I never wanted to leave his side. On other days, he was irritable and almost reminded me of the way he was when he'd been high, even though I knew he was clean now. Thomas assured me that it was normal, that he was just stressed out and tired of being in the rehab center, and that made sense.

It was after one particularly rough day that I bumped into Thomas in the hall of the rehab center.

"Where are you headed today?" Thomas asked, eying the book poking out of my bag.

I smiled. "I always carry a book with me."

"Dylan told me that. He said it was charming."

"Great."

"He also asked me to keep you company, hence my question."

I sighed.

"He's just worried about you, Lily. He feels bad."

"He should feel bad. He scared us half to death." I shrugged my bag higher onto my shoulder. "And he's not worried I'll get bored. He's worried I'll cheat on him. He's been paranoid lately."

Thomas gave me a quirky grin. "Well, are you? Cheating on him?"

"No, Thomas."

"Well, if you don't have another date, we might as well hang out today. I'm worried about you, too. Dealing with Dylan can take a toll on a person."

I shook my head. "I'm headed to Jersey to visit my grandma in the hospital. Nothing exciting. Sorry."

He perked up. "Sounds perfect. I have been hoping to spend some time in a hospital," he joked, glancing around at the fading white walls of the hospital-like facility we were currently inside.

"You don't have to do that. She's pretty miserable now. She's still in a lot of pain, and the medication makes her even more foggy than usual. She gets confused really easily, and then she gets angry if you try to correct her. I'll have my phone with me if you need me."

I started off down the hall and immediately spotted Tim, the driver Dylan and Thomas both used when they didn't want to drive. He stepped out of the car, walked around, and let me into the back. I frowned. Usually, when it was just me and Tim, he let me ride in the front seat. It felt less weird then. I didn't feel like questioning him this morning, though, so I climbed in the back. I leaned back into the seat and closed my eyes for a nanosecond, and then the other door opened and Thomas climbed in.

"Are we driving you home?"

"Nope. I'm going with you."

"Thomas, you don't have to."

He laughed. "I know, but I am."

I shrugged and pulled *Gone with the Wind* out of my bag.

"You know that's a movie," Thomas said.

"I prefer the book."

"But you've read it before." He paused. "In fact, you read everything more than once. Why not try something new?"

"I like what I like. There's no reason to waste my time reading something I might not enjoy when I know I'd love reading something else."

"But it's so depressing. Doesn't he dump her in the end?"

I nodded. As I thought about it, I realized that, while I liked my favorite books precisely because they were so romantic, none of them had the traditional happy ending.

"You're right," I said finally.

"So you go into a book and get all attached to the characters, knowing all along that they're going to be miserable and end up hurt and alone?"

"It does seem odd when you put it that way," I conceded. But still, in my current read, I was at a happy part. Rhett and Scarlett had just wed—and despite the logic, I felt optimistic for them.

"People change," I finally said.

Thomas frowned. "No, they don't. And besides, these aren't people; they're characters, frozen in time. Nothing will ever change in the books and you know it, yet you read them again anyway." He snorted. "I bet you still cry at the endings, too."

"If you're just going to mock me, I think I'd rather spend the day alone."

His expression softened. "I didn't mean to tease you, I was only musing aloud. You're a fascinating woman, Lily." He paused. "Your faith in people is amazing."

I gave him a look to let him know he was still mocking me.

"Okay, okay. But just tell me, do you think everyone can change, really?"

I considered this, then nodded.

"What about Hitler? Do you think he would've changed if they'd let him live?"

"Thomas, now you're just being obnoxious. I think everyone has the capacity to change, not that they necessarily will. Hitler was horrible and has absolutely nothing in common with the characters in the books I read."

He laughed, then changed the subject.

We made small talk on the lengthy drive, and then Thomas took a twenty minute phone call, so I started reading. Despite all the reading I'd done on the subway over the years, I still got a little queasy reading in cars. So I was relieved when we finally pulled up to the hospital. I had a brief moment of panic when I spotted my mom's car, debating how best to explain Dylan's absence, but Thomas flew out of the car too quickly for me to decide on a plan.

My mom was on her way out when we passed her. She smiled happily at me and waved, then paused, a curious look on her face.

"Why you must be Dylan's brother," she finally said, leaning awkwardly close to Thomas. "You look just like him."

"Thomas," he said, holding his hand out to her.

"Pleased to meet you. Dylan's told us a lot about you."

He raised an eyebrow suspiciously. I shrugged.

"Where is Dylan?" my mom asked. Since I'd been visiting alone for days, I knew she wasn't asking so much why Dylan wasn't with me, but rather why Thomas was.

"I needed to drop off some band papers nearby, so Lily let me carpool. Figured I'd rather come along inside than wait out in a car."

My mom smiled warmly and I was immediately impressed with how casually the lie came to him. "Well, I told your father I was on my way, so I better get going. Don't feel like you have to stay long, dear. Just pop in and say hello. She's not too with it today."

I nodded and noticed how tired my mom appeared. Watching someone she loved suffer and degenerate was clearly taking a toll on her. I hugged her before Thomas and I took off down the hall.

My grandma was in her wheelchair when we arrived, an excessively loud game show blaring on the television.

"Hi Grandma," I said cheerily, turning down the volume and hugging her.

"Lily, dear, how are you?"

"Good. How are you feeling today?"

"Rotten," she replied with a smile. "Hi there," she said to Thomas.

He greeted her warmly.

"Grandma, this is Thomas Parker, Dylan's brother," I explained.

"I know who he is. I'm not crazy. I've met him before, remember?"

I frowned. She had to have been thinking of Dylan, but it didn't seem worthwhile to argue with her.

"How are the wedding plans coming along?"

"Oh, well, you know how the band has that tour coming up, right? We're going to wait until after the tour to have the wedding, so I probably won't start planning much of anything for a while."

She turned to Thomas. "What about you? Are you going to help with this planning?"

He smiled, embarrassed. "I s'pose I'll probably end up involved somehow."

My grandma laughed at this. "Of course you'll be involved. You're the groom. You're not going to make us all go to England, are you? I'm too old to fly."

Thomas glanced at me. "I'm sure the wedding will be here in the states," he said.

We played a quick game of gin rummy with my grandma, which, surprisingly, Thomas won, and then I said we probably needed to get going.

Grandma bobbed her head, then grabbed an unsuspecting Thomas by the hand. "You better be treating my granddaughter well," she said.

He nodded sternly. "Of course."

She frowned and attempted to whisper to him. "Are you sure everything is okay with you two? I see the way you're looking at her like you still care, but something's off. Last time I saw you,

you couldn't keep your hands off her. You haven't even kissed her since you've been here."

"Grandma, I told you, this is Thomas."

"I know who it is!"

I sighed, then caught poor Thomas off guard by kissing him on the cheek. "See? Everything is fine."

Her eyes widened. "Oh, Lordy. That ain't a kiss. You're calling off the wedding, aren't you? I knew it. I told your mother you could never make a serious relationship last, but she just insisted that this time…"

My grandma kept talking, but I stopped listening as soon as Thomas grabbed my arm, pulled me close, and pressed his lips into mine. He pressed his hands into my cheeks, holding my face against his. It was a long and convincing kiss. No tongue, of course, but it still managed to make my knees wobbly.

When he ended the kiss, Thomas turned to my grandma and winked. "Nothing to worry about, I assure you," he said, and then he led me by the hand out of the room. I stumbled as we walked, too confused and disoriented.

We climbed back into the car, and Tim started to drive. Thomas pulled out his cell phone, but I snatched it out of his hand before he could call anyone.

"What was that?"

"What?" he asked innocently.

I stared pointedly.

"Oh, right. I just thought it would help your gran not worry, and it seems I was correct. She seemed pretty relieved."

"So that was just acting? For my grandma?"

He nodded.

It hadn't felt like acting. "Thomas, it didn't…"

He placed his hand over mine and nodded towards Tim. "We'll chat later, okay?"

I sighed.

When we got back home, we picked up a pizza and Thomas

came over to Dylan's apartment to eat. We joked and laughed while we ate, and I almost forgot the reason I was spending the evening with Thomas instead of my fiancé.

And then a song by Sierra came onto the radio and we both grew quiet. The sound of Dylan's deep, smooth voice instantly sobered us both.

"I don't understand you two," I said.

"Me and Dylan?"

I nodded.

"Why would you waste an entire day with your brother's fiancée just because he asked you to, especially after what he's done?"

"You should give yourself some credit, Lily. You're not exactly a chore to be around."

I smiled. "Okay, well, what about the kiss then?"

"What about it?" He shrugged. "You could hardly even call it a kiss. We were just pretending for your gran's sake."

"It didn't feel like pretending," I said.

"I don't know what you want me to say, Lily. I was just trying to help you out." His tone was final and dismissive.

I closed the pizza box and stared back at him quietly. "I've never been able to figure you out, Thomas. I always thought you didn't like me, but then you've been so kind to me lately." I noticed the way he was watching me. "And that, the way you look at me, with that pitiful expression. Am I that pathetic?"

He expression grew more serious. "You are many things, Lily, but pathetic is not one of them."

"Oh? Well, what am I then?" I folded the pizza box and placed it on the counter.

"You want the truth?"

"Of course."

"And you won't tell Dylan?"

This intrigued me. Why would he even care? I didn't answer

him, and he continued, so maybe confidentiality wasn't a priority.

"You're funny and smart and you really care about people you love," he said.

I smiled at the unexpected compliment, and he continued, standing up.

"You're so passionate about books and music, and your enthusiasm is contagious." He paused again. "And you're gorgeous. You have the most mysterious eyes I've ever seen and a smile that could melt icecaps."

I knew I was blushing now, but I couldn't help but smile at him. It was the sweetest thing he'd ever said to me, and I could tell he was being sincere. What I didn't know was why he was telling me all this or what possible motivation he had.

He was staring at me still, but he'd stopped talking.

"So you don't think I'm silly and boring," I said.

He smiled. "Is that what you thought?"

I shrugged. "You never seemed to like me very much. I know you said that wasn't true that day when…" I paused instead of reminding him about the fight he'd had with Dylan, "but then since then it didn't seem much different."

Thomas exhaled hard. "Lily, I'm sorry if I've behaved strangely around you. The problem, I guess, well, I just don't know how to act. You're my brother's fiancée and we're supposed to be friends." He laughed.

I didn't have any response for this, so he continued.

"If all goes as planned, you'll be my sister-in-law." Thomas shook his head as though that were the craziest notion he'd ever heard.

"Why is that bad?"

"It just complicates things."

"How? I don't understand." And I didn't. He was confusing me now more than ever.

"Lily, do you remember what I told you the day I learned you planned to marry Dylan?"

I nodded slowly. It was hard to forget a scene that ended with a black eye. Thomas had told me then that I was wrong to think he disliked me, but that he still didn't want me to marry his brother.

"You really didn't grasp what I was telling you?"

"Of course I did. You don't think Dylan and I are good for each other, but you don't hate me. I'm not stupid."

Thomas laughed. "You're definitely not stupid, Lily, but you certainly can be dense about things you don't want to acknowledge. And of course I don't hate you."

He stared back at me again, as though waiting for me to guess.

"Lily, I'm in love with you," he finally said, his voice quiet.

The shock of his words riddled me. "Since when?"

"I don't know. Since always. Since the moment I saw you. Since before we even met. What does it matter?" He shook his head. "I hate that I've hurt you."

"How have you hurt me?"

"Oh Lily, I know how Dylan is. I knew he could destroy you, and I pushed you to stay with him just because I wanted to be near you. And it never made any sense because you chose Dylan. You love Dylan." Thomas laughed.

I was still too dazed to speak.

"Hell, I love Dylan. He's my brother." Thomas added before pausing again. "But I love you more. And it's killing me to watch him torture you."

I didn't know what to say. He broke eye contact and glanced down at the floor.

"I'm sorry," I finally said. "I had no idea."

Even as I spoke those words, I realized how ridiculous it sounded. How had I not known? He'd done everything but told me that day before the fight. And now that I knew, well, every aspect of his behavior made more sense—the way he always tried to protect me and care for me, the gaze that lingered just a moment too long, the disgust when Dylan kissed me…and of course he didn't always like being around me. Why would he want to see a woman he loved be so happy with another man?

Moreover, this explained Dylan's behavior. Dylan wasn't just paranoid for no reason. Whether Thomas had told him or not, Dylan knew how his brother felt about me and that was what had fueled his recurrent bouts of jealousy.

"Yes, well…" Thomas cleared his throat. "I should go."

He quietly exited the apartment, leaving me standing, flabbergasted, in the kitchen.

CHAPTER NINETEEN

"Love, which in gentlest hearts will soonest bloom, seized my
lover
with passion for that sweet body from which I was torn
unshriven to my doom.
Love, which permits no loved one not to love, took me so
strongly with delight in him
that we are one in Hell, as we were above. Love led us to one
death.
In the depths of Hell, Caina waits for him who took our lives."
Dante Alighieri, *The Divine Comedy*

I visited Dylan every day he was in the hospital,
generally arriving early, leaving to pick up lunch for
us, then returning until around dinner. I didn't tell him what
Thomas had said, of course, and I assumed Thomas hadn't either.
With Dylan gone, I was already too overwhelmed to dwell on
Thomas' words anyway. So, I didn't. After that night, I simply

pretended the conversation had never happened. I shelved it away with all the other clues from Thomas' behavior over the past year.

When I visited Dylan, we could almost pretend we weren't in a hospital, that he hadn't nearly killed himself with a toxic combination of drugs and booze. We'd take turns reading to each other, then we'd snuggle on the bed and listen to music.

But when I went home each evening, to the cold, empty apartment I was supposed to be sharing with him, I felt tired and spent. There was a heaviness surrounding me that I couldn't shake, an anxiety that I'd been ignoring, and a painful urge to cry combined with the inability to actually shed any more tears.

On Wednesday, I left the hospital early. I hadn't been to the store since I'd gone to stay with my parents, and I was beyond desperate for food at the apartment. It felt oddly normal, shopping at the market for groceries. I enjoyed the appearance that my life wasn't falling to pieces around me, even if it was just a mirage.

As I reached the apartment building, the heaviness returned. I sighed, and scurried through the lobby.

"You've been avoiding me."

Even though I recognized the voice, it startled me, and I nearly dropped the bag I was carrying. I turned slowly. Thomas grabbed the bag from me and followed me into Dylan's apartment.

"I haven't been avoiding you," I answered.

He stared at me skeptically. "You have so."

"Maybe."

Thomas peered into the bag. "Groceries?"

"I realized I haven't been eating particularly well since Dylan's been…gone."

"How's your grandmother?"

"Same. I think she's going to move in with my parents for a

little while. My mother doesn't think she has much longer, and she doesn't want her to be alone."

"She's not exactly alone in a nursing home, though."

"I know. And it's going to be tough on my mom, having her around all the time, especially with how needy she is now. But my mom feels like it's her duty to take care of her."

Thomas laughed. "So it's genetic then?"

"What is?"

He shook his head. "Nothing."

I put the last of the groceries away. I was torn. On the one hand, it was awkward being alone with Thomas. But on the other hand, I was lonely. I had nowhere to be, now that I was unemployed, and no one to talk to since we were trying to keep Dylan's current location secret. I knew Jill wouldn't tell, but still, I'd promised Dylan I'd keep quiet. I planned to keep my word.

"I went to see Dylan this afternoon," Thomas said. "I actually thought I'd see you there."

"I went by earlier," I said.

"How'd that go?" Thomas had a curious grin on his face as he spoke.

"Fine."

"Really? The nurse told me he threw a book at you and told you never to come back."

I swung around to face him. "If you already knew, why did you ask me?"

"I dunno. Why did you lie?"

"He already apologized," I said, retrieving the loaf of bread I'd just put away from the cabinet. "And I think we could give him the benefit of the doubt. He's not feeling well and he's under tons of stress. This stupid tour is just weeks away, looming there, and Dylan knows if he lets one thing slip, he'll ruin it for all of you. That's a lot of pressure."

"What are you doing?" Thomas asked incredulously as I opened the jar of peanut butter.

"Making dinner."

He slid the knife out of my hand, grimacing. "You can't be serious."

"What?" Now that he was just taunting me, I was no longer torn. I wanted him to leave. I could watch TV and feel sorry for myself in peace.

"Lily, this is just depressing. The apartment's all dark and quiet, you've been shuttling back and forth between two hospitals all week, you're avoiding everyone you know, including me, your fiancé is being an arse, and now you're eating processed nuts from a plastic jar for dinner."

He twisted the cap back onto the peanut butter. "I can't stand to watch this."

"Then go," I suggested.

He gave me a quick once over. "I'm coming back in a half hour. Shower and get dressed. I'll take you out to dinner."

"Thomas, I can't just go out to dinner with you."

"Yes, you can, Lily. I'm literally the only person you can talk to now, aren't I? Unless you'd rather go out with Ari tonight."

I rolled my eyes. "Fine."

He swiped the jar of peanut butter off the counter. "Just so you're not tempted," he said, leaving the apartment.

A half hour later, I had showered, dried and straightened my hair, and changed into black skinny jeans, boots, and a turquoise button-down sweater. Thomas, not bothering to knock, was still wearing jeans and a fitted, hunter green sweater with the sleeves rolled up. I was admittedly relieved that he hadn't changed. I didn't want to risk it *looking* like we were on a date, and, in light of what he'd told me days before, I didn't want the meal to *feel* like a date either.

We went to a decent seafood restaurant and managed friendly small talk while we ate. Thomas filled me in on the details of the tour and made me laugh with tales of past mishaps involving the tour bus. We split a bottle of wine, and by the end of the meal, I was relaxed enough to know the alcohol had served its purpose.

The waiter offered us a dessert menu, which we politely declined, right as someone came up to get Thomas' autograph.

She fit the bill of most people who sought out an autograph from either Parker brother—she was late teens or early twenties, blonde, and cute. Actually, she reminded me of Thomas' last two girlfriends. I wondered if her name started with an H too.

Thomas signed an old paper she handed him, and then the girl paused and stared at me. I could tell she was wishing it was her, seated at a nice restaurant sharing wine and laughing with a sexy rockstar. I knew that because I used to think that whenever I saw musicians out and about. I was always even a little jealous of the groupies—just because they had that intimate connection of sorts with these magical people that created such awesome music.

If only she knew the reality, I thought.

Suddenly, the girls' eyes widened. She turned back to Thomas. "Oh my God, are you engaged? I thought that you were single. I swear I read that somewhere. This is so unfair!"

I saw Thomas swallow nervously, and then a peculiar grin crossed his face. "Well, this is awkward," he said to me. The girl watched him expectantly.

"This is my brother Dylan's fiancée. Rest assured, I am quite single." He paused as visible relief washed across the girls' face. "But probably too old for you anyway, and about to go on tour, so it's really not the best time…"

The girl nodded eagerly and made her way back to her own table. Thomas and I both laughed.

"You're not that old," I reminded him.

"I'm older than you," he replied.

That was true. I was two years younger than Dylan, meaning Thomas had a full three years on me. Thomas came across as much older than Dylan, though, or perhaps just more mature. He always seemed to be in control, calm, and prepared. Thomas never let his emotions get the better of him. Dylan, in contrast, well, he was a hot mess. His passions ruled him, and nothing he did ever seemed to be based on rational thinking but rather on emotion.

The waiter brought the bill. Thomas reached for it, but I shook my head. "I owe you," I said. I started to put a credit card out and then I hesitated, thinking cash might be a better idea.

Thomas pulled the bill away from me and quickly paid it. "Jesus, Lily, does Dylan actually monitor what you spend?"

I winced, wishing he hadn't known that was the reason for my waver. "He'd know I couldn't eat this much on my own," I finally said. "And he's been so jealous lately. I just don't want to stress him out any more."

I considered reminding him that it was Dylan's money anyway, now that I was unemployed, but when I glanced up and saw Thomas staring at me, a pitiful look in his eyes, I kept quiet. We left the restaurant and decided to walk back to the apartment building.

"You must think I'm insane," I mumbled once we seemed to be alone on the street. "You don't see what I see in him, and you don't know what he's like when we're alone. He's really not a bad guy," I said, hating that I felt I had to justify my relationship to Thomas, of all people.

"I don't think that at all, Lily. I know exactly what you see in him."

I glanced at Thomas, hoping he wasn't about to infer I was with Dylan for his money. He was staring straight ahead, hands in his pockets. I shivered and started walking a little closer to him.

Thomas noticed my cold and offered me his jacket, draping it across my shoulders and lingering with his arm on my back.

"And what is that?" I finally asked.

"The same thing we all see in him. Dylan is, well, you know. Magnetic."

I nodded. I did know. Dylan had one of those personalities that just drew people in. I supposed that Thomas understood better than anyone else would.

Then I caught myself wondering what if... what if I'd met Thomas that day in the rain instead of Dylan. Dylan turned out to be everything I'd feared in a musician and Thomas was none of those things. But would I have even talked to Thomas? Would we have hit it off? Surely I would have been attracted to him, but I didn't know if that attraction, without the persistence and charm Dylan had shown, would have been enough to overcome my no-musician rule.

And so what if we had hit it off?

I couldn't let myself consider it, couldn't wonder about all the ways our lives might be different if I had dated Thomas and not Dylan. It was a moot point and always would be. I chose Dylan. Whether or not I'd picked the right brother, I'd made my bed and now had to lie in it.

"Dylan's been my best friend my whole life," Thomas finally continued, drawing me out of my daydream. "Even when we were kids, and we'd have some fight and I just couldn't wait until we were older and I could get away from him for good, he'd always end up winning me over again sooner or later."

I laughed. "I could see that."

"He's a charismatic person," Thomas said. "There's something about him that just pulls you in. Like a spider web."

"There's a flattering analogy."

"Oh, you know what I mean. Once he's gotten under your skin, you just can't get away."

Clearly, Thomas wasn't just talking about me. I wondered how exactly he'd come to work with Dylan, to practically live with Dylan, and to spend the majority of his time with Dylan, if he had such jaded opinions of his brother.

But then, my phone buzzed and startled both of us.

I looked down to read the message from Dylan. "I need u. Come back 2nite please."

I glanced at Thomas and knew that he'd read it as well. He turned to me expectantly.

The truth be told, I was exhausted. Seeing Dylan depressed in a hospital was draining me, and it wasn't like I wouldn't see him first thing in the morning. If I went back, I knew what would happen—we'd talk and maybe have sex, which was not something I particularly liked doing in a rehab room. Then, he'd get upset about something and I'd leave feeling worse than when I'd arrived.

We reached the apartment building and I paused to reply to the message. "Sorry babe. I'm so tired and about to go to bed. Call me tomorrow AM and I'll come then. I love you."

I couldn't tell if Thomas read my response or not, but the fact that I followed him back into the building probably conveyed the same message. We lingered in the hall outside the apartment and I realized I was dreading going back in. Staying at Dylan's apartment without Dylan felt wrong. I missed having my own apartment. I missed having Dylan.

"Come have a drink with me," Thomas said, interrupting my thoughts.

I silently followed him into his apartment, despite the nagging sensation that it wasn't a good idea. The layout of his apartment was similar to Dylan's, with an equally impressive view, but there were more hints of personality scattered throughout Thomas'. I'd been in his apartment many times, but I'd never really explored it. I wandered around the apartment staring at framed photos and unusual trinkets while he poured me a drink.

"That's South Africa," Thomas said, nodding to the picture I was staring at. He handed me a mostly clear drink with a hint of pink. "Vodka and cranberry," he explained. He appeared to be drinking whiskey or something in that color-group.

I thanked him for the drink and drained it within a matter of minutes, pacing around the room. "I can't wait to see Rome," I said, eying a photo of the Coliseum.

"I think you'd like Egypt too," he said, taking my empty glass. "Another?"

I nodded. "You've been to Egypt?"

He poured the drink. "Hasn't Dylan told you?"

I shook my head and started on the next drink.

"I don't believe it's on this tour, but I'm sure you could make a side trip out of it. Dylan would go anywhere for you."

Suddenly, I felt resentful of Dylan.

All day, all week, and for the past few weeks, I'd been feeling sorry for him, and now I was just irritated. This was all Dylan's fault. If he'd just stop using, everything would be perfect. We could travel the world together, he could write songs and perform, I could spend my days reading. Everyone would be happy. Maybe even Thomas would be happy if he saw how happy we were.

Why couldn't Dylan just stop? Wasn't I worth it to him? Wasn't life worth it?

I went to take another sip of my drink but found it was empty. "More please," I said to Thomas.

"You sure?"

I nodded. "It's not like I have a long drive home," I tried to joke.

He still looked uncertain, but eventually he went and refilled it, although I noticed this drink was much weaker than the last two.

I rolled my eyes at him. "Yeah, I'd hate to be hungover when I head out to the detox unit tomorrow."

Thomas nodded without a hint of a smile. He bent and picked up a guitar and carried it across the room.

"Don't you have four others like Dylan?"

Now Thomas laughed. "No, Dylan is unique in his insistence

on keeping five guitars with him at all times. He has a knack for breaking strings unrivaled by any other musician."

I chugged the drink, set the empty glass on a coaster and exhaled dramatically. "You know he's going to ruin the tour, right? There's no way he can handle all that."

Thomas frowned and set down his own drink. "I realize it seems that way, but I think you're wrong. Dylan's at peace with himself when he's on stage. The writing—that's when he gets too reclusive. And the business side of things stresses him out. Performing, that he can handle."

I sighed. The more time Dylan spent with me, the more he seemed to need the drugs. Traveling the world with me didn't exactly seem like what he needed, and I wasn't sure I could handle watching Dylan spin out of control for much longer. I couldn't deny that over the past month, I'd seen the Dylan I loved less and less, with the unpredictable, high Dylan taking his place more often than not.

"A long tour is exactly what he needs right now," Thomas said, as though reading my mind.

The promise of exotic travels wasn't so alluring anymore. I wasn't sure I could handle being in a foreign country while Dylan continued his downward spiral. It was lonely enough in the city I knew intimately, let alone some strange town where I didn't even speak the language. But at this point, I hardly had a choice. I was trapped.

I stepped closer and turned to Thomas. "And what about the rest of us, and what we need?" I paused. "What do you need right now?"

His eyes locked on mine and I knew his answer. The green circling his pupils seemed even brighter than usual, especially in contrast with his thick, dark lashes.

I reached my hand out and gently grazed Thomas' smooth cheek, realizing he must have shaved since I saw him earlier in the day. I tried to think of why he would do that, but before I could reach a rational conclusion, my lips were on his.

He hesitated for a moment before kissing me back. His lips were warm and welcoming, and the scent of his cologne soothed to me. His arms wrapped around me, his hands pressing into the small of my back. I reached my own hands out, nervously skimming across his firm butt before settling on his back.

The kiss went on and on. We kissed until my mind went completely blank, until I was no longer dizzy and overwhelmed by the constant flurry of concern and what-ifs, until I simply felt at peace. We kissed in a way that made me forget where I was, why I was even with Thomas instead of with my fiancé in the first place.

As long as I could stay frozen in this moment, with Thomas' warm body and welcoming mouth pressed against my own, I didn't have to hate myself for loving Dylan, didn't have to worry about his next relapse, and didn't have to consider what his future—or mine— might hold.

Thomas was the one who ended the kiss, pulling his mouth inches from mine so that his hot breath still fell against my lips but I could no longer feel the dampness of his tongue against my own. He left his hands clasped gently behind my neck, but his eyes had already told me exactly what he wanted.

I stared back at Thomas for a moment, determined not to think about any of it, but just to be there, in the present, with him.

I stepped back, lifted my shirt over my head and tossed it onto the ground. His eyes never left mine, not even as I started to pull off his sweater, and not even when I reached around to unclasp my bra. When we were both naked from the waist up, I turned, and walked slowly to his bedroom.

I didn't turn to check if Thomas followed, but as I stretched out on my back on his bed, I saw that he had. But now he was frozen in the doorway, still undecided. He was watching me though, his eyes filled with longing.

For a brief flash, I knew this was all horribly wrong. But I wasn't ready to accept that yet. I unzipped my jeans and slithered out of them, tossing my panties on top of them on the ground.

Thomas opened his mouth to say something, then shook his head instead. He slowly stepped closer, his eyes scanning my naked body before locking on my eyes, waiting for me to change my mind.

When I didn't move or speak, Thomas stripped off the rest of his own clothes. I watched him undress, calmly, not fully relaxing until he climbed on top of me in the bed. We made love slowly, and almost silently. His every touch felt painfully familiar and yet wonderfully different at the same time.

I whispered his name as the physical sensations took over and Thomas responded in kind. His eyes stayed on mine, the greenish hue nearly hypnotizing me by the time he turned away to kiss my neck.

I knew I was crying by the time we finished, and I turned my head to the side so he wouldn't see, but I was too late.

"Lily, I…"

He began, but I raised my hand to his lips, begging him not to finish the sentence. "Please don't make me leave yet," I said.

Thomas frowned, then rolled onto his back and pulled me on top of him, wrapping his arms around me protectively.

I saw my tears trickling onto his chest hairs and knew he must think I was a mess, but I couldn't bring myself to move. I was safe there, in Thomas' arms. If I could just stay there forever, then…well, I didn't know what, but I was unwilling to think of an alternative.

I lifted my head and kissed him again, and this time there was no hesitation on his part. We made love a second time, and then Thomas pulled the comforter up over us, nestling my body against his. He sang to me, quietly, a song that I hadn't heard them perform, but before I could ask him the name, I fell asleep.

I slept soundly, dreaming about my childhood. It was a pleasant dream, where my mother, father, grandma and I all strolled along a stream in the meadow on a sunny spring day. It wasn't a memory, exactly, since even in sleep I knew I'd never been to that spot with my family. I recognized it as the spot Thomas and I had settled in while Kate and Dylan were chatting during out last trip to England.

The dream was soothing that I felt my entire body relax further into sleep.

* * *

WHEN I AWOKE, it was still dark out and my head was pounding. I sighed and settled further into Dylan's body, yearning to fall back to sleep. But as soon as I caught a glimpse of the arm wrapped around me, it all came back to me.

I sat abruptly, and Thomas followed suit.

"Lily," was all he said.

Still, that was enough to remind me of everything I'd done and everyone I hurt.

"Oh my God, Thomas. I'm so sorry. I didn't mean…"

He shook his head. "I know. It's not your fault."

"I can't," I began, my voice wavering, and then I looked into his eyes. I saw the glimmer of hope disappear, and he nodded solemnly.

"I know. This doesn't have to change anything. He won't ever know." Thomas's voice was quiet, but convincing.

"You won't tell him?"

"Of course not, Lily." Thomas seemed surprised that I'd even ask. "It would kill him."

I bit my lip. *Shit*. He was right, and we both knew it. Worse yet, we'd both known it the night before and it hadn't changed anything.

Thomas slipped out of bed and returned with my bra and shirt. I had nearly finished putting my jeans on by that point. He pulled on his own pants, handed me my purse, and walked me to the door.

As I unlocked Dylan's door, I glanced back at Thomas. He flashed a fake, but polite smile, and I shut the door behind me. I barely made it to the kitchen sink before vomiting.

Oh God. What had I done?

CHAPTER TWENTY

Blessed is the servant who loves his brother as much when he is
sick and useless
as well when he is afar off as when he is by his side, and who
would say nothing
behind his back he might not, in love, say before his face.
~St. Francis of Assisi

*W*hen I went to visit Dylan later that morning, he was listening to headphones and didn't hear me enter his room. His eyes were closed and his lips were moving, but no sound came out. I inched closer, not wanting to startle him, then waited. After a moment, his eyes popped open and he smiled.

"My Lily," he exclaimed, as though surprised to see me. Then he frowned. "What's wrong? You look terrible."

The blood rushed to my face. I hadn't realized my guilt was that obvious.

He stood up and pulled me in for a hug. "That came out

wrong. You look gorgeous and perfect, just maybe a bit on the tired side." He kissed my forehead. "I shouldn't have bothered you last night."

"You never bother me. I love hearing from you." I paused. "I miss you." I sat on the edge of his bed. "Were you practicing?"

Dylan laughed. "If you can call it that." He paused. "I spoke to Ari yesterday, and I think I'll check out tomorrow so we have time for some final adjustments to the set before we leave for tour."

"You can check out tomorrow, just like that?"

He nodded. "Why not? There's no medical reason for me to be here. It's just stressing everyone out and keeping me away from you."

I tried to smile, and probably should've bitten my tongue, but I had to ask him. "But it's also keeping you from using, right? Shouldn't you stay here until you're..." I wasn't sure how to finish my sentence.

"You wouldn't have them keep me here forever, would you, love?" He stood in front of me and leaned down, pressing his forehead against the top of my head and rubbing my back. He rose back up quickly. "It's fine anyway. I spoke with the doctor, and it's all out of my system now."

I must have looked concerned, because he sat beside me and squeezed my hand.

"Lily, don't be so alarmed. I thought you'd want me to come home. We're not going to have a lot of privacy or downtime once the tour gets underway, you know."

"Of course I want you home. I just want to make sure you're okay. You really scared me that night."

He nodded. "I know. I completely miscalculated. I had the right amount and then it didn't seem to do anything, so I did some more."

He shrugged casually, like he was discussing a botched batch of cookies. "The doctor said it's more common than you'd think.

You know, you build up a tolerance and so you know you need a little more for the same effect, but then you overestimate or maybe it was just impatience. Who knows? Either way, lesson learned."

I stood up. "Dylan, stop. Do you hear yourself? The lesson you're supposed to have learned was not to do drugs ever again, not just how to avoid overdosing."

He held up his hands defensively. "Don't worry, Lily. I got it."

I started to protest, steadfastly certain he "got" nothing, but he kissed me, effectively shushing me. A minute into the kiss, there was a tap at the door, then a voice.

"Hope we're not interrupting." It was Ari, jokingly covering his eyes. Thomas stood behind him, staring pointedly at the ground.

Dylan grinned excitedly. "I was just telling Lil the good news, about me coming home tomorrow," he said to Ari.

"Tomorrow?" Thomas repeated. He glanced from Dylan to me then back to Dylan. "Yesterday you were throwing things, today you're manically happy, and tomorrow you're going home?"

"Did you rat me out?" Dylan asked, turning to me.

"The nurse told me," Thomas said.

Ari seemed perplexed, but kept quiet.

"Lily needs me back anyway," Dylan said.

"As does the band," Ari added.

"What'd you do last night after you ditched me, anyway?" Dylan asked his brother.

Thomas went pale.

"Actually, babe, he took me out to an early dinner," I jumped in.

Dylan seemed intrigued by this, but not bothered. He patted my thigh. "I hope you were nice to him," he teased.

I laughed. "Why don't I come back later, if you guys are going to discuss band stuff now?"

Ari and Thomas both jumped at this suggestion, but Dylan shook his head.

"You just got here," he whined. "We won't talk shop for too long. Can't you just read or something? I've got some books Thomas dropped off."

My eyes followed his gesture to the stack of novels by the bed. I smiled at Dylan, then grabbed the top one from the stack. It was *The Sound and the Fury*, and though it had been a while since I read it, I immediately realized the irony of Thomas bringing that for his brother to read. Nonetheless, I settled down in a chair in the corner and attempted to ignore the discussions about the tour.

Nearly an hour passed before they finally stood to leave.

"Hey Thomas, tell the nurses not to bother me till Lily leaves, would you?" Dylan said with a wink as his brother left the room.

Thomas looked sick, but nodded.

Dylan turned to me with a mischievous grin. "I think that should secure us at least a half hour," he said, pulling me out of my chair and onto his lap on the couch.

"Dylan, no. Anyone could walk in. You'll just have to wait until tomorrow."

He pouted. "That didn't stop you last week."

I vividly recalled the prior week. His mood had been alternating between sullen and hyper, and a part of me had worried he'd go crazy if I'd refused him then. Since that day, though, I'd conveniently timed my visits so as not to be alone with him for long. "Dylan that was right after you'd gotten here, when I nearly thought I'd lost you."

He slid off the bed and led me to the bathroom. "But now you're so grateful that you've got me, right?" he asked, his dimples popping.

He kissed me hard, and I knew he wouldn't give up. I missed his kisses, missed feeling how much he wanted me with every brush of his tongue. I unzipped his pants, lowered them slightly, and reached for him with my hand.

As his breathing quickened, I considered the irony, of this simple act making me feel slutty, in light of what I'd done less than twelve hours prior. Clearly I was the one who belonged in counseling.

Dylan's hand slipped under my skirt, frantically tugging at my panties. I grabbed his hand and held it firm.

"Dylan," I whispered in protest.

He pulled away. "Please, Lily. I miss you." He hoisted me up onto the counter beside the sink and kept lowering my panties. "I want to be with you. I need to be in you." His eyes pleaded with me and I knew I couldn't say no. How could I, after what I'd done?

I lifted my hips to help him with my panties then pulled him close for a kiss.

CHAPTER TWENTY-ONE

She was an honorable woman who had bestowed her love
upon him,
and he loved her, and therefore she was in his eyes a woman who
had a right to the same,
or even more, respect than a lawful wife. He would have had his
hand chopped off
before he would have allowed himself by a word, by a hint, to
humiliate her,
or even to fall short of the fullest respect a woman could look for.
Leo Tolstoy, *Anna Karenina*

*D*ylan returned home exactly three weeks before we were scheduled to leave for the tour. He seemed glad to be home, and stayed remarkably serene, sweet, and sober. He reminded me a little of the Dylan I'd first met, minus the mystery, I suppose. Thomas avoided both Dylan and I, but I was probably the only one who perceived his efforts.

Dylan was desperate to keep me excited about the tour and all of the new places we could visit together. I think he picked up on my nervousness and attributed it to being away from my home and my family and my friends for so long, but in reality, I was accustomed to being lonely from them after keeping secrets for so long. It was more a fear of being with Dylan and Thomas, together, in a close space over a lengthy period of time.

I didn't doubt that Thomas would keep his promise and never tell Dylan the truth, but I still knew it would come out somehow. Secrets never stayed hidden for long. I couldn't stand the thought of the two brothers that had overcome so much together finally ripping each other apart over something stupid I had done. And I also had a nagging fear that we'd all end up in a trashy tabloid.

A week before the tour, I made a decision. I wasn't going to leave with the rest of the band for the tour. I'd stay behind for two weeks and help my parents move my grandmother into their house. That would give me some time to myself, and then Thomas and Dylan could spend some time alone together before I rejoined the picture.

Surprisingly, Dylan was supportive of the plan. He offered to postpone the tour for me, surely knowing I'd refuse, but then even arranged my travel so I could meet up with them in Vancouver.

The week before they were set to leave, I went to run some errands. When I returned, Thomas was waiting in the lobby. I waved politely at him before starting for the elevator. He hurried onto the elevator with me, started to say something, then paused as another woman stepped on behind him. His obvious frustration amused me, and I laughed.

The woman got off at the fifteenth floor, but Thomas hardly had time to say anything before the elevator reached our floor.

"I need to talk to you," he said. "Come with me for a minute."

I glanced at Dylan's apartment, then followed Thomas into his.

"I'll be quick," he promised, sighing.

"No, it's okay. I owe you an apology. I was really upset that night, and I shouldn't have done what I did, and now I've fucked up everything with you and Dylan."

Thomas smiled. "That's precisely what I planned to say to you."

I shrugged and reached for the doorknob.

He grabbed my hand. "Wait, Lily. There is more. You need to know that I meant what I said. I'll never tell Dylan, unless you ask me to. And since he doesn't know, you can't keep blaming yourself. You were already too much of a martyr for him. What he doesn't know isn't hurting him. Just forget what happened between us. Nothing's changed."

I rolled my eyes.

"I mean it, Lily." He paused and caught my eye again. "But if you ever change your mind, I'm here."

"Change my mind about what?"

"About Dylan, about me." He sighed again. "I know I can't compete with him, and I know you don't love me, but I want you to know I still love you, and if you're feelings for me ever change..."

"Then what, Thomas?" I shook my head furiously. "It doesn't matter how I feel, and it never will. You said it yourself. If Dylan knew what happened, it would kill him. You can't possibly be this naïve, Thomas. Regardless of how you or I feel, there is no possible scenario here where you and I just ride off into the sunset, happily ever after."

"Lily, I'd protect you."

"I don't need protection, Thomas. What I need is for you to accept reality. Dylan is my fiancé. Dylan is your brother, your best friend, and your band mate. Everything else is irrelevant. You and I can never be together. You have to know that."

He winced and pulled away, and I immediately regretted the harsh tone behind my words. I'd already hurt him enough, and I hadn't meant to make it worse. But I'd been going over it all in my head, and what I was saying was the only truth there was.

"Lily, I know you're trying to spare my feelings here, but I need to hear you say it. I need to know that you're in love with Dylan, that he's the one you want to be with."

My breath caught in my throat, but I looked him in the eyes. "I love Dylan. And I'm so sorry about everything."

Thomas smiled. "Don't be. No regrets, right?" He winked, reminding me again of the irony of the name they'd chosen for the tour. He glanced out the peephole, then opened the door.

"Remind Dylan to call Mom sometime," he called casually to me as I walked down the hall. "It's her birthday today."

* * *

ONE WEEK LATER, I sat on the bed and watched Dylan zip his last bag shut.

"You sure you don't want to send any of your stuff with us?" he asked.

"I'm sure. I can fit everything I'll need into two suitcases anyway, and it'll just complicate things if I have to figure out what I'll use this week and what I won't need until I join you." I glanced at him. "Are you nervous?"

He laughed. "Not in the least. Tom is, though. He's been acting strange lately."

I stood and made my way to the closet. "You sure you don't need any of this other stuff?"

Dylan came up behind me and wrapped his arms around my waist. "We'll only be gone three months at a time, love. It isn't like we're moving."

"But then you leave again," I reminded him.

He laughed, his breath tickling my ear. "Are you nervous? You've been acting odd, too."

He was right, but the nervousness didn't stem from the

upcoming tour. Although, it did seem to be worsening the closer we got to the tour. I knew it was probably just guilt that was filling my stomach with butterflies, but it seemed like the nausea was increasing by the day.

Dylan kissed my neck then swiveled me around to face him. "Come on now, we have an hour till I need to leave. Are we really going to waste it talking?"

I smiled and acquiesced to his familiar touch.

The next hour flew by, and before I knew it, I was kissing him goodbye in the lobby of the apartment building. Ari was there, as was Thomas, but they were meeting the rest of the band at the airport. I watched as they loaded everything into the van that was taking them to the airport. Dylan hovered over his guitars like they were Venetian glass, insisting on placing them in the van himself.

"Dylan says you're meeting up with us in Vancouver," Thomas said.

I jumped at his voice, not having realized he'd approached me. "That's the plan," I replied, unintentionally vague.

The band was flying to southern California and working their way around the Pacific southwest, slowly heading up north and then east with the tour. That way, they could limit their time in the tour bus, although after watching the debacle of them trying to load their instruments into a van for a flight, I saw some definite perks to the tour bus.

I turned to Thomas. He was standing a respectable distance from me, his hands wedged into the pockets of his dark blue jeans as I spoke. "I'm sorry about everything. This wasn't your fault. I'm the one at blame for what happened."

He shook his head. "Lily, you have all the reason in the world to hate me. So does Dylan, he just doesn't know it."

"He never will," I promised. Our eyes met briefly, and I saw behind his thick green irises that there was something else he wanted to say. Instead, he leaned forward and gave me an awkward hug.

"Take care of yourself, Lily," he whispered.

I nodded just as Dylan approached.

"See, that's what performance anxiety looks like," he teased, gesturing to his brother.

I forced a smile as Thomas climbed into the van.

"I'll miss you," I told Dylan, squeezing his hands. He kissed each of my hands in turn, then released them. I reached forward and lifted his sunglasses off his eyes. I just needed to see him one last time.

"You're crazy," he said, his eyes smooth as hot chocolate. "In another month's time you'll be sick of me and the whole band."

"Maybe," I replied.

We kissed again, then Ari reached over the driver and honked. Dylan hopped into the van and waved as they drove off.

When I went back into the apartment, I still couldn't shake the funny feeling. I knew it was probably just stress about the tour or Dylan's sobriety or the fact that I was the worst fiancée ever. But then I decided that maybe I'd just eaten something that hadn't agreed with me. I opened the cabinet under the bathroom sink in search of some Tums, but my eyes immediately settled on something else—an unopened box of tampons. I held my breath and tried to do a mental math calculation, but I was quickly interrupted by a knock at the door.

I closed the cabinet and leapt up, curious as to what Dylan forgot. I swung the door open eagerly, but it was only Charles, the doorman.

"Hi," I said. "Dylan's already gone, if you were looking for him."

Charles shook his head and smiled. "No, it was you I was looking for." He held a small package out to me. "Mr. Parker asked that I hand-deliver this to you after they left."

"Oh. Thanks," I said, accepting the package and closing the

door. It was typical Dylan to leave me with a parting gift, and I was eager to see what it was. It was a padded envelope, which I tore open carefully. As soon as I did, a large stack of hundred dollar bills fell out. My jaw dropped, and I quickly collected the cash and wedged it back into the envelope, glancing around me as though some invisible intruder might be watching me.

I flipped through the money slowly, counting fifty bills in total, making five thousand dollars. When my heart stopped pounding uncontrollably, I noticed there was a note with the money. As soon as I saw the handwriting, I realized my mistake.

The package wasn't from Dylan, but from Thomas.

I moved my lips as I read the note:

Dear Lily-

By the time you're reading this, Dylan and I should be on our way to the airport. I'm telling you this by letter because I don't think I'd have the courage to say what I need to say in person. I know you don't owe me anything, but please do me the courtesy of reading to the end.

I want you to know that I meant it when I said I love you. I've been selfish by trying to keep you around longer, but I've also been struggling to tell you what you need to hear when the truth may hurt Dylan. I know you love him, and I know he loves you. But Lily, he's abusive, and he's an addict, and he's not ready to change. You've been good to him and you don't owe him anything. You need to leave him.

I'm his brother; I'm the one who needs to stay and take care of him. I'll be with him every day of the tour, and I promise you he'll be fine. Maybe someday he'll be better, and then you could come back. But until then, I know you're better off without him, even if it means I have to go without you too.

Nothing that Dylan has done or that has happened to him was your fault. He's always felt things too deeply. I guess the same qualities that make him such a gifted songwriter also leave him feeling tormented.

You have spent the last year putting him first and never considering the consequences for your life, and that has to stop.

Take the money in the envelope and get yourself a new apartment. Find a job. Start your life again. Just don't join us on the tour. If Dylan's better by the time we return, then you can blame all of this on me and you two can live happily ever after. But if not, then you won't have wasted another nine months of your life taking care of someone who shouldn't be your burden.

I'm sorry it took me so long to tell you all this, and I'm sorry I couldn't do it in person. I'll be thinking about you.

Regards, Thomas.

I READ the letter four or five times in all and then recounted the money. Then I wedged the entire envelope into the bottom of my suitcase, under the books I'd already selected for my trip. I locked up the apartment and ran out to the drugstore, certain I couldn't even begin to process what Thomas had said until I knew one thing for sure.

CHAPTER TWENTY-TWO

"She had not known the weight until she felt the freedom."
Nathaniel Hawthorne, *The Scarlet Letter*

Two weeks later, after saying goodbye to my parents and grandma and enjoying one last smoothie-date with Jill, I was at the airport. I had two large suitcases in addition to my duffel bag and purse, and I struggled to drag them both up to the ticket counter. The desk attendant's eyes widened in horror.

"You'll have to pay extra to check both of those you know."

I nodded and lugged them onto the rack, one at a time.

"Ticket," she said expectantly.

"I have a ticket, but I can't go on this flight," I said, handing her the ticket. "Can you just refund this ticket onto the original credit card and I'll buy a new one now?"

She scanned the ticket and shook her head. "This one is nonrefundable, but for a fee, I can modify the flight and you can just pay the difference and the fee for changing the ticket." She eyed my bags again. "I assume you're looking to travel today. Where are you wanting to go?"

"Well, the original ticket isn't on my credit card."

"That doesn't matter. You're the listed passenger, so you can modify the ticket. You'll have to pay the difference on a different card, of course."

"If you modify the ticket, will the new destination show up on the receipt? I mean, is there any way that the person whose card it was on could find out how the ticket was modified?"

She frowned. "I don't understand."

I took a deep breath. I considered just paying for a new ticket out of pocket, but if this worked, it would certainly save me a big chunk of change, and since Dylan couldn't get a refund anyway, there didn't seem to be any harm in it.

"Someone bought me this ticket to Vancouver so I could meet up with him there, but I can't go there. I'm moving to Michigan, and it is very important that the person who paid for this ticket never knows where I'm moving," I finally said.

The woman nodded quickly, and I immediately saw the look of pity in her eyes.

"I can just pay cash if it won't work."

She shook her head. "No, I can do that."

We went over the remaining details for my new flight, I paid the fees, and she checked in my bags.

"Have a good flight," she said.

I nodded in lieu of smiling and started to back away when I thought of something. "Do you have a lost and found bin?"

"Yes."

I pulled my cell phone out of my purse. "Can you put this in there, please?"

She nodded, and I went to wait for my flight. When I reached the gate, I sat down with my worn copy of *The Scarlet Letter* and flipped to the folded down page. My breath slowed with the rhythm of the words and I gradually felt calmer with each page.

As I read the familiar passage about little Pearl frolicking through the forest, I rubbed my stomach peacefully. I felt a sudden flutter, and just like that, I knew that everything would be alright.

EPILOGUE

a *true love story never has a happy ending. The lovers may be happy, but the story never ends. True love goes on and on and on. That's how it happened for me, anyway, or at least the part about no end. I never forgot the girl, and I never shook off the guilt.*

The pain lessened with time, but it never went away. To some extent, it was comforting, my private reminder that it had all been real. Course, perhaps it was supposed to remind me of something altogether different, of how I'd betrayed them both.

I had gotten the call from Lily the previous night, and I hadn't slept since. After nearly four years without so much as a word from her, I couldn't imagine why she was possibly contacting me now. She asked me to meet her at a local park, and I quickly obliged, doubtlessly surprising her with my eagerness. Still, I knew that while time hadn't changed my feelings for her, I'd be a fool to hope that it had somehow changed her feelings, or at least her willingness to admit them.

I was circling the park the next day, having arrived early, and I kept my eyes peeled for Lily. It hadn't occurred to me that she might've aged or changed her appearance since I last saw her, but it didn't matter.

Before I even spotted Lily, I stopped dead in my tracks at the sight of a ghost.

I apologized to a woman who bumped into me following my abrupt stop, then I stepped closer to the apparition, rubbing my eyes with disbelief. There, sitting on a metallic owl-shaped teeter totter contraption on the playground was my sister Lucy. I knew it wasn't real, that it actually wasn't her, but I couldn't force myself to look away, knowing I had to cherish whatever brief time I had the privilege of viewing this beautiful hallucination.

She was just as I remembered her, not when she died, but when she was younger. She had dark brown hair that fell across her shoulders in thick waves and blue eyes that stood out even from fifteen feet away. She was giggling, obviously thrilled with her adventure, and her dimples popped.

"Thomas."

I turned abruptly at the sound of my name and came face to face with Lily. She smiled warmly at me, and I noticed that, aside from a hint of experience in her eyes, her face and hair were the same, gorgeous as always. Normally, I'd have stared at her longer, but these were extenuating circumstances. I turned back to the playground, desperately hoping the ghost was still there. She was.

"It's Lucy," I explained, realizing Lily still wouldn't understand my odd behavior.

I glanced briefly at her, confirming that the confusion I'd expect from her was indeed written all over her face. She opened her mouth to speak, then hesitated. I turned back to Lucy.

"It's impossible," I said, unable to blink.

Lily squeezed my hand then and cleared her throat. "Thomas, that's not your sister Lucy. That's my daughter."

My breath caught in my throat as I considered her words. What Lily said made sense. Of course I wasn't seeing my dead sister. But why... my mind reeled as I put it all together.

"Her name is Lucy," Lily added, I suppose by way of acknowledging my confusion.

I struggled to take a deep breath, then turned briefly to her. She was watching the girl now as well. "So Dylan's the father?" It was a pointless question, since the only explanation for the girl's striking resemblance to Lucy was a blood connection.

"I don't know," Lily said after a pause.

I didn't doubt for a minute her sincerity, or the likelihood that she knew I was now contemplating the only other possible candidate.

"How old is she?"

"She just turned three."

"So..."

"It's possible," she said. "I never found out. I didn't know how, and I didn't want to know, honestly." She bit her lip. "In terms of the timing, it could be either of you. I was on the pill, but when I left Dylan and went to my parents' house for a few days, I forgot to take my pills with me. I figured it didn't matter at the time, since I was leaving him anyway, but then when I came back, I forgot all about it when I found Dylan and he was in the hospital."

I had a nagging sensation that I should feel betrayed by this news and angry at Lily, but instead, I felt relief. It explained so much to me, and I couldn't really fault her actions.

"That's why you left," I concluded. "When I sent you that note, I thought you'd move out, maybe even leave for a short while, not leave for good, or cut me out too. But I guess that explains it."

She nodded, then waved at little Lucy as the child raced towards a climber, glancing around to confirm her mother was still watching. "I thought you already knew about Lucy," Lily finally said.

I turned to her, now feeling the pain gnawing at me. "How could you say that? You think if I had known I would have done nothing?"

Her dark brown eyes narrowed. "Of course not. But I..." her voice was nervous. "I assumed Dylan told you."

Another stab of pain. "You told Dylan?"

"No," she quickly assured me. "I don't know how he found out, but he's known since she was a baby. My best guess is that he hired someone to track me down and they took a picture of me with Lucy." She paused, clearly wanting me to respond, but I had no words.

"He's been sending me money," she finally continued. "I returned it the first time and he sent back twice as much, with a note saying that if I didn't keep it, he'd come find me. Find us."

"He threatened you?" My voice did little to hide my disgust at my brother's actions.

She shrugged. "He has every right to be upset with me. I left him and never told him about Lucy. I planned to keep her from him indefinitely."

"You didn't tell me either," I reminded her.

"I know. And I'm sorry. I wanted to. There were so many times I thought about calling you, but..." She shook her head, wiping an invisible tear out from under her thick eyelashes. "I've already made you keep too many secrets from your brother. And Lucy's a very happy child."

"I can see that."

"You know how he was when I left. I didn't want that for her. I didn't want any of that in her life."

I grabbed her hand. "Lily, I understand why you left. I don't blame you for that. I was relieved when you didn't meet us in Vancouver."

She sniffled and nodded.

"But you could've told me. I wouldn't have told Dylan. I would've helped you, regardless of which of us is her father."

Suddenly, Lucy ran towards us. My stomach lurched when she stopped just a few feet away. Even up close, she was the spitting image of my sister. She glanced furtively at me, then back to her mother. And then she asked Lily to push her on the swing and I laughed.

I couldn't help it. The sound of the girl's voice was so unexpected that laughter was the only reaction I could muster. She sounded exactly like Lily, not like her namesake. Her words were soft and flowed easily, coming across nothing like those of my sister who'd never actually heard herself speak.

Lily seemed confused by my reaction, but smiled. She crouched down to face her daughter and I realized that she'd filled out some in the years since I'd last seen her. She was still thin, but her face seemed softer, her hips less sharp, and her breasts more rounded.

"Lucy, this is my friend Thomas. Can you say hello to him?"

The girl blushed.

"You have a very pretty name," I said.

"Thanks," the girl whispered.

"Sweetie, why don't you go down the slide a few more times and then I'll come push you on the swings." Lily said. The suggestion apparently appealed to Lucy, who scampered off.

"Why did you call me?" I asked, my voice sounding harsher than I'd intended. I held my breath, praying she'd say what I wanted to hear, but of course she didn't.

"I wanted you to have the chance to know her, if that's what you want."

I gazed down to the pavement. I saw my own feet, clad in brown work boots and scuffling the gravel nervously, then noticed that Lily was wearing bright red shoes, just like the first time I'd seen her.

"And Dylan?" I asked.

She nodded. "As long as he stays clean."

"You never told him about us?" The question was pointless. Obviously, I would've known if Dylan had even suspected the truth. He would never have accepted that level of betrayal without consequence.

"No. You?"

"No," I said. That meant Dylan must believe Lucy was his. Probably, she was. I wondered what my rights were, whether I could somehow force Lily to find out the truth. I quickly dismissed the thought, already aware of the severe consequences such a thing would have on the lives of all four of us involved.

"Did you move back here?"

"We're staying with my parents until I find an apartment. My mother watches Lucy while I work." Her lips curled upwards into a gorgeous smile. "I went back to school and now I'm teaching high school English." She paused. "So basically I get paid to read Wuthering Heights and Scarlet Letter over and over."

Her smile was contagious, but I still had to ask. "Are you happy?"

A peculiar look came across Lily's face as she considered this. "Yes."

I glanced at her hand. "You never married?"

She laughed lightly. "God, no."

I didn't understand her reaction. She was an attractive, entertaining woman who'd surely be a catch for any man, so there was hardly anything laughable about my question.

"You know my track record," she finally explained. "I can't risk making that kind of choice now that I have Lucy."

I frowned. "So you just don't date?"

She shrugged. "I wouldn't say never. There was only one serious relationship." She giggled again. "He was a CPA."

Now I laughed. I couldn't imagine Lily with a business man. "You must have been bored to death."

"He's a really good man, but not the one for me," she said.

She gazed at me as she said this and I was certain I saw something that gave me a glimmer of hope.

"Have dinner with me tonight," I asked.

Lily smiled, but shook her head. "I don't think that would be a good idea."

I accepted this, for the moment. I realized that she hadn't asked about me, whether I was happy, whether I was married, but then again, she probably already knew. Much of my life was an open book, readily visible to anyone with internet access or a nearby newsstand.

She'd probably been following both Dylan and me over the past few years, reading the gossip in the tabloids, buying our albums, watching us on TV. Surely that was how she knew she'd waited long enough, that Dylan was clean and had moved on romantically.

"What did you mean when you said I could get to know her? You're not going to tell her the truth, are you?"

Lily laughed again, her voice like a mockingbird. "What, tell my three year old that her father is one of two brothers that are sort of famous? No, I think not." She paused. "But she plays the piano. Really well, for her age."

I gazed over at Lucy, as though I hoped to somehow see the talent in her fingers as she clutched the ladder of the climber.

"And you know I'm not very musical, so she needs a teacher," Lily continued.

Now it was my turn to laugh. "I have four albums, five Billboard chart songs, two Grammys and an Academy Award for a score, and you'd like me to teach your preschooler to play chopsticks?"

Lily smiled again, bringing the sparkle back to her eyes. "Oh, she's way past chopsticks," she said.

"You realize I have no teaching experience?"

She nodded. "Yeah, so I figured we probably wouldn't pay you for your services, given that you're not exactly qualified."

I grinned. "Did you already ask Dylan?"

Lily shook her head. "I figured he was probably too busy with his new wife."

I nodded again, though I felt confident we both knew that wasn't the only reason she came to me. Suddenly, I was uncomfortable, and Lily clearly sensed it.

She placed her hand on my arm. "Thomas, I know this is a lot to take in. You should think about it all and call me." She paused, breaking eye contact. "I promise not to change my number and run away this time."

"Okay," I agreed. I stood beside her for another moment, watching Lucy for just a little longer. "I'll call you," I said, starting off down the path.

It was a long walk home, probably more than three miles, but the exercise felt good. With each jolt from my feet hitting the pavement, I felt more alive and more certain that this would all work out.

By the time I reached my building, I knew I needed to confront Dylan. I reasoned that he never knew my feelings for Lily, and certainly never knew I was intimate with her, but still, it struck me that my own brother hadn't bothered to mention his discovery that he'd fathered a child with his long-lost fiancée and that he was secretly blackmailing her into accepting unofficial child support payments.

Dylan answered the door quickly when I knocked, a look of innocence on his face. I glimpsed past him into the apartment, then asked if his wife Patty was there. He shook his head, so I asked if he had a minute to talk. He nodded, his face still calm and unknowing.

He retrieved a bottle of water from the fridge and offered one to me. I shook my head and sat on the couch. I took a deep breath, and began. "You wouldn't believe who I just ran into," I said.

Dylan raised his eyebrows in response.

"Lily," I said, gauging his expression. Tellingly, it remained calm. "You knew she was back in town?"

He nodded.

"Was there anything else you know about her?"

"I haven't exactly kept up with her since she left," he said.

"But you knew she had a child," I said.

Dylan's eyes darkened and I caught a glimmer of a smile cross his face before I realized he'd stopped breathing.

"You never mentioned that," I said.

He shrugged, clearly trying to appear nonchalant, but I knew he was still holding his breath. "You never asked." He sat on the chair across from me.

I nodded, conceding that point. "Does Patty know?"

Dylan shrugged again.

"Dylan, I'm your brother. You didn't think I'd want to know you had a child?"

He frowned. "I don't."

"You don't what? You don't think I'd want to know?"

Dylan laughed. "No, Thomas. I don't have a child. It's funny you should bring this all up now, though, because Patty and I were just discussing adoption."

I opened my mouth to ask him about his first statement when I processed the second one. "Why would you be adopting?" I felt the anger rising in my chest before he even answered.

"I can't have kids, Thomas. I thought you knew that."

My breath caught in my throat as he spoke and I realized what that meant, for me, for Lucy, even for Lily. And then I turned to face him, *my loyal brother whom I'd blindly defended and protected for so many years.*

"You've seen her," I said. "Her daughter?"

"Lily's child? Lucy?" He nodded in response to his own question. "I've seen photos."

"Then you had to know. You knew all along and you never told me." My hands were shaking and my vision blurred. I wanted to hit him, but I couldn't bring myself to even stand up. "How could you do that to me?"

Dylan's face hardened. "How could you do that to me? She was my fiancée. You knew how much she meant to me." He shook his head with disgust. "I was in rehab, for Christ's sake. You want to talk about betrayal? Fine, let's have at it. I have four fucking years of it stored up."

I felt my lips move, but no words came out. We were both quiet, probably for more than five minutes, contemplating our dilemma. "It was just one..." I finally began.

"One time?" Dylan said skeptically.

I nodded. "One night," I clarified, subtly, I hoped. "We were drunk. Lily was upset about you. You'd been so hard on her." I paused. "We were talking about you, actually. And it was all my fault. Don't be mad at her. The last thing she wanted was to hurt you."

I prayed he wouldn't ask me for details, that he'd just let it go. It wasn't that I couldn't tell him, or that I didn't remember, because I did. I remembered every moment of that night, from the delicious smell of Lily's skin to the way her tears gathered on her dark eyelashes before dripping to her smooth cheeks. I could still feel her soft hands on my body, still hear her breath quicken as she whispered my name, still taste the liquor on her lips.

I held on to my memories of the moments with Lily like the priceless ancient artifacts they were quickly becoming. In the years she'd been gone, when I hadn't known if I'd ever see her again, the vision of her smiling when she gazed into my eyes was all that kept me going on some days.

My mind drifted back to the conversation at hand and I saw Dylan watching me, his eyebrows pursed.

"Did she love you too?" Dylan asked, and I knew he'd read my mind. I wasn't sure if he'd known all along or if something in my expression just now had given it away, but I was certain at that moment that my brother understood exactly how I felt about his former fiancée.

"No," I said softly, my throat dry. "She loved you." I should've shut up then, but I didn't. "She loved you and you hurt her over and over. She couldn't trust you and she was scared to raise a baby near you so she left, and in the end we both lost her."

He exhaled through clenched teeth. "No, Thomas, I lost her. You never had her."

"For one night I did," I retorted.

Dylan flew out of his seat and lunged forward. I braced myself for the hit, but it never came. Dylan froze, mid-air, then eventually sat back down. We resumed our silent staring match.

Suddenly, I remembered something Lily had said. "Why did you send Lily money if you knew Lucy wasn't yours?"

He inhaled sharply, then smiled. It was a genuine, happy smile, completely unlike the demonic smile he'd flashed earlier. "She's my niece, Tom. And Lily named her Lucy."

Dylan shook his head before completing his confession, and I almost thought I saw a hint of a tear. "I didn't want to punish the child. I was sure you'd support her if you knew she existed, but I couldn't let you or Lily know the truth. Neither of you deserved to know."

"Lily deserved to know. You already hurt her more than she possibly could have hurt you."

Dylan's face remained unchanged.

"So you'd fork over thousands of dollars to support a child that isn't even yours just to hurt me," I summarized.

He swallowed, and our eyes locked. "Now we're even."

Neither of us spoke again until long after it grew dark. I didn't know how much time had passed and I didn't care. None of it was relevant now.

Finally, a car alarm suddenly beeped outside, and it must have jolted us both out of our thoughts because we stood, in unison.

"Are we practicing tomorrow?" Dylan asked.

I knew he hadn't forgotten, that he wasn't truly asking about our schedule, and so I understood the ramifications of my nodding yes in response. Dylan seemed relieved, and I realized I was, too. I started for the door.

"Please tell her I'm sorry for everything," he blurted out. "I never meant to hurt her."

"She knows that," I said, and I understood that he wasn't apologizing for his lie of omission but for everything that had come earlier.

Maybe this was his way of finally accepting blame for the situation we all found ourselves in years ago. Or maybe it wasn't his fault at all.

"Lily asked me to teach Lucy piano. She said Lucy's a natural talent," I added.

Dylan smiled. "I'll have to hear her play someday."

I stepped into the hall, feeling noticeably lighter the moment his door closed. My stomach growled, and I glanced at the clock in my own flat, not surprised to see that I'd spent nearly three hours in the staring match with Dylan which ultimately resulted in a stalemate.

I weighed my options, then called Lily to schedule our first lesson.

ACKNOWLEDGMENTS

Phew...this book has been an adventure. I'm so appreciative for all the support and encouragement my family, friends, beta readers, and fellow writers have provided during the years it has taken me to finalize and polish this story.

Thank you to JD Book Designs for this amazing cover. I adore this design and can't wait to see what you come up with for the sequel.

Thanks to my patient and detail-oriented editor, Kimberly. I appreciate your painstaking review of my work and tolerance for my countless questions.

As always, I'm so grateful to my readers, book bloggers, librarians, reviewers, booksellers, and everyone else out there who reads and promotes books.

Finally, thank you to all of the amazing writers who came before me...it gives me chills to see your carefully scripted words quoted on the pages of my book.

ABOUT THE AUTHOR

Liza Malloy writes contemporary romance, new adult romance, women's fiction, and fantasy romance. She's a sucker for alpha males, bad boys, dimples, and muscles, and she can't resist a man in uniform. Liza loves creating worlds where her heroine discovers her own strength and finds her Happily Ever After. When Liza isn't reading or writing torrid love stories, she's a practicing attorney. Her other passions include gummy bears, jelly beans, and the occasional marathon. She lives in the Midwest with her four daughters and her own Prince Charming. *The Brothers' Band* is her fourth published novel.

Visit her website at www.LizaMalloy.com

Join her email list at
    http://eepurl.com/gnuROD

Available for purchase through Amazon, Barnes & Noble, Apple Books and Kobo.

For Love and Italian

* * *

Forbidden Ink

Loving the bad boy never felt so good!

Ashley Kensington has it all—affluence, status, and the perfect boyfriend. Sheltered by her exclusive southern island community and overprotective father and brothers, Ashley has never strayed from the path her parents chose for her.

Until now.

When Adam Bricker rolls into town with no money, no family, and no ambition for the future, there's no reason that Ashley Kensington should be attracted to him; yet she is. Adam doesn't mind that the locals can't see past his collection of tattoos and his New England accent. Everyone assumes Adam isn't good enough for Ashley, but he's certain he can make her happy and he's ready to fight for what he wants.

For a while, Ashley believes nothing can shatter their epic romance. But when the unexpected happens, Adam is forced to accept that maybe everyone else was right about him from the start.

Available for purchase through Amazon, Barnes & Noble, Apple Books and Kobo.

Forbidden Ink

* * *

PRAISE FOR LIZA MALLOY

Reviews of *For Love and Italian:*

"A fun, lighthearted and steamy romance, *For Love and Italian* is sweet, romantic, and naughty in the best ways. I was entertained the entire time and was quite sad when it was over. Liza Malloy knows how to write addictive and satisfyingly charming romance stories that will surely give you plenty of swoons and feels...I can't wait to see what she writes next."
   - Karen Jo Custodio, Book Blogger.
   www.SincerelyKarenJo.com

"Perfect summer read! Great writing & great characters! Can't wait for more books from this author!"
   - Amazon Customer Review

Praise for *Forbidden Ink*:
   "Get comfortable, you won't be able to put the book down!"
   - Amazon Customer Review

Praise for *Sixty Days for Love*:

"A perfect late-at-night after the kids are in bed escape. The heroine is fun and likeable and the hero is sexy and loveable. What more could you want?"

   - Verified Amazon Review

"This was such an enjoyable read, I had a hard time putting this book down. It has the perfect blend of romance, humor, and character development!"

   - Verified Amazon Review